KEEPING TIME

DAVID BEAR

ST. MARTIN'S PRESS
NEW YORK

With Adria

First Edition

Library of Congress Cataloging in Publication Data

Bear, David.
Keeping time.

I. Title.
PZ4.B367Ke [PS3552.E155] 813'.5'4 79-16368
ISBN 0-312-45110-5

"There are more things in heaven and earth, Horatio,
Than are dreamt of in your philosophy. But
come;"

HAMLET, ACT I, SCENE V

"Every body will persist in its uniform state of rest or
motion in a straight line unless compelled to alter that
state by forces impressed upon it."

FIRST LAW OF MOTION

1

Had he entered my office without knocking, Ivory Wightman would have found me on my knees in front of my desk trapping cockroaches under teacups. The Dresden-blue cups were wedding presents, but they had spent the last fifteen years in a box under the kitchen sink. This new use for them was a recent discovery of mine.

The roaches, however, were constant companions. They were absolute wonders, the latest models hot off an evolutionary assembly line that had invested a hundred million or so years perfecting its products. As big as black olives and quicker than sneezes, they thrived on exotic powder so deadly I had to wear rubber gloves just to open the can it came in. The roaches were also strong, which is the reason I started trapping them under the heavy cups. The bastards would have walked off with anything lighter.

Wightman's knock gave me just enough time to get up off my knees before he filled the doorway. He caught me standing there with a row of cups lined up neatly at my toes. "You are, I assume, Jack Hughes." His voice, small, precise, well-tuned, like the tick of a fine watch, could have belonged to a cultured elf. Instead, it belonged to a pillar of a man who had to duck his head to get through the doorway. He must have weighed well over a hundred kilos, with a black mountain for a head and a canyon cut through red clay for a mouth. He was dressed in a gray winter tunic that fit his powerful body the way a tailored tent fits a circus.

"That's what it says on the door," I answered with my usual aplomb.

The huge man nodded papally, the tight sheath of flesh that lined his long neck doing a fair impression of a well-oiled concertina. He gave my office one more critical glance and finished squeezing himself through the doorway.

"That's some climb," he huffed. "I'm not used to steps. What was it? Six floors?"

"Only five."

"Elevators were a marvelous convenience." He smiled and showed me a double row of beautifully maintained teeth.

"Only as marvelous as the system that powered them. No electricity. No elevators. But you get used to the climb. Wonderful exercise. Keeps a man feeling young."

"Perhaps, but I prefer to live closer to the ground," he answered, sliding into my desk chair.

"Who wouldn't," I said. "But, these days in New York, only rich men can afford the ground." I sat down in the stiff-backed chair that faced the desk. "You must have had a good reason for making the climb, Mr. . . . ?"

"Wightman," he said with rich satisfaction. "Ivory Wightman." He smiled patronizingly, as if there was a connection I should have been making.

"Sorry. Should I know you?"

"There's no particular reason you should." He looked slightly disappointed. "I thought perhaps a person in your profession . . . You still do private investigations, don't you?"

I nodded. "Come to the point, Mr. Wightman. I'm a busy man."

"Yes," he said, surveying the spartan furnishings. "I can see how busy you are. Very well. I'd like you to investigate something." He leaned back in my chair as if he owned it and smiled as if that explained everything.

"What will this investigation entail?" I asked after a few seconds.

"Entail?" he said in a suddenly sarcastic tone. "If I knew what it entailed, why would I need you? If I knew how to slaughter a pig, Mr. Hughes, would I hire a butcher?" I looked for something in his face to tell me to be insulted. I did notice his lips tighten for an instant. It might have been a sneer. It might also have been gas.

"I'll need to know a little more about your . . . situation before I can help you."

He nodded. "Certain items, magnetic tape cassettes to be exact, have been taken. I wish to hire you to recover them."

"You could go to the police for that. You don't have to hire me."

"Come now," he pouted, laying both of his war-club fists on the desk top. "Give me credit for a few brains. Little these days is of sufficient value, or shall we say irreplaceability, to warrant the public expense of a competent investigative staff. The police forces are controllers of mobs and hungry people. They have their hands full enough without my burdening them with stolen objects to recover. Besides, I don't have any faith they would return anything they recover. No, I'm afraid I require your services."

"Why me, Mr. Wightman? There are detectives who live nearer the ground. Some of them may be cheaper."

"Not as many as you think," he answered too quickly. "And, you have a reputation that precedes you. One of honesty. Tact. And, of course, a certain social grace that might allow you access to my clients." His eyes turned toward the row of diplomas on the wall. He smiled and got up to inspect them more closely. "Very impressive. Harvard Law School. Do you still practice?"

"No," I said simply.

"So many of us spent our time learning trades that have become useless."

"What was yours?"

He looked back at me and smiled. "Basketball."

"Sorry, I never followed the game."

He shrugged and looked back at the wall. I used the opportunity to reclaim my desk chair.

"Is this your family?" he asked, pointing to the framed photograph that hung next to the diplomas. "Your daughter takes after your wife."

"It used to be my family. The picture's sixteen years old. They're all dead."

"Sixteen years," he said evenly. "You've aged well. Except for the gray in your hair, you might be the same man."

"Yes, I might be."

"I'm curious why you keep these relics of a long dead era?"

"It hasn't been that long."

"Not that long? Sixteen years! Mr. Hughes, you should take all these down and hang a simple calendar instead." He pointed his thick index finger at me and started to curl and uncurl it as if it were a cheap paper noisemaker. "This is 1999. A new millenium is upon us. The Apathera is long gone. Out with the old. In with the new."

"If you don't mind, I'll do my own decorating." I swiveled my desk chair to the right and watched the December afternoon sun give new life to the blots of last summer's mosquitoes on the wall. The first time I saw the sun play that trick, I thought it strangely beautiful. Now it was only sunshine and squashed bugs.

I looked back at Wightman. "This isn't getting us anywhere. If I'm going to help you, I need to know a little more about your problem." I felt as if I were repeating myself. "What business are you in?"

"Personal banking."

"Not a thriving field either. The credit transfer business is a government monopoly."

"I don't deal in money." The man drew himself to attention and watched a fly circle the hard-boiled egg I had been eating prior to the roach hunt. The pink tip of his tongue poked out from between his lips, and I almost expected Wightman to launch it after the fly. "My clients, Mr. Hughes, save something of far greater value than money. They save time."

"That sounds like a good idea," I said after a few moments. "What do you do? Time and motion studies? That sort of thing?"

"No, Mr. Hughes. I run a time deposit bank." He stuck his hand into the pocket of his tunic and pulled out a wafer of silver metal the size of a poker chip. "This little marvel is a transduction disk. When surgically implanted here," he said, tapping the back of his neck, "the transduction disk can actually elasticize time, just like heat elasticizes glass. Once time is made fluid, it becomes possible to draw off small amounts to be stored for later use. A minute here. A minute there. Time adds up quickly."

I studied the man's face for a second, to see if I was talking to an incipient lunatic. He was grinning like a man who's been given too much change, but I saw only the normal brand of madness in his eyes. I had to assume he was as sane as I was.

"You claim you can store time like grain?"

"Not claim. There are three hundred happy depositers who'll vouch for the fact. Time accounts are very much a reality. They have been for three or four years now. Though, for reasons that must be obvious, the fact hasn't been made public."

"Just out of curiosity, what happens if you take thirty minutes from an hour? Wouldn't you notice a blank space?"

"It would be impossible to draw away that much time. The maximum would be more in the range of three or four minutes an hour. And, to answer your question, time, the eternal healer, heals itself. It thins slightly, as does blood when you donate a pint."

"What's thin time like?"

"Disorienting at first, I'm told. But once a person grows used to the feeling, the sensation is more a dilution of, shall we say, perception." While he prospected for the right word, Wightman generated small, hypnotic circles in the air with his huge hands. "The effect can be pleasant, relaxing, similar to the glow of alcohol when used in moderation. Think of the huge amounts of time even the most efficient person wastes during a day. Time that is otherwise useless, dead, a burden. But my depositors can take those minutes and store them for when time is at a premium or greater concentration is needed."

"A rainy day, so to speak," I said to keep him talking. "And if you exceed the proper limits?"

Wightman's eyes rolled in opposite directions, and his right hand massaged that chiseled ridge of a jaw. "Just as if too much blood were taken away; unconsciousness, coma, eventually death. But that eventuality is, I assure you, quite impossible. You're dwelling on negative aspects. Think instead of precious time piling up. How worth an infinitesimal risk is that?"

"And an infinitesimal expense?"

"Of course, the cost of my service is beyond the means of all but our wealthiest citizens. But there are so few true luxuries these days."

I picked up the transduction disk and balanced it on the end of my finger. "How do you turn this thing on?"

From that same pocket, Wightman produced something that was the size and general appearance of a personal computer. "This is the transducer, a marvel of microelectronics. The red sensor controls the absorption circuit. One click, and time is drawn out and stored on magnetic filaments in the transducer. Another click, and the circuit closes. The black sensor operates the transfusion circuit in the same manner. It's beautifully uncomplicated. A child couldn't misuse it. The red light indicates that the transducer has been activated."

Wightman saw me looking warily at the disk I held. "No cause for alarm, Mr. Hughes. Each transducer is coded to its owner's brain waves and can only be activated by that person."

"What happens to all this stored time?"

"The owner must periodically bring his transducer into

the bank and we transfer the stored time to an account cassette."

"Those are the cassettes that are missing?"

He nodded.

"You've got a bank robber on your hands." I smiled sardonically. "Probably the first in a dozen years."

"No, Mr. Hughes, more than a simple thief. Time, unlike blood, is non-transferrable. It is useless unless transfused back into the life of a donor. Why, I asked myself, would someone steal something he couldn't use or sell? And that's why . . . " Wightman stopped talking and stared down at the floor. He paled noticeably, slapped both arms across his chest, and leaned heavily against the wall. For a moment, I thought the man was having a coronary. But then he righted himself and regained his ebony sheen.

"Are you all right?"

"Yes . . . I . . . I thought I saw those teacups jiggling."

"You might have. What have you got against jiggling teacups?"

"I lived in Los Angeles, and barely escaped the quake with my life. As it was, I spent eight months in a body cast."

"You were lucky."

"I was. Geomorphic security was the prime reason I chose to live in New York City when I got out of the hospital."

"There was certainly nothing to go back to."

"Nothing at all." Wightman sat down across the desk from me.

"Don't worry about the teacups. I was trapping super roaches. The place is infested with them. Park Avenue isn't what it was."

"What is? But what can you expect? Garbage lining the street. Sewers caving in. No one observing even the simplest rules of hygiene."

"Some of us call it home. I got this apartment back in the early Apathera. I hoped it would blow over. All that's blown over is hordes of Jersey mosquitoes."

"We had a similar problem in L.A. A council of citizens

was formed and the entire area was dosed with low-level radiation." He rubbed his hand across his smooth expanse of forehead. "Better bald than bitten, they say."

"Didn't it also leave a lot of people sterile?"

"Some of us saw that as an added benefit. There were too many hungry babies as it was."

Something in Wightman's attitude made me slightly ill. Getting used to a house without children was the hardest part for me, and I wasn't anxious to hear Wightman's opinions on the subject. "We were talking about stolen cassettes."

"Quite right. And now you can see why I've come to you. Time is irreplaceable, and once it is extracted, it is lost if not introduced at another point in one's life. Many of my clients have months on account with me."

"And now you've lost the bank."

"Not all. But five of the tapes are missing."

"Since when?"

"I don't know. We only discovered the loss yesterday. I expected to get a message asking for ransom. That would be the only reason someone would steal those cassettes. But I haven't heard anything."

"Perhaps the thief contacted the owners directly."

"Someone would have asked me for verification."

"Perhaps. Who are the five people?"

"I can't tell you until we come to some agreement. My clients all pay heavily for their privacy."

"I understand. No one wants the world to know when he's been had." I was on the verge of telling him what I thought of his whole story. Clearly, it was a con act, and half of me wanted to tell him to get out. I knew he wasn't hiring me to get those tapes back; these days no one seriously expects to get results from an expert. He wanted off the hook, out from under the responsibility of the tape loss. It was a losing proposition as far as I could see.

But the other half of me, the half that worried about paying bills, that kept track of how many days it had been since I'd had anything better to do than hunt roaches, the half that kept reminding me of things I had tried to forget the day before, that half of me knew I couldn't afford to turn business away. "But that's their problem, isn't it, Mr. Wightman? You're familiar with my fees?"

"Your sign on the wall makes it quite obvious. A thousand dollars per day is cheap enough. But perhaps you'd be willing to work for the right to open a time account? That can be arranged and would be worth far more than you're going to earn otherwise."

"If it's all the same, I think I'll stick with the money."

"If you wish. Half in advance is usual, I believe."

I nodded as I pulled the pad of contracts from the desk. "This states that for the agreed amount of one thousand dollars per day, I agree to investigate for a period of two weeks—"

"No. Four days is all you have."

"Four days won't be nearly long enough. It takes that long to get a case going. Two weeks is minimum."

"That may be, but four days is all you get. I won't support an investigation after Tuesday. Take it or leave it."

I silently tallied up my options in my hand. The man was cutting his losses. I couldn't blame him for that. As far as I could see, it was going to be easy. What kind of trouble could I get into in four days?

"All right, four days it is."

"And none of these disclaimers eschewing responsibility for inconvenience incurred during the investigation. I won't sign any of these." He inked through line after line of the contract until there wasn't much left but the places for our signatures. I needed the money too much to argue. There are some very basic things only money can buy. He used his own pen to sign the credit transfer for two thousand dollars and slid the paper back across the desk.

"That, I believe, completes our business for the moment." He stood up. "I'll leave you to assemble the case. If need be you can reach me here." He handed me a card and turned toward the door. Halfway there, he stopped and returned to the desk. "How foolish. Of course, you'll be needing this. The five victims."

I took the piece of paper he offered, looked at the names, and let out a low whistle. "Are these your normal depositors?"

"As I said, Hughes, my clients must be able to pay for the services I offer." He was out of the office before I could say another word.

After a few minutes, I walked around the data console to the window. As usual, not much moved on Park Avenue; a few faltering electric cabs and a dozen cyclists meandered between the endless rows of snow-covered garbage dumpsters which lined the curb. Looking out the window is another way I pass the time between cases. It is an easy way to lose myself in thought about things I can no longer see from the window. Sometimes, it is too easy.

2

Carlo Mountain, Gregory Darling, Lea Dark, Victor Sieg, Allison Bashcock: For a good half hour after Wightman had gone, I contemplated the five names on the list he had left. They were five pillars of society, or at least notoriety, the sort of people who cross my path these days as often as white whales dancing the fandango. They definitely weren't the sort of people you'd associate Wightman with. But the rich and the powerful are sometimes the most susceptible to con artists. They, better than most, know how little happiness money can buy. But they're just as hungry for it, and they have the money to waste looking. They also have a lot of empty time to contend with.

Among other things, the list told me why Wightman had chosen me instead of one of my few competitors. Once upon a time, I would have been right at home sipping Scotch and talking shop with any one of the five names on Wightman's list.

Two of them, in fact, I had known personally. Victor Sieg and I had worked on more than one case together. That was twenty-five years ago, and recent rumors had Senator Sieg running hard for the presidential nomination.

Lea Dark had earned her reputation as an acid, unfeeling bitch well before I had known her. Lea had used marriage the way most people use steps: to get out of the cellar. The stairs she used to climb from nowhere were Alexander Hamilton Dark, a senior partner in the venerable law firm of McCraken, Dark, and Dimeswell. For nine years in the late seventies and early eighties, Jack Hughes, the young lawyer, was a junior partner at McCraken, Dark, and Dimeswell. During those years, I had ample opportunity to observe Lea Dark's cruelty at its very best. But that's another story.

The other three names on the list were also grist for the daily rumor sheets, even though I had never had the pleasure of meeting them.

Although Gregory Darling was past seventy and hadn't made a film in twenty years, his name still turned up regularly in the gossip columns. Darling was a man who stepped on toes, wherever he went. More often than not, the toes belonged to some woman's irate husband. Of course, I only kept up with Darling's antics because newspaper editors bury the gossip columns back with the comics.

But Carlo Mountain's domain was strictly page one. He was an inventor extraordinaire, entrepreneur in the classic sense, and president of Mountain Industries. He also had a hundred million dollars for each of his eighty-three years. His reputation as a mover and shaker was as well deserved as it was publicized. The more Mr. Mountain shunned public attention the more one seemed to read his name.

I recognized the fifth name on the list, Allison Bashcock, but only vaguely. A quick trip to the data console solved that. According to the file, Miss Bashcock was the twenty-nine-year-old author of three novels, as well as a staff masseuse at Melray Johnson, a public relations firm that specialized in creating new public images for tired old faces. A bit young perhaps, when compared to the other names on the list, but Miss Bashcock still qualified as an overachiever in a world that gives an A plus for mediocrity.

It wasn't difficult to see why Wightman wanted to protect himself from these folks by going through the motions of hiring me. Any one of these birds could fill the coop with feathers if they got ruffled, an unpleasant prospect for Wightman, who was clearly a fox on the make. Just to make sure, I ran Wightman's name through the files, and, for my efforts, got a list of aliases long enough to fill a phone book and a history of dubious-sounding ventures that told me that the same person had put the "A" in alibi and alias. Wightman was once a forward for the Los Angeles Lakers but got drummed out of the league for selling snortables to his fellow players. Since then, he had run a series of operations which verged on the illegal, though he had never actually been convicted of anything. After the Quake, he transferred his operations to Manhattan. The file mentioned nothing about the time deposit bank, which meant only that it was a recent development.

I was having the first of my many second thoughts about taking the case. It wasn't that I resented Wightman using me to cover his retreat. That's why I'm in business, and if I was above helping thieves, I would never have made it as a lawyer. It was the prospect of shuffling through a garden of old memories that bothered me most. Still, Wightman's scheme was one of the more original cons I'd ever heard of, and the prospect of money stifles a lot of second guesses in a hungry man.

I shooed the lone fly off the egg I had been munching on before the roach patrol. To the victor, so they say, go the spoils.

After flies and taxes, spoils is the perfect word for what's left.

Wightman claimed he had over three hundred depositors, but only five tapes had been stolen. I began by assuming there was some special reason why those five were taken. Once I figured out why I'd be well on my way to figuring out who had taken them. I've read all the detective manuals. I know how things are supposed to work.

So I killed a half hour and came up with a dozen ways the five victims might fit together. I could have come up with another dozen with no trouble. Wealthy people move in curiously tight circles, and trying to surmise just which circle was the right one was a pastime for idiots. There was really only one way to get the case rolling.

I pulled the phone book from the drawer and quickly found not one of the five names was listed. But that, in itself, wasn't odd. Manhattan isn't the bustling place it once was, but enough pettifoggery still transpires to make a little exclusivity a desirable thing. As a result, the once proud Manhattan phone book has shrunk to the size of a condom catalogue.

I put the names through the data console and, for each one, got a handy little file that briefly covered the last ten years of each one's life. The data consoles are great little machines. Cheap, quick, quiet, and equipped with batteries that suck the scant electricity from the city power lines like a cactus drinking between monsoons. Every home should have one. If they had been perfected ten years earlier, every home would. The data console's only real drawback is that, given the right subject, it can bury you with information. You have to know how to ask the right questions because they have the right answers. All of them. That's why I requested only the most recent brief report on each person. I could have wasted all four days of my case just digesting the information the data console would give me if I wasn't specific.

Just for the hell of it, I dialed the number the file gave for Carlo Mountain. One doesn't expect a billionaire to answer his own calls, but the tone hadn't sounded twice when a man with a voice like a growl in a gravel pit picked up the phone.

"Hello?"

"Mr. Mountain, please."

"This is Mountain," he answered impatiently. "Who's this?"

"Name's Hughes, Mr. Mountain. I'm working—"

"And you should be glad for that much. Where the hell did you get this number? What am I paying all this money for if any fool who wants to can call me whenever he gets the urge?" The man's voice stank of power and domination. I knew the answers to all his questions but still had to think twice before I spoke.

"I'm a private investigator, Mr. Mountain. It's my business to have information like this. What I'd like to know from you—"

"A private investigator? A detective? Gumshoe? Be damned, I didn't think there were any divorce chasers still around. Though, now that I think about it, I don't know why there shouldn't be. People are as malicious as they ever were. Even if they haven't got enough energy to wipe their own asses. What's your problem? You've got fifteen seconds to tell me."

"I was hired by a man named Ivory Wightman. He claims he's got some of your life stored on magnetic tapes. Is that right?"

Mountain said nothing for a few seconds, but even his silence had a sharp tongue. "I've made more money in these five seconds than you have in your whole life," it said.

"I was under the false impression that I paid Wightman for privacy. What kind of poll is the man running? He probably sold his list of depositors to a mail-order house."

"I'd rather not talk about it over the phone. Could I see you this afternoon?"

"Ha! You stand a better chance of seeing Saint Peter. For me, you have to make an appointment. I might be free sometime in the next century."

"It's important."

"Important! Do you know what I'm doing at the moment? Closing in on the final design for a perfect solar cell, one that will transform sunlight into plentiful, easily stored electricity. One that will work on your rooftop or your car. One that will cost a tiny fraction of what we're spending on this orbiting solar station. Now, is what you have to say that important?"

"Maybe not to mankind, but perhaps it is to you."

"Listen, I don't know how much you know about me, but a little research might do you well. All my life, I've been a saver. That's why time deposits fascinated me in the first place, and why I've spent so much money on them. I can save something no one ever could before. Not Solomon, not Midas, not Rockefeller. I don't intend to waste any more of my precious resources on you. My secretary will decide if what you have to tell me is so important. Don't take it personally. My feelings would be the same if you were the president. I haven't got the time—"

"Neither has Wightman," I cut in.

"What do you mean?"

"There's been a robbery. If you care about that time you've saved, you'd better find a few minutes to talk to me."

"Is this a threat?"

"Nothing of the kind. Wightman hired me to get back what was stolen."

A man doesn't earn a billion dollars or, for that matter, live to eighty-three if he needs everything spelled out for him. "This afternoon is impossible. So is tomorrow. Try Sunday around three P.M. Since you have my private phone number, I also assume you've got my private address."

"They're part of the same package."

"I hope, for your sake, that package has a better guarantee than the privacy I pay for. In fact, if you . . . "

The fading connection cut Mountain off in mid-sentence. I waited a few seconds, hoping he'd come back, but I knew he wouldn't. When I heard the faint buzz of the dial tone, I knew the phone company's brownout had turned black. Phone work is a perpetual liability for someone like me, someone who saves his best blows for last. It wasn't the first time I've been left chewing a mouthful of useless words. I had been planning to tell Mountain even his billions couldn't buy him immunity from either the Apathera or a con man like Wightman.

Of course, the phone company said it far more eloquently than I could have. The trouble is I never got the chance to tell him myself.

For a few months, when I was a kid, I carried a picture of Gregory Darling in my wallet. The picture showed a man in his early twenties with intensely blue eyes set in a lean face the color of polished copper and topped by a rich mat of auburn hair. In that picture, Darling already sported the famous pencil-thin mustache that had never gone out of style on his face even though it always looked ridiculous on me. Darling always wore that mustache with the confidence of a man who knows he's handsome from any angle.

The picture had come inside the new wallet, but I told my friends the handsome young man was a cousin of mine who lived in California. Of course, that was before Darling hit it big, before vistavision turned his face into a national monument. Then, as now, Gregory Darling looked like a relative everyone wants to call his own. A more recent photograph came with the data file. It was a couple of years old at the most, but it showed a man who had aged only a year for every ten that had passed since that wallet picture had been taken. It requires more than a shot of vitamin E and an occasional, haphazard dab of shoe polish to keep a man looking that young. I know.

As I dialed the number listed in the file, I noted the letters corresponding with the numbers spelled out DARLING. Coincidences like that cost money. But they don't keep the phones working any better. The blackout was still on, and there was no way of knowing how long it would be before normal power came back.

East Ninety-third was only thirty blocks uptown from my place, and I hadn't been out of the building in days anyway, so I decided to see how recent the address the file gave for Darling was. I locked my apartment behind me and walked to the elevator. I always walk to the elevator, and I always go through the motion of pressing the button, though I can't even remember the last time the elevator answered my summons. It's a little ritual of mine, a harmless tribute to a time when we took things like elevators for granted, a time before electric power became so uncertain that a five-floor elevator ride often turned into a ten-hour wait in a dark closet. I shouldn't complain. Before the Apathera, fifth-floor apartments in this area were called penthouses and cost a monthly mint. Now, they give them away to anyone willing to make the climb.

Down in the lobby, I wheeled my old Schwinn out of the closet and onto the street. The bike was a present for my daughter's second birthday. She never got old enough to use it, and the bike had spent most of the last twelve years in a closet. Only recently did I realize Schwinns make lousy shrines.

Little traffic moved uptown, but an accident at Seventy-second Street and a stiff headwind made the going slow. North of Seventy-second, however, the wind collapsed, and then minutes later, I was braking in front of 177 East Ninety-third, a prosperous-looking brownstone on a well-kept block. Only the small nasal shriek of a dozen rooftop wind generators rustled the otherwise peaceful street. I leaned the bike against the iron railing that curled around the tiny front yard. There was no name under the brass street numbers on the door, but the expectant face that appeared for an instant at the front window when I rang the bell belonged, without a doubt, to Gregory Darling.

The pickle-faced maid who actually answered the door had no time or interest for me. She wore high, black plastic walking boots and a gray parka, and wasn't at all subtle about wanting to get rid of me. When I told her I wanted to see Mr. Darling, she said he wasn't home without even blinking an eye.

The woman didn't seem the type to be swayed by argument, and calling her a liar would get me nowhere. So I said, "Thank you very much," backed away from the door, pedaled the Schwinn half a block east, and parked it where I got a good view of Darling's front door. Sure enough, two minutes later, the maid appeared at the door, gave the street a quick once-over, and then trundled west, pulling a wire carryall loaded with clothes behind her.

This time, when I rang the bell, I made sure Darling knew I saw him at the window. Still, I had to ring for a full thirty seconds before he understood I wasn't going to go away. When the door opened a crack, I flashed my I.D. at him.

"Mr. Darling. I'd like to ask you a few questions regarding the account you have with Ivory Wightman."

The famous face looked at me and then again at the I.D. The surgeons had done a fine job keeping the bloom in those tight cheeks and chin, but no one has yet found a way to erase the glaze of age and disappointment that stained Darling's eyes.

"I suppose you'll have to come in." His voice still creaked with the plush, easy comfort of a well-used leather couch. He undid the chain holding the door closed and stood aside for me to enter. "I apologize for the charade." He smiled sardonically. "I'm expecting company. I told Gail to get rid of you."

Darling's body seemed to be as tight as his face. His worsted tunic flowed gracefully over his still strong arms and trunk. It surprised me to see he was only centimeters shorter than

I. Movie actors usually turn out to be dwarfs in real life.

"No problem," I said, laying my hat and coat in his hands. We both stood there for a moment while he decided what to do with them.

"We can talk in there." He pointed through a doorway, and turned to hang my hat and coat in a closet to our left across the terrazzo hallway.

I walked through the doorway and found myself in what I assumed was the living room. I say assumed because it didn't look like any living room I had ever seen before. The tufted pile on the green-and-gold tessellated carpet was ankle deep, almost engulfing the white satin couch that circled the center of the room. The walls, covered with the same satin fabric as the couch, were barely visible through the cascade of flora that hung suspended from the ceiling. A single translucent bulb, a plant light, I supposed, was mounted at the top end of a milky colored glass pole two meters high and of such grand proportions that it took me a second look to recognize it was shaped like a phallus, complete with a pair of brass balls at the base. But the finishing touch in the room was the thick, two-meter-wide disk of clear glass that hovered knee high in the green-and-gold lagoon created by the encircling couch. From the magnum of what claimed to be French champagne chilling on the floating table, I surmised Darling wasn't expecting the grocery boy.

When he entered the room, Darling caught me trying to figure out what kept the glass in the air. As far as I could tell, there was no support underneath or above that might keep a hundred kilos of plate glass suspended.

He flashed me that same beamish grin I had seen magnified to twenty times its size by the miracle of vistavision. "An electromagnet in the ceiling creates a selective magnetic field. Lodestone filaments are embedded in the glass. This," he said, flicking a wall switch next to the door, "controls the process." Sure enough, after a second, the plate of heavy glass drifted gently to the floor, landing so smoothly it didn't ruffle the champagne. From the way the carpet underneath was mashed, it was an easy guess that was where the table spent most of the day.

"Clever," I commented appreciatively.

"I suppose. Of course the damn thing is as impractical as a cold-water tap in hell. You have to keep metal away, and I can't tell you how many times I've had the ceiling repainted because the magnet sucked make-up out of someone's purse. It uses so much electricity, it'll drain the house batteries in two hours. Of course, back when there was city current . . ." Darling shrugged his shoulders. "It's a relic, all right. I bought it many years ago. A sculpture by Dionelli. He also did the lamp. They were called functional art back then. Times change." We both regarded the table for a moment. It was a symbol of an age that needed no more symbols.

"Mind if I sit down?"

He looked at me curiously. "No, of course not."

I settled my tail onto the soft couch, and Darling dropped into a lotus position on the tabletop. "Am I correct in assuming Wightman hired you to find my tape?"

"Wightman didn't tell me anyone else knew the tapes were missing," I said, slightly surprised at his knowledge.

His eyes perked up. "Others are missing? He didn't tell me that yesterday when I discovered my compartment empty. The son of a bitch probably took them himself."

"You don't trust him?" I wanted to add "either" but didn't.

"I've known Wightman too long."

"Why do you use his bank?"

"Mr. Hughes, it's the only game in town. Wightman may be a crook, but his bank is an absolute miracle. I don't think I could live without it."

"The gizmo really works?"

"The world would be a happy place if a fraction of it worked as well. I take it you haven't experienced the pleasure of a transducer. It's warm. It's comforting. It's sublime. It's peace which passeth understanding, to coin a phrase. It's a still moment in a chaotic world. Boredom and frustration lose their sting. Have time on your hands, Mr. Hughes? Press the black button, and it's gone. Want to savor a particularily gratifying moment? Press the red button, and it will last forever."

Something about the faraway look in his eyes reminded me of other addicts I have known. The man wasn't talking to me as much as to the object of his adoration. Darling was an actor, a good one by some accounts, but there was real emotion in his idle histrionics.

"You like the idea," I said lamely when he had finished his soliloquy.

"I can think of many things I can more easily do without." He reached into the pocket of his tunic and hauled out a transducer which except for its silver case was identical to the one Wightman had shown me. "I've been frantic these last several days without my time."

"I'm not sure I understand, Mr. Darling. What do you mean, 'without'? Can't you use the transducer without the account tape?"

He shook his head with excess energy. "Well, yes. Strictly speaking, I can. I can take time away, but without my account tape, I am unable to put any back in my life. That means I can't accent any of life's sweeter moments." He smiled sheepishly. "I'm afraid I've developed quite a sweet tooth."

"Couldn't you save up some time during the day? Just enough to tide you over till we get your tape back?"

"No, I'm afraid not. The movement of time between the body and the transducer is an osmotic process. Time flows only from an area of higher concentration to an area of lower concentration. That's why a transducer must be continually drained of its stored time, why, for example, one can never take too much time out or put too much in. As the concentration of time in the transducer rises, the siphoning process slows. But, conversely, if you want to put time back in your life, you have to increase the transducer's concentration above that of the body. To do that, you need a large reservoir of stored time, the account tape. Without my account tape,

I can't drain off the time I've stored since yesterday. My transducer has reached a state of equilibrium. It won't accept time from my body; it won't put any in. I can turn the thing on but it won't do a damn thing."

"You know a bit about how a tranducer operates."

He chuckled. "I should. I was one of Wightman's first depositors. I've always been fascinated by the hidden processes of life. An understanding is critical, Mr. Hughes. The more profound our understanding of life's mysteries, the less susceptible we are to unwelcome surprises. Through sensible, enlightened analysis, synthesis becomes possible, and thus, the future palatable. Man's ability to anticipate is all that separates him from the animal world. That, and his respect for the past. I'm not bragging when I say I understand the process of time transduction better than Wightman."

"Didn't he invent the process?."

"I should say not. The man is as scientific as a gumdrop, a licorice one. The transduction principle and application is the work of a genius."

"Who might that be?"

"I haven't the faintest idea. I've questioned Wightman a hundred times. He won't say. Whoever the person is, he should be canonized. Wightman's another type of genius entirely." Darling glanced toward the front window. When he looked back at me a moment later, he seemed disoriented, as if his train of thought had left without him. He stared at the champagne bottle a moment before he spoke. "Sometimes I grieve because the world has lost its taste for imagination. I always felt radio drama was more imaginative that any visual medium. It required more participation on the part of the listener. Without participation, there is no imagination. Without imagination, no anticipation. Without anticipation, no joy. That's what's kept the Apathera going all these years. A lack of imagination." Darling combed his hand through his heavy shock of red hair.

"I was under the impression the Apathera ended a few years ago."

"Don't believe it for a moment. The pervasive apathy continues. Only the name has lost its vogue. Well, no matter, the blight will be over soon enough."

I admit the man had me mystified. He sighed and settled back into his thoughts. It was as if he had left the room.

"Over?" I asked, not really knowing what else to say.

"Of course. In three years. It's information anyone could see if they took time to examine the evidence. It's all in the numbers. Everything, Mr. Hughes, moves in specific rhythms geared to predictable numerical sequences. For example, the western droughts this past summer. Forecast thirty years ago by numerologists who understood the numerical dynamics at work. Wind currents in the upper atmosphere shift every twenty-two years. When they shift, they bring serious droughts. Nineteen thirty-three, 1955, and 1977 were all drought years. Any fool could have predicted that 1999 was going to be one too. But was anything done? Someone should have anticipated these crop failures. Now, millions are going to starve. Needlessly. All because numbers were ignored. Really, if mankind was as willing to accept the predictibility of disasters as it was their inevitability, we wouldn't get caught ass-naked every few years. This Apathera thing. Anyone could have seen that the years between 1991 and 2002 were going to be difficult. That's a transmillenial palindromation of prime integers."

"Run that last one by me again. The transmillenial whatever it was."

"Palindromation. That's all the Apathera is. You remember what happened during the last transmillenial palindromation, don't you?"

"I might if I knew what one was."

"A palindromation? That's the period of time between two years which are themselves palindromes. The years 1551 and 1661, for example, are palindromes. They read backward the same as they do forward. Normally, palindromes occur every one hundred and ten years. But, at the extremities of the millenia, the palindromations are concentrated in a few years. These periods are always times of great turmoil. During the last one, from 999 to 1001, the seeds of the Dark Ages were sown. Anyone could have predicted this malaise they call the Apathera had they paid attention to the numbers at work. When did it begin? 1991. When will it end? 2002, of course. And the severity of the crisis could have been forecast as well. This palindromation is eleven years long."

"That's bad?"

"Eleven is always a bad number, Mr. Hughes. It's the lowest binomial integer which is itself a palindrome." He was getting a dangerous gleam in his eyes, and I felt myself tense automatically. I've seen that look in too many deep-enders. "Eleven spells disaster," he continued. "I have a wonderful book for you to read. It will explain everything. You will understand why a transmillenial palindromation spells catastrophe. The proof of the numbers is everywhere. Never, not in all of history, not in the darkest of the dark ages, not even when Christ was on the cross, which was, by the way, during another transmillenial palindromation, has mankind been so totally without direction. All of our expectations crushed, all our futures deflated. Our wonderful science and culture is as chaff before a gale of numbers."

"Well," I said after a second. "It's good to hear things are going to be getting better soon. I've about had it."

"You're not alone in that feeling." Suddenly Darling seemed very sorry for himself. His age flowed over him like a drift of damp snow. He looked ninety instead of his chronological seventy or usual forty. It was a shocking glimpse that lasted only a second before the doorbell rang. And then, as if someone had flicked an internal switch, Darling sprang from the ashes of his age. He shed those fifty years and regained that youthful bouyancy he so consciously cultivated.

He pranced coltishly to the front window, peeking through the curtain as he must have done when I rang. When he turned back to me, his face was a mask of sly expectation. "My guest," he explained needlessly, starting for the door. "It would be better if she didn't see you. She's a shy one. That's why I gave the maid the evening off. I'm sure my Jeanette would prefer thinking no one knew she was here. You understand. I'll take her into the dining room and you can slip out."

"I still have a few questions. . . . "

"Later," he twitched nervously. "We'll be done by nine. Come back then."

I nodded, realizing I had no other choice.

"Well, then." Darling closed the living-room door behind himself only to open it a second later. Smiling sheepishly, he flicked the wall switch. "She's never seen my table down. It makes a better impression if it's erect." Without a sound, the heavy glass bore itself and its load of champagne smoothly into the air.

I waited only a moment before going to the window, but Darling had already let his visitor in. The thick wood of the door muffled all but the faintest buzz of voices in the hall. I kept my part of the bargain and waited until that buzz faded into the rear of the house. Then I found my hat and coat in the hall closet. Next to them hung a woman's coat, dark gray fur with a natural swath of black across the back. Out of habit, I gave the still cold coat a once-over but found no quick clues to its owner's identity. Then, with all the stealth of a critic sneaking out of the theater at intermission, I let myself out the front door. I didn't think it was important enough at the time to search for the slower clues to the coat's owner. I assumed this was a normal incident in Darling's life. I was wrong, of course. Dead wrong.

3

While Darling was busy explaining the mystery of numbers to me, the afternoon had died. The frail blue of the mid-December sky had been swallowed whole by a chill western wind, shrouded by a heavy, charcoal gloom that meant snow.

I buttoned the flaps of my hat tightly under my chin and began pedaling west toward the park and Wightman's place. Central Park north of Eightieth Street has been timbered flat, and there was nothing but me and the occasional stump of a defoliated statue to slow the fierce wind slashing across the barren fields. Fighting that wind took me the better part of a half hour, and when I finally emerged into the lee of Central Park West, I felt like an old lily.

A long block in from the park, I found the address on Wightman's card. 103 West Seventy-seventh was one of those flat, stone-faced, four-story buildings that, thirty years ago, were costly cooperative apartments. But the buildings were too close to the riot grounds of the park for comfortable living, so, in the late eighties, they had been turned into low-rise offices. Wightman's bank was on the ground floor where a tarnished plaque announced, "I. Wightman: By Appointment Only."

I used the bell next to the door to announce myself. But, instead of the door opening, the letters on the plaque began to dissolve, and I realized it was actually a security screen. A second elapsed while the image on the screen focused into the face of a young woman who filled the screen with the insouciance of a bubble-eyed waif. The nubbin she wore for a nose complimented her blue eyes, and her soft mouth was drawn up into a smile that said welcome and get lost at the same time. Top it off with a fluffy bun of hair the color of polished maple, and she was a picture of chic innocence halting just enough on this side of cute to be believable.

Pleasantly the young woman asked for my name, and pleasantly I gave it to her. When I returned the question, she ignored me, asking instead, still pleasantly, if I had an appointment, both of us knowing quite well I didn't.

I explained my purpose and she seemed to understand, but when I had finished, she told me absolutely no one could come in without an appointment. I tried once more but realized I was getting nowhere. Some days, just getting a foot in the door is a full-time occupation. I said thank-you to the cute lady and watched her smile freeze back into a line of polished bronze letters.

I was unlocking my Schwinn when a public pedicab, bearing my latest employer, pulled up at the curb.

"Mr. Hughes," Wightman said cheerfully. "How reassuring to see you on the job."

"Actually, I was just leaving. I couldn't get past your lockmaster."

As he caught my meaning, he clapped his broad approval heartily on my back. "Jeanette's a marvel, isn't she. As beautiful as she is absolutely incorruptible. A perfect watchdog, wouldn't you say?"

"Perfect, unless she frightens away the help."

"Now, now," he snorted, the twin gromets of his nostrils flairing slightly. "You'll find her most cooperative once she understands exactly who you are. She's a bit overcautious at the moment. The poor girl is plagued by an almost neurotic sense of responsibility. She's taken this theft far too personally."

I followed Wightman to his office and waited while he laid his meaty palm on the security screen. The screen read his palmprint quickly, and the door slid to the left.

Wightman had obviously put some money into decorating. His office was cosy, designed to either put you at ease or take you off your guard, depending on how you feel about the ambience of plush-plastic. Soft indirect lighting, the kind that is so expensive to own and operate, played off windowless walls textured the color of creamy coffee. I'm talking about creamy coffee back when cream was a thick, rich, velvety liquid that came in cartons decorated with contented cows rather than the colorless, freeze-dried pellets which turn pseudo-coffee even grayer. Every piece of Wightman's office furniture was pearly plush-plastic and form-adjusting, a dream to sit in if you're built like a forward like Wightman or a long-distance swimmer like me. The room reminded me of another office in which I had spent three hours every week for six years when I still felt responsible for the way the world was falling apart.

On one of those soft, sensuous, contoured chairs sat the blonde cherub checking a compuprint. When we entered, she looked up, smiled ever so sweetly, and touched a button that retracted her chair into the wall. She was clad in a glittering body stocking highlighting all the places a lonely man would like to warm his hands. She resembled one of those diaphanous dream virgins you only find on barbershop calendars, and I admit she had me thinking things I hardly ever think in public anymore.

"Jeanette," Wightman began. "My dear, this is Jack Hughes, the investigator I've hired to help us recover the tapes. I want you to help him in any way you can. Mr. Hughes, this is Jeanette Dobbson, my assistant. Her friends call her Trigger."

The two of them, for some reason not obvious to me, found that immensely amusing. Instead of guessing why, I busied myself finding a chair where viewing Trigger would be easier than watching Wightman.

"There are several things I need to know before I can recover any tapes."

"Such as?" Wightman asked.

"Such as how and where those tapes were stored, how

they're processed. Things like how someone might have gotten into your vault."

It didn't seem to me I had said anything so strange, but both Wightman and Trigger looked alarmed by my request.

"I see," Wightman said, seating himself heavily in the chair next to mine. "I suppose that's only logical. Trigger, open the vault."

"Ivory, do you think that's smart?" Jeanette's voice was oddly tinny. A less sensitive fellow than I might have called it shrill.

"Perfectly, my love. Mr. Hughes is a professional. After all, he won't be able to do his job properly without our complete trust. Isn't that right, Mr. Hughes?"

I started to nod, but realized neither of them was paying me the least attention. Jeanette had already started pressing a series of switches on the console behind her. When a green light began blinking, she laid her palm on a scanner next to the light. Immediately, the wall behind us split in two with a soft, hydraulic hiss. The lower half dropped into the floor and the upper half disappeared into the ceiling. The exposed alcove was about two meters square. All three interior walls were lined with metal doors, each the size of a thick book.

Wightman whipped himself out of his chair with all the fluid purpose of a used-car salesman and strutted across the room. "As you can see, our little vault is quite secure: an electronic locking system that responds only to the palmprint of either Jeanette or myself; a wall that will stand up to anything short of a nuclear attack; and a dividing partition that seals itself automatically if anyone attempts to tamper with the controls. The vault is airtight and, as you can see, every centimeter of it is visible from any point in the room. It would be as impossible for anyone to break into the vault as it would for anyone to hide inside when it was closed."

"Why?"

"When this partition is closed, Mr. Hughes, the inner atmosphere of the vault is charged with a cyanide gas necessary to keep the tapes from decaying. It is also quite lethal. But, even if someone did secret himself in the vault, it would do him no good. Each compartment is locked individually and can be opened only by pressing a six-number sequence on the control plate which, as you see, is outside the vault itself." He shoved his finger toward a securidial mounted on the wall next to me.

"What powers it all? I haven't seen such a dependence on artificial energy since the family planning exhibition at the last World's Fair."

"We have a battery of wind turbines on the roof to take advantage of the bad weather and a bank of solar panels to take advantage of the good. A costly solution, I admit, but we find it worth the price. Better than freezing in the dark, as the gas rebels used to say. As you see, we are well pre-pared."

"Then why do you need me? Somehow someone got five tapes out of your vault." I tried to keep a professional atti-tude, but it wasn't easy amid so much smugness. "Any sign of forced entry?"

He shook his head. Wightman's security system was good, state of the art, in fact, the best that money can buy in a time when security is a highly priced commodity. But even the best systems are only as secure as the people who operate them are vigilant. The better systems eventually give their owners a false sense of security, and when that happens, there's a good chance for a quarterback sneak. The first logical assumption was that the thief was a person with nor-mal access to the vault, either Wightman, his assistant, or a depositor.

"When a depositer comes in, does he get his own tape from the vault?"

Jeanette answered quickly. "Only the customer knows his securinumber. He brings the tape to the console for pro-cessing, but one of us watches him every step of the way."

"But all depositors have complete access to the vault when-ever they want. Assuming they knew the proper numbers, anyone could open any compartment."

"Well, I suppose, but nobody could bring someone else's tape up for processing. Each cassette is coded with the owner's palmprint. If the print of a person attempting a transaction doesn't match the cassette record, the tape is locked in place and an alarm is triggered. It's a precaution to prevent time getting on the wrong cassette, but it also insures the identity of every depositor. The alarm has never been triggered."

I digested those facts, still sure that unless Wightman or his assistant was guilty, the thief could be found among the list of depositors. That narrowed my possible suspects down to three hundred, a small number compared with the two and a half million people who still inhabit Manhattan.

"May I see a cassette?"

Jeanette reached into a drawer and handed me a cellophane-wrapped cassette. I tore the wrapper off and let the cassette slide onto the desk. "It looks like an audio tape," I said after examining it.

"Except for the special coating that makes it sensitive to temporal impulses, it is normal tape."

"If you fill up one tape, do you get a second one?"

"That," Wightman said officiously, "would be unlikely. That tape in your hands will store over a billion seconds. Thirty-five years. No one will ever save that much in one lifetime."

"No, I suppose not." I walked over to the securidial, and punched out the six numbers of my birthday, 12/29/49. No reaction. Then I tried the last six numbers of my social identity designation. Also no reaction. "My guess is your thief is a depositor who took the tapes out one by one over a period weeks. It's obvious he must have had knowledge of the securinumbers of his victims. From which compartments were the five missing tapes removed?"

I walked to the vault and sniffed carefully before I entered. Both Wightman and Jeanette joined me, and suddenly the vault was a tight fit. A close, curious knit of odors filled the narrow alcove. There was the sweet perfume of Jeanette, the sour musk of Wightman, a faint tinge of cyanide, and a hint of rancid butter which I hoped wasn't me. Jeanette pointed out five compartments in the gridwork of doors.

"All five are on the same wall. I'll bet we find our thief somewhere along here too." I ran my hand along the cold metal doors.

"Your logic is impressive, Mr. Hughes," Wightman said after some seconds. "You might even be right, but I don't see how that gets us closer to recovering the tapes. You've managed to, at least circumstantially, narrow the field down to a hundred or so people." I could detect a smirk in his voice. "I'd still call those long odds."

"Not so long. Assuming we eliminate you two."

I hit a sore spot of Jeanette's. She looked at me with that sneer librarians reserved for over-loud children.

"You're not suggesting one of us took the tapes, are you? Ivory, why did you hire him if he doesn't trust us?"

"I'm not accusing anyone. I don't know five things about you, Trigger, but your boss has a history misty enough to make me think twice about his intentions."

"You're doing a thorough job, Mr. Hughes," Wightman said benignly. "You know, my love, I am beginning to suspect that if we give Mr. Hughes a chance, he might just get our tapes back."

"I'd feel guilty accepting your money if you didn't think that."

"Yes, I'm sure you would. Trigger, we've got ourselves a zealot. Don't worry about me, Mr. Hughes. I have no outstanding debts to society. Mine were all the mistakes of a young man. I paid for them with a broken career and shattered illusions."

"Everyone weeps about the past, Mr. Wightman, but no one carries any Kleenex."

I left the vault and picked up my coat. "I've seen enough for the moment. When I have more ideas as to the thief's identity, I'll be back." It was the right time to leave. I had

put on a good show, something which always impresses customers, who, after all, are paying for the illusion of com-
petence.

Of course, I had to wait for Trigger to point out the door,
because it was impossible to see in the uniformly colored wall.
I'm sure Wightman planned the room that way. He seemed
the sort who likes the last laugh himself.

4

The weather front had shifted. Dark, lantern-
jawed clouds were now storming in from the east
like an army on the move. Pedaling hard, I nearly made it
back across the park before the first slap of snow and freezing
rain caught me full in the face. I got to Seventy-second Street
and had worked my way in to Madison when a red light
convinced me to wait the storm out in a doorway of a restaurant that had been closed for repairs as long as I could
remember.

Ten minutes blew by while I considered what a pure waste
it was to power traffic signals on a night so foul only a fool
would be out. Then I noticed the feeble gleam of a cyclist's
headlamp racing toward me on Seventy-second Street. Anyone out riding in this gale was either a person in a hell of a
hurry or some kid so charged by the awful pressure of the

wind at his back that concerns like double pneumonia didn't matter. The cyclist didn't even slow for the red light that should have stopped him dead at Park Avenue. With pedals flying, he reached Madison as the red light was turning green. The cyclist had timed this change perfectly.

Except for one thing.

A city bus, charging at full speed up Madison, tried the same trick the cyclist had pulled off at Park. The cyclist never saw the bus. It caught him broadside. He caromed across the street and was dead before he hit the window of the restaurant. The drama unfolded before my eyes so quickly there wasn't a thing I could do.

The bus needed the better part of a block to stop, and I had already picked my way through the splinters and broken glass before the driver got there.

"I never saw him. Reflection of my lights blinded me in the snow."

I looked up out of the gruesome rat's nest of twisted bicycle parts, detached limbs, bloody silverwear, and shattered glass. The bus driver was huge, ugly. She had a face like a worn saddlebag and a build like a lady wrestler. Steam was billowing everywhere, and for a moment, I thought it was boiling off the driver. Then I realized that in flying though the window the cyclist had sheared off a radiator.

"Why the hell were you going so fast?" I couldn't be of any help inside so I stepped back through the broken window and stood, clapping my hands over my arms in a vain attempt to locate some warmth in my body.

"Dead?" The driver asked stupidly.

"If the bus didn't do it, the window did."

I'm a meter seventy, but the bus driver had to look down at me when she said, "Which was it?"

"Which was what?"

"Guy or lady?"

"No way left to tell."

The driver jerked her head suddenly to the side, and I

thought she was going to be sick. But she wasn't, and, for the next moments, we stood with our hands buried in our pockets watching the wind chase steam in a thousand directions. I wanted to be somewhere else. Anywhere would do. I wasn't particular, as long as it put me far enough from that corner so I could read in tomorrow's paper about the fatal accident on Madison at Seventy-second, shake my head, and go on to the comics. The bus driver was probably thinking the same thing, but there wasn't a wish in either of us strong enough to make that dead cyclist disappear.

I turned toward the driver. "One of us has to call the police."

"Is there a phone inside?" As she spoke, she shifted heavily from one foot to the other.

"Not one I saw." I looked up Madison for a booth and noticed the row of blank faces staring back at me through the steamed glass of the bus's rear window. I couldn't tell if it was fear or boredom I saw in those faces, but not one looked the least interested in doing anything but getting the bus moving again. I could visualize them talking in the morning about the excitement of the night before. Their impassiveness gave my already twisted stomach one more twist.

The driver was now doing a little dance, bouncing from one foot to the other like a candy foot in leaky shoes. "There's a phone on the corner of Eighty-eighth that may work. I could call from there."

I looked at her face. I didn't have to look hard to see that the few traces of compassion which had bubbled to the surface were already frozen over. I knew that she was thinking even though she cowered behind a mask of concern.

"You do that thing. And tell them to send an ambulance. But don't look long for change. I've got too good a memory to forget a face like yours."

"Trust me," she said not at all convincingly.

"Trust you? I don't trust myself not to forget about this as quickly as I can."

She looked like she wanted to pick me up and add me to the heap inside the restaurant. She was big enough to have done it.

"What the fuck are you, Charley? A concerned citizen? I got responsibility to the people on that bus. That's what I get paid for. I don't have time to get mixed up in something like this."

"It's too damn bad about those good people. There's someone here you killed, and I want to see you get up in front of Lady Justice and explain why you ran that light. You'll have a good story worked out by then, but, if you try to run off without reporting this, you sure as hell will need a better one."

"Well, you chauvey pig fucker, I said I'd call, and I will." She turned and stomped back to the bus. Not five seconds later, the door slammed closed, the air brakes hissed, and the much-dented vehicle moved on up Madison, its battery compartment lid slapping in the gale.

I waited in that same gale for three quarters of an hour before a battered prowl car with only one headlight pulled up to the curb. The cop in the driver's seat shut down the electric motor, pushed open his door, and waited for his partner to come around from the other side before getting out. Neither cop looked cold, neither looked as if he had spent the better part of an hour baby-sitting the various members of a freezing corpse. They strolled over to me as if they were at Jones Beach in July.

"You the one called about the suicide cyclist?" The larger of the two cops shined a light into the doorway where I huddled.

"No. Who said it was suicide?"

"Who, hell? The person who filed the report, that's who."

Then the smaller cop spoke. "Chick. Let me introduce Jack Hughes."

The short cop was hidden behind his flashbeam, but I didn't have to see his face to know who he was. "Little far uptown, aren't you, Slovinsky? They finally transfer you?"

"On a night like this, Hughes, you're lucky you get anyone. Union frowns on us going out in inclement weather." He stepped close enough for me to see his sallow, pock-marked face. "You still trying to compete with us? If you want to be a cop, get yourself a badge? It's easy enough."

"I was never competing with you, though it wouldn't be hard. What's it take to get help in less than an hour? A presidential assassination?"

Slovinsky patted me on the shoulder. I only know a few cops very well, and Slovinsky wasn't one of them. But I did know he was neither the best nor worst one around. I didn't know his friend from a fishstick.

"What happened to DiAmico, Slovinsky?"

"Billy got crushed by a deep-ender doing sixty klicks up the sidewalk in front of headquarters about a month ago. Chick Mangelli here's my new partner. Real efficient cop."

As if to prove the claim, Chick stepped forward and, in a low, official voice, said, "Where's the meat?"

I nodded over my shoulder, and Chick hopped through the broken window. Snow had shrouded most of the evidence, but I didn't need Chick's flashlight to see the snow was no longer white.

"Whoever it was done a permanant-type job. Slovinsky, better get a slush sack out of the trunk. Christ, I wish these deep-enders would pick neater ways to stiff themselves."

I followed Slovinsky back to the car. "I saw the whole thing. The cyclist was traveling fast, but the bus ran the red light. It was a tough read, but I don't think the cyclist was out to deep-end himself."

Slovinsky looked up at me from the trunk of the patrol car. He smiled a queer sort of smile and winked at me. "Bus? I don't see any bus. Hey, Chick," he called back over his shoulder. "You see a bus around here?"

"No bus around here."

"It was the bus driver who phoned in the report," I said with a sinking feeling.

"No bus driver called," Slovinsky said, pulling a black plasticized sack from the roll in the trunk. "The report was filed by a concerned citizen who wishes to remain anonymous."

"Yeah, well to hell with that anonymous business. I could pick that lady driver out of any crowd."

"Hughes, let it be. Suicide is suicide. Who reports it don't matter. Details like that are unnecessary complications. We got enough reports to triplicate as it is. That right, Chick?"

Chick had stepped back outside the restaurant and was wiping gore off his hands with a white tablecloth he found somewhere inside. I didn't say anything, but the pockets of his uniform were bulging in a way I hadn't noticed earlier. When he had finished with the tablecloth, he wadded up the linen and drop-kicked it back through the window. "That's right. Don't see any point in bothering innocent people."

"Wait just a minute! Don't tell me you two are going to turn a clear accident into a suicide to save yourselves some paperwork. You can't be that lazy. Or is it because both the cops and the bus drivers share the same union? That's it, isn't it? Teamsters sticking together."

Slovinsky turned toward me and tried to look as menacing as he could. "No, that's not it. Old man, you know how many stiffs like this we see every day? A dozen. Sometimes more on a busy Sunday. You and I both know we're nothing but corpse haulers. What do you want from us? Justice? The first hundred of these hamburgers you see, you do your job the way it's written. You spend half your life running to hell and back with forms, answering questions before grand juries that couldn't give a fly shit for justice. They're just looking for a way to justify their day's pay. Just like you. I shouldn't have to tell you there ain't no justice. Hell, you're lucky if you find justification. So, if nobody cares, why should I? And if I don't give a damn, why should you? You want some advice? Pedal home and forget what you saw. Those pansy poem ideas about the way things should be don't do anyone any good at all."

Chick slid his steroid-stuffed body between Slovinsky and me, but I was the one who got the little shove. "Just move along, fellow. You're not doing anyone any good being here. Not me. Not Slovinsky. Not the bus driver you think you saw. Not the burger in there. And most of all, not yourself. Look at it this way. We need someone to involve in this mess, it'll be a whole lot easier to nominate you. After all, we found you with the deceased."

"Since when is that a crime?"

"Manslaughter's always a crime."

"How did I do that good a job on him? Swat him off the street with a brick wall?"

"All I'm trying to say is the only thing we got is your story of what happened and one mashed corpse. We could put that two and two together in a couple of ways."

It didn't take eyes to see they were going to file the report the way they wanted, and nothing I could do or say would make them change their minds. The worst part was, they were absolutely right. No one who mattered would give a damn. Fifteen years ago, maybe even ten, I could have written a letter to city hall or one of the newspapers. Someone would have read the letter and gotten excited enough to do something.

Maybe that cyclist had been out to stiff himself. The way he treated the red light on Park Avenue didn't speak of caution. There were plenty of people grabbing themselves a quick ticket out every day. The last time I counted one day's crop of deep-enders in the newspaper, I quit at forty with a bridge jumper named Grabenstein.

But how many of those people were really deep-enders, and how many were sacrifices to bureaucratic efficiency? Nothing justified falsifying the facts. The bus driver ran a red light and killed someone. How many more lights would she run before someone else got killed? I didn't see the situation as a question of morality. It was a question of self-preservation. Or common decency. I told that to the two cops.

I might as well have told the cyclist.

Slovinsky, looking as cold and tired as I felt, licked the

snow from his mustache. "Listen, Hughes. I'm not arguing that point with you. The situation is rotten, but that's the way it is. I only want you to see reality. Nobody, but absolutely nobody gives a damn. Sure, you can jump and scream if you want. It's still a free country. But no one's going to listen. And the next time, maybe it'll be something really important to you. You think anyone's going to pay attention to a screamer? You'll be yelling at the deaf and dumb. Don't trump a penny pot. It creates bad feelings. In your line of work, you need friends. Let's just let Chick and me handle this the way we know best. We'll owe you one small favor. Maybe you'll live to collect it."

There was no menace in his voice anymore. Every tired, freezing millimeter of me knew Slovinsky was right. He wasn't a bad cop by any means and was only doing what he saw as his job. I don't know. Maybe every millimeter of me agreed with him.

Every millimeter but one. Not much to show for fifty years of life, not by the standards where I came from. But, considering where we have all been, I suppose I should have been proud of even one millimeter.

I walked aimlessly a few blocks down Madison Avenue, mad at the cops, myself, the cyclist, and the rest of the world, in that order. But the empty street gave me no place to focus my real fury; no place except the dark and staring rows of apartment windows, each as empty and uncaring as the humanity that existed behind it. It terrified me to realize how much shit a man can swallow if he does it one tiny bite at a time.

I was crossing Sixty-fifth before I realized I had left the Schwinn parked in the doorway of the restaurant. Numbly, before I could think twice about it, I began retracing my own fresh tracks in the snow back to the scene of the crime.

The two missionaries of justice were nothing if not efficient. I used maybe fifteen minutes covering those seven blocks twice, but Slovinsky and Chick had already cleaned up and gone. Except for the table cloth tacked across the shattered window, they left nothing to make this corner different from the others I had just passed. It was empty, anonymous, quiet, except for the slow, monotonous click of the traffic light still beating out its weary rhythm though the dancers had all gone home.

One of the dancers had helped himself to my Schwinn.

5

And, just like that, I was crying. I felt like a fool reassuring myself the tears weren't only for the bike. I'm sure I made a fine sight, a man a few weeks shy of fifty standing in a snowstorm and bawling because someone's taken his bicycle. Even though I knew it was bye-bye Schwinn, I spent a minute looking around before I started wandering toward Park Avenue, the tears freezing in snail's tracks down my cheeks.

I didn't feel like going back to my empty apartment, and it was still too early to return to Darling's, but I didn't have many other options open to me. There aren't many neighborhood bars or restaurants left in that part of town. I did remember a little diner called Augustino's on Lexington at Eighty-first. The place had a reputation for keeping odd hours, but when I got there, the door was locked and the lights were turned down. I was about to leave when I saw someone move in the dull glow of the kitchen. I knocked on the frosted window until someone I assumed was Augustino appeared at the door. I took a few sips from an imaginary cup I held in my trembling hand. After a second, he got the idea and opened the door for me.

"Power's down, and I locked up 'cause I didn't think anyone'd be out on a night like this."

"Don't worry. No one else is. What have you got that's hot?"

The short, swarthy man looked around appraising his restaurant with the slightest hint of dissatisfaction, a painter viewing a prized canvas in imperfect light. He shrugged his rounded shoulders. "Dunno. Some coffee. I got microwave. If there's any juice in my batteries, I could heat something up, I guess. If you're not particular."

"Do I look like I'm going to be particular?"

"Nah, you look like you've been crying."

I slid through the door, and Augustino sealed out the night behind me. The diner wasn't large, seating maybe fifteen along the single counter that ran back through the narrow, brick-walled room. It wasn't fancy either, but I wasn't looking for fancy either. Neither was it warm, and I was looking for that.

"Don't you have any heat?"

"I turn the gas off when I lock up. Don't make no sense to heat this whole place if all I'm using is the kitchen."

I drew myself up on one of the iron stools nearest the kitchen, and Augustino put down a cup of coffee in front of me on the speckled white formica counter. I slopped out half the brown liquid getting it from the cup into my mouth. Not that I was missing much. The brew that spilled on my hands warmed me as much as the brew that made it to my lips.

Augustino called out from the kitchen, "You're in luck. I got one Augustino's Thanksgiving Special left. You want it?"

"Last Thanksgiving or the one before?"

"It's frozen. What difference does it make?"

I told him to put it on and went back to spilling my coffee.

Science has produced some absolute losers over the years. Roach powder was one. The dinner Augustino dished up was another. It took him all of forty seconds to microwave a frozen slab of unpalatable nutrition into a steaming mush of unpalatable nutrition. He set the limp tray in front of me on the counter, padded back into the kitchen, and hid there the entire time I was eating. Not that I blamed him. I know I couldn't have kept a straight face watching a person toss down that soupy mess.

Still, I took my time with dinner, and, when I had scooped up the last glob, I sat contemplating the empty tray. Only after Augustino saw I was going to get neither violent nor violently ill did he leave his shelter, bringing a cup and a coffee pot with him.

When he asked, "Finished?", I detected a certain amazement in his voice.

"Why, you got someone who wants this seat?"

He smiled and I smiled. There was no point in frowning. Then Augustino picked his cup up and said, "You know, I've seen you in here before. You must be a glutton for punishment."

I nodded and he smiled again.

"Live on the block?"

I shook my head. "Park and Fifty-third."

He nodded appreciatively. "Up high?"

"Five stories."

"That's not bad. I used to live down in that neck of the town, but on the twenty-second floor. Moved up here in July of '89."

"You've been in business a long time." I pointed with my nose at the empty tray between us.

"Lot of places serving better food didn't make it." He grinned and showed me a set of broken teeth. "Hard to believe, isn't it." He took a sip from his cup. "You wouldn't by any chance remember a place called the Venice, would you? On Lex at Fifty-first."

I lied with a straight face. "Yeah. Pizza shop."

Augustino nodded heavily. "Before that. According to the 'Times' critic, the Venice was the best Italian restaurant north of Mulberry Street. I owned it." He spoke without emotion, as if about a pair of socks he lost in the laundry. "Went broke serving good food." He scratched the spare gray stubble that framed his face.

"Happened to a lot of people," I offered after a moment.

"Dunno about other people, but it happened to me. We had fantastic food. Fair prices. Genuine decor. No plastic. All the right things that make a successful restaurant. But I couldn't pull in the burger crowd, so I tried the switch to fast food. Almost made it. Know what killed me? City regulations." Augustino put down his cup. "That's what killed a lot of places. City regs. Got so they could close you down for just about anything. Me, I'm so small now, half the time I don't think they know I'm here. You know the old saying, to find a successful restaurant, ask a rich city health inspector." He took another sip. "I wouldn't have let slop like you just ate in the back door of the Venice."

"What made you open a place like this?"

"At least I don't claim to make good food. People get what they expect, they stay happy." Augustino swept slowly over the counter with one hand. "Fifty-three years. I guess running a restaurant's all I ever knew. Maybe the world'll change again." He nodded toward the window. "Maybe people will start throwing crap like this in the street instead of their faces." He stowed my empty tray under the counter. "If that happens, maybe I'll try quality again." He peered over the edge of my cup. "More coffee?"

"Thanks, no." I chewed grains of undissolved creamer and put down the empty cup. "Know the time?"

"Why, you got some place to go?"

When I nodded, he rubbed at his mouth with a finger and

slowly shook his head. "Must be important to get you out on a night like this."

"Yeah."

He shrugged, rocked back, and peered through the hatchway into the kitchen. "Ten past nine."

"I'd better get on the road. I was supposed to be there at nine."

"I was you, tomorrow would be soon enough. Play gin? I got a deck of cards."

"I play, but another time. This is important."

"Nothing in years has been important. Not even the poker game we hold here Tuesday evenings about seven. You're welcome to join us."

I nodded, stood up, and put on my coat. Augustino handed me my hat from the counter.

"What do I owe you?"

He rubbed his chin with a tired hand. "Dunno. Suppose twenty'll cover it."

I snorted in disbelief. "Twenty dollars? Who are you trying to kid? I know what things cost. Just the electricity to heat that meal cost twenty dollars."

"Like I said, twenty will cover it." He looked at me with dark cow's eyes. "I'm glad to get the shit out of here."

I slid my card on the counter, but he shook his head. "Sorry. I can't take plastic. They lifted my plates."

"Why?"

He shrugged. "No one ever said why. One day a couple of months ago, two city inspectors came in and lifted the plates. That's the last I heard of it."

"Didn't you find out why?"

"What good would finding out do me?"

I located three paper tens in the bottom of my jacket pocket and stuck them in Augustino's hand. He looked at them and shook his head. "Don't give me a hard time, mister. I said the meal only cost twenty."

"The extra ten's for being open when I needed you. But don't worry. Some Tuesday soon I'll take it back in poker."

Augustino looked at the bills, grimaced, and stuck them in his pocket. "I owe you," he said.

"What?"

"A good meal."

"That I'll be sure to collect." I gallantly snapped the flaps of my hat down over my ears and waited while Augustino shuffled around the counter to unlock the door.

"I'm here all the time. Got a cot in the kitchen. God knows there's no place else worth going. Just bang on the glass. I'm a light sleeper."

I shook the hand he offered and stepped outside. A chill swirl of wind whipped around the corner to welcome me back into the night.

I trudged north along Lexington. The worst of the gales had passed, but now snow was falling in that slow, steady drift of the all-night storm. The street was white to my ankles, and getting whiter. But the frigid cold had left with the wind. The city was quiet, hushed as a city is only when it's slowly being buried.

This real estate was once some of the liveliest in Manhattan. Right up to the early nineties these streets had been real bazaars twenty-four hours a day. Anything one's little heart desired could be done or had. For a price, of course, but the price was always the biggest part of the thrill.

Now everything and everyone was asleep, locked up tight. The whole world, it seemed, had fallen asleep ten years ago and was still waiting for its handsome prince to come along.

Certainly no one was awake at Darling's when I finally arrived. The house looked dark, but I had walked off most of my gloom. I felt flush and forgiving, and picturing the sexy little tableau that lay behind those dark windows even made me warmer. In my mind I could see an empty champagne bottle lying amid the clutter of a mutually successful seduction. Darling, the still potent clown, wrapped between the long legs of his latest conquest.

I turned to go, not really wishing to disturb the post-coital tranquility inside. Augustino was right. Nothing was so important it couldn't be put on ice for another day. Then I noticed Darling's front door wasn't quite closed.

I gave it a tentative pull, but the dead bolt kept it from locking, and suddenly I was curious. I remembered closing the door tightly on my way out, which only meant someone had used the door since me. But who? Darling's guest? I didn't want to interrupt Darling's recreation, but, if he was alone, we did have an appointment.

I used the bell first, but after a minute when no one answered, I knuckled the door lightly. It swung open and cautiously I stepped inside, mildly aware of the slush puddles I was leaving on the beautiful stone floor of the darkened hallway.

The house was absolutely quiet. Too quiet, as they say. To break the perfect, unnatural tranquility I was tempted to announce my presence with a shout. But I kept my mouth closed and waited while my eyes adjusted themselves to the gloom. Then I moved toward the living room. Enough feeble light sifted through the window to give me a glimpse of what looked too much like a body on the floor to be anything else. Instantly, I knew it was Darling. It had to be. It had been one of those days.

I found a lamp, switched it on, and immediately wished I hadn't. Darling was on his back caught from the waist up under the heavy glass table. The weight of the glass stretched the skin of his cheek so that, in the harsh light, the hairline scars of a dozen facelifts stood out like termite tracks in a terrarium. His head was turned, and his hair stiffly parted by that same weight.

All those scars were pretty compared with the expression on Darling's face. His eyes and mouth were pulled open by the glass, his lips drawn tightly over his teeth, his face frozen into a gargoyle's scream. Except for a skimpy pair of lavender briefs, he was naked, and both arms were tensed across his chest, their veins and sinews distended into bloated filigrees on his now-crepey skin. The fingers of his right hand were

splayed into a stiff claw which he had dug into his chest mat.
His left hand was pressed into his throat by the weight of
the glass which covered him. His legs were drawn up tight
at an impossible angles, as if his knees had burst their joints.
In the bright light, Darling looked shriveled, distorted, a
cruel cartoon of that imaginary relative whose picture I had
once carried in my wallet.

I've seen my share of death. Who hasn't? It's only one
more joy of growing older. A person gets used to it. The
cyclist, for example, was unnerving, but the blood and the
mayhem, as grim as it was, somehow helped reduce even that
death to acceptability. But I had never in my life seen death's
bloodless stain like on Darling. His was unholy death, unnatural, not grannies passing away soundlessly in old-age
homes, not gore and guts, but purest death, a distillation of
most perfect agony, the personal and private horror that,
unnamed and faceless, reaches out for us from the groaning
pit of our blackest nightmares.

I was lucky. My legs reacted before my stomach. I recoiled
into the hallway until I hit the opposite wall. Sliding to the
floor, I sat there a good minute before realizing I was chewing
a hole in my own cheek. It took me longer than a minute to
calm my breath and retrain my lungs to breathe in rhythm.

I sat huddled against that wall, as far from the grinning
specter of Darling's face as I could get, for fifteen minutes
before I knew I wasn't going to lose that fine dinner of
Augustino's. All that time, I kept trying to convince myself
that this didn't affect my case one bit. I failed miserably. I
suspected someone was playing this game for blood.

6

Even after the fifteen minutes had passed, all I could do was stand, and with my toes feeling what my eyes weren't ready to see, make my way back into the living room. Peeking just enough to see where to throw, I buried Darling's face under my coat.

Then I found the phone and dialed the number I wanted. The connection was instant, but the tone still sounded thirteen times before anyone answered.

"Yeah? Midtown East."

"I want to report a murder."

"Okay," the man at the other end responded unenthusiastically.

"Send a car to One Seventy-seven East Ninety-third."

"Can it wait till morning? We're on short shift now. I don't know if you're aware of the fact, but it's snowing. I doubt I can even get a car up there. East Ninety-third. That's Manhattan?"

"Yeah, right across the river from Queens. Can't miss it. It's the island with all the tall, dark buildings."

"Listen, chuckles. You want some help or don't you? I don't have to take this crap from the public anymore. Our union . . . "

"I know all about your union. I also know I can file a complaint with your sergeant if I don't get some cooperation."

"I am the sergeant."

"That must impress somebody. See if you can find a car to send up here tonight."

"I'll do what I can."

I put down the phone knowing it would be hours before anyone showed up. I gave myself the choice of having a look around the house or sitting on the couch watching Darling's corpse. At that point, I was telling myself Darling's death, however unsettling, was only incidental to the job I had been hired to do. As far as I was concerned, I had already seen more of Darling than I wanted to.

I felt my way out into the hallway, switching on every light I could find. Conservation of energy is one thing, but preservation of sanity takes precedence. The house batteries of a dead man don't come into it at all.

Darling's house, like many old brownstones, was built on a lot that was no more than eight or nine meters wide but was a country mile long. The entrance hall ran along the left side of the building to a junction of heavy wooden stairs. I took the low road first and walked down half a floor to the kitchen and, beyond that, to a dining room as conservatively decorated as the living room had been high potency. A round walnut table, polished to a mirror finish, dwarfed a set of four perfectly matched Early American cane-backed chairs. A demi-fireplace was neatly framed by a pair of delicate French doors which led out to a small terrace. The heavy, red velvet curtains were parted enough to let me see the iron gates covering the doors were locked with massive bolts that looked as if they hadn't been opened in years.

The table, set for two, revealed the ruins of a roastlet nestling on a bone china platter. From the copious remains on both plates, both diners obviously had activities other than eating on their minds. The empty champagne bottle lay floating on its side, but the only glasses on the table were filled with water.

The other room on the lower floor was a pantry/kitchen which, while well stocked, looked more like a storeroom in a bomb shelter than a rich man's larder. Cases of dried fruit lay covered by a thick layer of dust. From the prices marked on the boxtops, I surmised the fruit had been there for a long time. You haven't been able to buy a box of dried apples for fifteen dollars in that many years.

I left the lower floor and walked back up the steps, still not searching for clues as much as avoiding them. That face under the glass loomed around every dark corner, and I had to clench my fists to keep it from greeting me.

The second floor was laid out along the lines of the first. The large, dark room in the front was a study of some sort. Astrology charts and what I assumed were numerologist's tables covered one whole wall. An ancient manual typewriter was waiting on a wooden desk the size of a billiard table. I checked the drawers one by one, and found nothing that shouldn't have been there.

A stack of typewritten pages lay next to the typewriter, a pair of gold-rimmed spectacles serving as a paperweight on top of them. I didn't have to read far to see the pages were the early chapters of an autobiography that would never be finished. Too bad, for Darling had a good sense of himself. The title of his opus was *The Steel Facade: Prospects and Broken Promises*. Other books, a curious mixture of beautifully bound vellum editions and cheap, coverless paperbacks, were scattered randomly around the floor. I found several loose-leaf binders packed with yellowed clippings and dog-eared photographs. I turned through the most recent reviews but none had been written in the last five years. I felt as if I were going through a dead man's pockets so I laid the binder down.

Next to an extention phone on a small table, I found what some people might call a real clue, Darling's fancy desk calendar. The page for that day, Friday, December tenth, had already been torn out. On Saturday's page was the notation, "Allison Bashcock, 1 P.M." On that page, I could just make out the impression of the previous day's memo. It was a set of initials which might have been J.D. or L.D., and the words "brings time." I tore Saturday's page out and stuck it in my pocket. Friday's page was nowhere to be found. I even checked the trashcan.

Darling's bathroom, directly over the kitchen, wasn't even as comfortable a room as the white tile closet I've got in my apartment, even if his hot-water tap looked like it occasionally still did what it had been designed to do. I checked the shower stall and the toilet seat, which, incidently, was up, the way a man would have left it. But that was circumstantial evidence. So was the medicine chest, which was chock full of some potent mixtures. None of the seals on the bottles were broken. One whole shelf was filled with unopened aspirin bottles. That fit. Figuring on assuring himself a lifetime supply Darling probably stocked up when you could still get the stuff. On the top shelf, I noticed an empty can of my brand of roach powder.

A halo of rose color ringed the inside of the sink. Many things could have caused the stain, and it wasn't nearly red enough to be blood. I picked two crumpled tissues out of the waste can; one was smeared with a deep blue I assumed was lipstick, the other was too damp for investigation. I dropped both back in the can, neither being the sort of clue I was inclined to collect, and the shade of blue wasn't one you'd forget.

The rear room was where Darling slept and, judging from the decor, had also done some serious entertaining. A round bed three meters in diameter was set on the floor. One stepped into it over a bright, multicolored carpeted parapet half a meter high. A bank of switches on the parapet controlled the room lighting, the curtains, and a music center, the firmness and temperature of the mattress, and the mirrored triview screen in the ceiling. The bed was well rumpled, the dark-burgundy covers and pale-blue sheets twisted into a ball the way only one pastime twists bedclothes. One champagne glass lay tipped on its side on the shelf. I discovered the shards of the other on the floor when I circumnavigated Darling's playpen.

Compared to the bed, the rest of the chromette furniture in the room seemed sedate. Three chairs covered by plush silver lamé surrounded a chrome coffee table at the far end of the room. Three walls were covered by mirrors. The fourth was a huge triptych of Darling in the three great roles of his career. Each panel slid open to reveal a closet stuffed with a selection of clothing which rivaled that of any store. Little of it, however, seemed the least bit worn. A few pairs of briefs, each a duplicate of Darling's skimpy funeral suit, lay in the top drawer of the broad dresser set into the middle closet. The second drawer was empty except for a white cardigan sweater. That drawer was lined with a front page of *The New York Times* dating back over fifteen years. The headline announced federal troops had finally recaptured a Louisiana gasfield after a week-long battle. The article went on to report that the retreating Louisiana National Guardsmen had sabotaged the wells. The victorious general predicted the wells would be back in operation within the month. They had never been repaired. After the natural gas rebellion, production was never the same.

Other stories on the page detailed more developments in that brief war. At the bottom of the page an insert lined in black reported the Yankees had won the World Series for the fifth consecutive year. Nothing on the page indicated why Darling had chosen this particular paper to line his drawer.

The bottom drawer was filled to the brim with old tennis shoes. Each was a left shoe and the sole of every single one was worn through at the big toe.

I sat in one of the plush chairs and contemplated Darling's bedroom. It reminded me of the kind of setup that might have once given a college freshmen wet dreams, but I couldn't imagine any adult seriously inhabiting such a place. I leaned back in the chair and felt something hard under my hip. It was the silver-cased transducer Darling had proudly shown me earlier in the day. I picked it up and weighed it most tentatively in my palm, feeling ghoulish at the slight possibility that I was holding a dead man's time. I slipped the transducer in my pocket and changed chairs.

I began to piece together some of the possible scenarios that might have been played out since my earlier visit. Darling and his visitor had obviously shared a quiet dinner before retiring to the bedroom. There they had finished the champagne and attended to the evening's main event. Sometime during the go-round, Darling had laid his transducer on the chair. Most likely, both Darling and his visitor had used the bathroom. Then something very important must have taken Darling downstairs. He had never returned.

I still wasn't in a mood for guessing how he had died. It must have been horrible. Someone could have surprised him downstairs, maybe even the woman. Robbery and crimes of passion do still occur occasionally, even if the motivation for either has become almost extinct. Nothing I could imagine would leave a body looking like that. Certainly not the table crushing him. I might have considered Darling's time deposit had gone haywire, but I had his transducer in my pocket.

I pulled the page of the calendar out of my pocket and looked it over. I still couldn't make out the impression from that day, but tomorrow's appointment was obvious enough. Darling, for some reason, was anticipating a visit from Allison Bashcock. The reason might have been innocent, or it might not have been. Finding out which seemed reasonably urgent. Almost two hours had passed since I had called the police, and I was running out of safe ways to entertain myself. I desperately wanted someone to take Darling's body out of my life. The thought of leaving before the police came crossed my mind, but I knew if I wasn't there to supply them with the right answers, there was a slight chance they might look for some of their own. The police are unpredictable like that. Sometimes, when you least expect it, they make a federal case out of a jaywalking ticket. Like any sleeping giant, law and order still occasionally stretches its long arms. If you happen to be in the way, well, that's your hard luck. My leaving the scene would make one of two consequences certain. Either Darling's death would be reported as a suicide or as a murder in which I would undoubtedly figure. I had left too many signs of my presence to retire anonomously. Neither choice was at all appetizing to a public-minded citizen like me.

So I stayed and, like it or not, was mentally listing all the ways people have found to die when I heard the door bell. I wasn't slow about getting downstairs to open it.

"Damn it, Hughes, you get around!"

"You two don't do so badly yourselves. Are you the only two cops on duty tonight?"

"I told you, Slovinsky. I said don't answer that call. We had only an hour worth of shift left. But no, he had to open his face and tell them we were still uptown."

I opened the front door widely, but neither cop seemed anxious to come inside. Slovinsky frowned at me after a second. "Sergeant said there was a stiff. Two in one night, Hughes? I hope you haven't developed any bad habits in your old age."

"Yeah, we only just finished cleaning up the last one." Chick pointed over his shoulder with his thumb. "This one better be in one piece."

I showed them into the living room. "There he is."

"Who's he?" Slovinsky asked.

"Gregory Darling."

"The old movie actor?"

I nodded.

"I seen him all the time when I was a kid," Slovinsky reflected solemnly. "My mother was nuts for him. It was his eyes that got her, I think. Who would've thought he was still alive?"

"You're a little late for autographs."

Chick had wandered into the lagoon created by the couch. "Why you got his face covered?"

With my foot, I shoved the coat off the glass and showed him Darling's face.

Slovinsky went white and turned away, but Chick just stared in openmouthed fascination. Neither said anything for a second. Then Chick swallowed greedily and asked, "Jesus. What did that? The bastard looks like he was trying to crawl out of his own skin."

"Put the coat back, Hughes."

I did as Slovinsky asked, but Chick was still fascinated. He got down on his knees for a closer examination. "What's the glass for?" he asked, tapping the table with his ragged fingernails. "That what stiffed him?"

"It's a coffee table. Floats in the air with electromagnets. No, I don't think it killed him. The glass is heavy, but not that heavy. Besides, it doesn't really fall to the floor when you turn it off. It sort of drifts. You'd have time to shave and shower before it landed on top of you."

"Oh, yeah?" Slovinsky glared at me, suddenly hostile. "How come you know so much about it, Hughes?"

"Darling showed me how the table works. I was here earlier in the afternoon."

"That sounds convenient. What were you doing here?"

"Darling was involved in a case I'm working on. You want to hear the whole story?"

Slovinsky held up his hand. "I'll take your word, Hughes. It's your problem, and, like I said before, we got enough of our own. We each got our job to do, right? What do you want done with the body?"

I spoke without thinking his question through. "They still do autopsies downtown? I'm curious what killed him." That was true, but more than that, it occurred to me they would report Darling's death as a suicide if I didn't stop them. I kept telling myself his death wasn't part of my case, but I didn't know it for sure. It never hurts to play safe.

"You sure like to complicate things, Hughes," Slovinsky answered after a second. "But I guess we owe you one. Chick, can we get an autopsy without too much paperwork?"

Chick was still inspecting the plate glass. He didn't look up. "Autopsy? I suppose. I used to date one of the coroner's assistants. She'll do him up for us without too many questions. You want thick slices or thin, Hughes?" He stood up and looked at me. "You say this table floats. I'd sure like to see that."

"Try the switch next to the door."

Slovinsky had already started for the door. "I'll get a sack for the stiff. Probably take an extra large. I hope we got one left."

Slovinsky wasn't moving at all slowly, but Chick beat him to the door. The larger cop flicked the wall switch, and the glass over Darling's body started to level itself. Chick waited until it just cleared the body before he turned the table off. It settled back down without a whisper. "Pretty cute little trick he had there. Wonder what a setup like this costs?"

I thought about showing Chick the upstairs. If he loved the table so much, he'd probably go crazy over the bed. But I was in as much a hurry to get out of there as Slovinsky. "They probably don't make them anymore."

My answer disappointed Chick. "Nah, probably not." He flicked the switch again and slowly started walking back to where I was standing. Suddenly, he caught himself in mid-stride, his face looking as if someone had just poured a pitcher of ice water down his back.

"Jesus, Hughes! Your stiff's moving."

I turned in time to see Darling's head, still locked in that endless howl of agony, turn slowly so that his unseeing eyes stared at me.

I'm sure I screamed, because Slovinsky was back in the room before either Chick or I moved. He was carrying a heavy plastic sack under his arm. "What's the matter with you two? You trying to wake the whole neighborhood?"

Chick licked his lips and answered. "The meat just moved his head."

"Both of you are doping."

"Like hell we are. Chick is right. Darling's head just turned. It was looking the other way before."

Slovinsky looked over at Darling and saw we were right. "Probably just a muscular reaction to the glass being moved. The guy's dead. He's not going anywhere, not by himself at any rate." Slovinsky pulled a portable encephalometer from his shirt pocket and held it against Darling's forehead. "See? Needle's flat. No brain activity whatsoever. Dead is dead.

He's stiff as a board. Stiff means dead. That's why they call them stiffs. Come on, Chick. You've seen a thousand." Slovinsky's bravado sounded just positive enough to be true.

"Yeah," the rookie cop said, unfreezing himself and quickly finishing the distance to Darling's body. "Let's get him in the bag. Sooner we get out of here, better I'll like it."

The two cops hurried Darling into the sack. Chick had to force the corpse's legs flat so they could stuff him in. When they finally got the velcro seals into place, I admit I breathed a little easier. Each cop grabbed the handle at either end of the sack and hoisted the still-rigid body like a log between them.

"Listen, Hughes, why don't you call it a day? We've had our fill of your handiwork."

"That makes three of us, Slovinsky. Just wait while I turn the lights off. I'd like a ride downtown. Someone stole my bike. You wouldn't have any idea who, would you?"

"No," Chick said much too quickly. "You think we got the time to chase down nickel-and-dime stuff like that?"

While the two of them lugged Darling out, I went around and shut off the lights. As I was walking out the front door, I remembered something else that needed shutting down. I was too late. Darling's table was already fading to the floor. He had been right about the amount of power the table drew from the house batteries. I switched it off anyway. Then I picked up my hat and closed the front door behind myself.

Half an hour later, Chick and Slovinsky dropped me in front of my building. The snow had stopped, but no one was clearing the streets. It was almost half past one. As I turned to go, Chick called to me through the prowl-car window.

"Hughes, call the morgue tomorrow afternoon. Ask for Mary Dietz. But don't bother her with too many questions. They don't like complications down there any more than we do."

I nodded. "I won't."

Chick smiled, rolled the window up, and the prowl car moved away, its electric motor a purr compared to the churning of its steel treads on the snow.

I went inside, pressed the elevator button, and walked up the five floors to my apartment.

7

About seven the next morning, I quit pretending to be asleep and hauled myself out of bed. Instead of worrying about the cause of my insomnia while the coffee water warmed, I busied my mind planning things I would do that day to justify the juicy fee Wightman was paying me. Everyone has rough nights now and then. Headache, backache, heartache, anything can bring one on. My personal ache was a particular sad story I seem to remember only at four in the morning. So sleepless nights never surprise me. Trying to digest two corpses in twenty-four hours without having them act up on me was too much to expect.

Wonder of wonders. There was some juice in the city lines. I pushed my luck and went for a boil. The last thing I wanted that morning was tepid coffee. When the water was bubbling, I poured half of it in a cup. With the other half, I poached an egg. I broke five saltines into a second cup, tossed in the egg, and sloshed the whole mess around until I couldn't tell what was what. I know better than to skimp on nourishment. There's a sore spot in my stomach to remind me of things like that. If this day was going to be anything like the one before, I wanted to have a good meal under my belt.

I waited until after nine before phoning Allison Bashcock. After several rings, someone picked up the receiver. I knew only because I could hear breathing.

"Allison Bashcock, please."

I heard the receiver change hands, and a female voice, clear and well rounded, full, and husky with morning sensuality, answered.

"This is Allison Bashcock."

"Miss Bashcock, my name is Jack Hughes. Sorry to disturb you this early but . . . "

"That's all right, Mr. Hughes. Rinaldo was just leaving."

"Yes, well, I'm a private investigator. I've been hired by . . . "

"A private investigator!" she said with what sounded like genuine amazement. "How lucky. Mr. Hughes, I know this might be an imposition, but I'd love to meet you. Could we get together soon? Perhaps this morning? I know a lovely place on West Twenty-third, just off Broadway. The Sands."

"I know where it is."

"Wonderful. I'll be there in an hour. Rinaldo!" I heard her stiffle a giggle. "Mr. Hughes, would eleven be too late?"

"No, but . . . "

"No buts, Mr. Hughes. Eleven o'clock. Ask for my table."

I did start to tell her why I had called in the first place, but realized I was telling my tale to a dead line.

That left two more names to be contacted, Lea Dark and Victor Sieg. It was no accident they were last. Both people were direct links to my past, and, as I said, I wasn't looking forward to seeing how well some old scars of mine had healed.

I dialed the office number listed for Senator Sieg and got an electrosecretary which informed me the Senator was still in Washington and wouldn't be back till Monday noon. I left my name and number and asked him to call me as soon as he got in. When the electrosecretary asked the reason for my call, I said I was an old friend of the Senator's. It wasn't a total lie. I was, after all, very nearly fifty.

Which meant Lea Dark was well past sixty. Lea's address was still 87 Riverside Drive. When Lea divorced Alex Dark, she drove him out of a house that had been in his family for over a century. Lea had an uncanny knack for wanting only those things someone else loved most dearly. Since the divorce, she had stayed locked up in that mansion fighting off the world. Everyone assumed Lea would sell the house after Alex's death, which was the earliest she could liquidate his estate according to provisions of the divorce settlement. Instead, she kept living there as if nothing had happened, attempting in vain to preserve through her home a class she had never earned on her own. I once heard someone say nobody knew where Lea Dark came from, but everybody knew where she was going. I never saw any reason to dispute that statement.

When I finally dialed the number listed for her in the microfiles, a butler with a voice as fine and friendly as a spider's web informed me: "Mrs. Dark is not accepting phone calls or appointments. Matters of utmost urgency may be directed through her daughter, who maintains offices at 342 East Forty-second Street." The hired hand finished his little piece, and I thanked him, feeling that same stupid feeling I always get thanking an electrosecretary.

I checked the phone book under Joan Dark and found, as usual, only cab drivers listed. The microfiles were a bit more helpful. I dialed the number they gave, but no one answered.

I didn't need the microfiles to tell me that, while Joan was the only child either Lea or Alex had ever had, she was always much closer to her father; not strange, considering her mother's disposition. In 1980, after her parents's divorce, Joan went to Paris to live with Alex. She must have been about fifteen at the time. It was Joan who tended Alex for those three years of alcoholic decline which ended in his death. The experience must have matured her, because I remember hearing that shortly after Alex's death, Joan returned to live with her mother, an act of self-sacrifice a child of eighteen couldn't have made.

Alex may have died of a rotten liver, but my memories of him were all good. He, or rather the firm in which he was a partner, hired me right out of Harvard, and Alex exhibited an interest in my career that exceeded the interest a partner normally shows for a raw recruit. There was always a cheerful greeting, and, on the many occasions when we worked together, he received my opinions as those of a respected colleague rather than a rank novice. Alex was a splendid lawyer as well as a scrupulously honest human being, a rare combination. I wasn't the only of his many friends who hated to see him get ripped to pieces by his wife's buzz-saw sensitivity. Alex had married Lea under questionable circumstances. The stories I heard all involved her being a waitress in a bar near where Alex had gone to law school, Emory University in Atlanta. He must have been drunk when he married her.

The character of the firm changed noticeably when Alex left, and, to a large degree, so did all of us who remained. Looking back, of course, it's easy to blame that unfortunate evolution on the pressures of a changing world and the Apathera in general. But, more than once, I've thought that if Alex had stayed around, the rest of us might have resisted those pressures a bit better. I know that opinion is probably naive in view of the way he chose to die, and it might have been different if I had seen him during those last years. But I hadn't, so in my eyes Alex Dark never quite lost that luster a master is assigned by a thankful apprentice.

It was well above freezing outside, which meant last night's snow was already slush. I pulled on a pair of waterproof boots and reminded myself to keep away from curbs. The three-a-day weekend subway schedules were in effect, a holdover from the days when weekends actually meant something. I had more time on my hands than money and decided a quick walk downtown would be better for me than an expensive cab ride. My bike wouldn't have done me any good on the slushy streets anyway.

The hike began well, but I ran into a delay on Lexington at Forty-sixth Street. The yo-yo temperatures of the last forty-eight hours had had their usual effect. The facade of an old building had come loose, and a torrent of bricks was cascading into the street. Building failures aren't as common as they were a few years ago, but weather changes still occasionally bring the inevitable structural responses. The laws of natural selection weed out any pedestrian who forgets the middle of the streets are safer than the sidewalk; more than one person has suffered the unanticipated indignity of premature burial that way.

The Sands is one of the few class restaurants that survived the end of the expense account. It was a gaudy, class-conscious place that served tasteless food in a tasteless manner. Once upon a time, in a former life, another client had taken me to lunch there, and I had been honestly shocked by the exorbitant prices they wanted for processed food. That was during the Apathera, but I didn't expect the intervening years to have improved matters.

The Sands, for no discernible reason, was still packing them in. Tables set outside on the snow-cleared sidewalks were crowded with chattering idiots who couldn't tell the difference between a mid-winter thaw and the Gobi in August. I went inside, hoping Allison Bashcock wasn't one of those prospective pneumonia cases. When I asked the dainty maitre d' if Miss Bashcock had arrived, he chewed a mouthful of tongue, looked at me as if I were a bad toothache, and shook his head.

"I was supposed to meet her here at eleven."

"If you've got a package for her, you can leave it with me."

"No package. She told me to wait at her table."

He glared at his watch and chewed some more tongue. You can always tell ex-smokers by their alternative compulsions. "I suppose she'll be in soon enough. Over there." He pointed to a corner near the window. "Her table." He waved blithely toward the empty space.

"She bringing the table with her?"

He looked at me once again and shook his head with clear distain. He reached behind his little stand and fiddled with a valve I couldn't see. Then he swept his hand toward the window with the same sense of drama that Moses reserved for occasions like the parting of the Red Sea. "Behold." The floor in the empty space divided, and, out of the hole, a table for two was slowly rising. It was, I admit, an interesting touch, though no one in the restaurant but the maitre d' and I gave it even a passing glance. When everything was locked in its proper place, the floor snapped shut with a hydraulic whine.

"That's handy."

"Yes," the maitre d' sniffed. "As long as the wind blows."

I nodded understandingly and went over to wait for Allison Bashcock. My wait wasn't long.

You just knew that everyone else knew when Allison Bashcock entered the room. Three dozen heads caught themselves halfway through a quick glance. Allison Bashcock is tall, maybe a meter seventy, and pure curved geometry. The second thing I noticed was how her carrot-colored hair, plaited in two long braids, crossed her breasts like bandoleers. If she owned a coat, she had removed it before she came in. Except for her hair, she was naked from the waist up, and not overdressed from there down. And yet, despite the frontal attack of supple flesh, she draped innocence over herself like a warm fur. The end result was the daughter all men dream of though are better off without.

Allison ignored everyone ignoring her and strolled over to me. "Mr. Hughes?"

"I hope so."

She sat in the chair opposite mine and stared soulfully into my eyes. While she stared, I tried using some of that sonar sensitivity we all use to gauge people at first sight, but I got nothing for my efforts but deep water working in her guileless eyes. There was no way to tell if she dressed like that for seduction or by ingenuous accident. After a moment, she pressed her lips together in a businesslike manner that seemed somehow a third side of her totally inconsistent costume.

"You look nothing like I pictured."

"What did you expect? Humphrey Bogart?"

She smiled. "No, of course not, but someone a little less attractive."

"Than?"

Allison cocked her head. "Why, than you sounded on the phone. For one thing, I thought you'd be much older." She straightened a little in her chair and crossed her arms under both breasts, lifting all four of us just that much. It wasn't hard to see why Gregory Darling had been looking forward to a visit from this woman.

"Our conversation was so brief," I began. "How did you deduce so many things about me?"

"Rinaldo told me. But he wasn't even close. That's unusual. He's usually so accurate."

"Does Rinaldo know me?"

"Only from this morning. He answered the phone."

I nodded, not caring to pursue the matter further. "You never gave me a chance to explain why I called, Miss Bashcock."

She stopped me by raising her hand in the two-fingered Boy Scout sign for silence, though I'm sure she hadn't the vaguest idea of that sign's origins. "Call me Allison and I'll call you Jack. And before we start talking, let's eat. I'm famished." She stood up dramatically. "I recommend the potage et poisson platter. The meat here is always synthetic, but the seafood is sometimes real."

I followed her over to the broad menu counter where several grotesquely over-colored meals were holographically displayed in glass cubicles. I suppose they had been designed to tease the senses, and all the food looked designed rather than cooked. I chose the fish and soup platter on Allison's recommendation even though I couldn't tell which half was soup and which half was fish. I started to slide my plastic into the slot marked "Pay," but the machine spit it right back in my hand.

"I'm so sorry," Allison said. "I always forget they accept only gold cards here. Please, let me buy lunch." She slid her high-priced disk into the slot and before you could say "Open Sesame" a hatchway opened and out rolled two blue plate specials the appearance of which was not improved by the fact they actually came on blue plates.

We were at the table again before Allison spoke. "Now, why did you want to see me, Mr. Hughes? You tell me. Then I'll explain why I wanted to see you."

That seemed equitable. "You're a client of Ivory Wightman's, aren't you?"

"I didn't know you could tell by looking. Does the scar show?" She shared a smile with me and then lifted her hair so I could see the white half-moon scar at the base of her skull.

"No, your scar doesn't show, Allison. I'm working for Wightman. He claims to have some of your life stored on magnetic tape."

"What of it?"

"Earlier this week, several tapes were stolen."

"And was mine one of them?" she asked placidly.

When I nodded, not even the slightest tremor rippled her calm face.

"That doesn't seem to bother you. Did you know about the theft?"

"No." Allison placed a morsel of food on her tongue. "Did you take them?"

Her question blindsided me, and my answer had too much quickness in it. "No, I was hired to recover the tapes."

"Why?"

"You'd like your tape back, wouldn't you?"

She popped another piece of fish in her mouth and shook her head placidly. "No."

"Then you must not have much time saved up. That, or you don't really believe Wightman's gizmo works."

"I'd be a fool to pay him all the money I do if I thought he was cheating me, wouldn't I? The time deposit works perfectly. And I've got over six months on account. I know because that Miss . . . " She orchestrated the silence with her fork for a moment. "The cheap spread Wightman lives with?"

"Jeanette Dobbson."

"I know because she made a point of telling me the last time I made a deposit."

"The thought of losing six months doesn't bother you?"

"Should it?"

"If I was told six months of my life was suddenly lost, I think it would bother me."

"That would depend on your reason for storing time in the first place." She looked me in the eye, and, without a trace of the cuteness which to that point had been one-third of her image, said, "I hope that six months is gone. As if it never was."

She paused a moment before she continued. "My attitude seems to shock you, Jack. It shouldn't." She rubbed at the hint of fuzz on her upper lip. "Your oily friend Wightman thinks he's selling a passbook to future happiness. The squid would charge twice as much if he suspected his transducer is all that makes my life bearable right now. Those months of mine on tape, Jack, are the wretched accumulation of thousands of boring and burdensome minutes. The transducer is my laxative, the way I unstuff my life, kill all that unwanted, excess time. I'd go absolutely crazy if I had to live fully each moment of every day. I just wish I could purge myself of more time than I can now. To quote our illustrious president, 'To hell with the future. Just get me through this afternoon.' My fondest wish is for a present so limp that every passing second doesn't rub me raw."

"Quite a statement coming from someone with a world of time to burn."

"Trite, Jack. Very trite. But then, so it is: Looks can be

deceiving. It's the light of that burning time that lets me see what makes the world work. Nothing. Inertia. Momentum. Look at all these people in here. Out on the street. Anywhere. They're all burned out. Or maybe they never got lit. I don't know. I can't remember a time when people enjoyed life as little as they do now. And I know what little fire the world has left isn't worth the spit it would take to put it out."

"Now, I bet you thought that up all by yourself." There was more cynicism in my voice than I wished, but I couldn't help it. Her neo-nineties attitude annoyed me. I couldn't see where someone with as much going for her as she obviously had could have developed it. I was tempted to say more, to tell her off, but I stopped myself. I had too many questions to ask her to start an argument. I also remembered what people always ask neo-ninetyites. If she felt life was so useless, why didn't she head for the back door? She remembered the same thing.

"Isn't this where you ask me why I don't do a deep-end?"

"I admit thinking something like that."

"Don't be ashamed, Jack. I've given it some thought, but it's too fashionable. Too glitchy."

I knew better than to respond.

"I'm too stable. Too smart." She waited for my reaction, but got nothing for her efforts. "Or, would you prefer to say stupid? But I do know when I'm on the transducer, I don't worry about anything. Nothing at all. It's better than drugs. It doesn't make you fat, bald, toothless, or sterile." Allison blew softly on the last forkful of her lunch. She swallowed without chewing. "Though I couldn't imagine why anyone would want children." Then she raised her head and passed me a frail smile. "You still haven't said why you wanted to see me, Jack."

"I thought you might give me a reason why these five tapes in particular were stolen." I reached into my pocket and handed her the list Wightman had given me. "Know any of the other folks on this list?"

She glanced at the paper for a moment. "Every one. Either

personally or by reputation. I doubt you'd have a hard time finding too many people not familiar with most of us."

"Can you think of something you might have in common with the others?"

She shook her head. "No, not offhand. But I could probably name something I have in common with each of them individually."

"Victor Sieg?" I asked.

"I voted for Mr. Sieg once when I was still voting. The company I work for handles his public relations. Once, I got a fan letter from his wife. She enjoyed my first book so much she just had to let me know it."

"Carlo Mountain?"

"He's old and so rich he can hire someone else to fart for him. Of course, he runs Mountain Industries and has invented a thousand things. But he doesn't get around much socially. I've never met him."

"Lea Dark?"

Allison frowned. "My mother detests her. I've met her once or twice, and I'll agree with my mother's opinion. As far as I can tell, Mrs. Dark has absolutely none of that southern class she advertises. She's just another phony iron butterfly. I think my uncle knew her. At least I saw an old picture of the two of them in one of his scrapbooks. He took it from me, tore it up, and refused to answer any questions about her. Strange, because he usually loves to tell me about his old lovers. I guess that's the sort of hidden connection you're looking for."

"What do you mean?"

"My uncle is Gregory Darling."

I started to nod, and kept it up for two reasons. I should have known without her telling me that she was Darling's neice. It's bad for business if people get the impression you don't know things everyone thinks you should, and business was bad enough already. I made a mental note to check the data-console files more completely before I went any further. That was one reason I kept nodding.

My other reason was much better. I could see from Allison's cool attitude that she knew nothing about Darling's death. I didn't want to be the person to tell her. I've had too many people go willy on me when I've been the bearer of bad news. I don't like the feeling at all. So I nodded as if I knew Darling was her uncle and kept nodding until I could think of something intelligent to say.

"Did you know any of these people had time accounts?"

"Only Gregory. He was the person who put me on to time accounts in the first place. Though we use them for quite different reasons."

"You never saw any of the other people at Wightman's?"

"I never saw anyone at Wightman's."

"How long have you had an account?"

She shrugged and disarranged the critical positioning of the braids across her chest. As she quickly readjusted the braid ends back into her pants, she looked up at me almost sheepishly. "It's a silly style and I haven't quite got the knack of it. I don't usually dress this way. It's for your benefit. Rinaldo told me you'd be a sucker for tits. He said all detectives were."

I nodded and tried to look professional. "How long have you been a depositor?"

"Two, maybe two and a half years."

"You've never used any of this time you've deposited?"

She shook her head slowly, more conscious now of not disturbing her hair blouse.

"So you don't know whether the system actually works?"

She shrugged. "I know all I need to know. The part I care about works well enough."

"And you don't plan on using this time when the world gets a little more friendly?"

"What makes you think the Apathera will ever be over?"

This was the second person I'd met in an many days who seemed to think the Apathera hadn't ended. "Apathera. It meant Apathy Era. Era means a period of time. That period of time came to an official end years ago."

"When? Tell me. Apathera was a clever name some television newsman gave to a problem, but just because everyone got tired of the name doesn't mean that the problem went away. The malaise is as strong even if it hasn't got a clever name."

"You know, I recently met a man who was convinced the Apathera was only a malfunction of chronology. He told me it didn't start until 1991 and wouldn't be over until 2002."

She nodded. "I know several numerologists too. I've also heard a thousand other stories about the causes of the Apathera, some more ridiculous than that one." She paused a moment, almost as if she were trying to catch her breath. "How old are you?"

"Forty-nine. Actually, fifty, in a couple weeks."

"Then maybe you can remember life being better than today. I can't. I was born the year the war in Vietnam ended, and, as long as I can remember, people have always been talking about how much better life used to be at some indefinite point in the past. I was ten when the fuel rebellion broke out, and I got to see people killing each other to protect natural gas reserves. Please, give me one reason to hope life's ever going to get better. You'll be giving me a gift no one has before. I know the Apathera offically began in 1987. But the fuel shortages didn't cause the Apathera any more than the food droughts, or the blackouts, or the nuclear plant meltdowns, or the climate changes, or even southern California sliding into the ocean. They were all just the death rattles of civilization. Why were the sabotaged gas wells never repaired? Or San Francisco? It burned to the ground once before in this century. It suffered other earthquakes. But it wasn't abandoned then. Why this time? The country lived through food riots before, but there weren't mass suicides then. The country once thrived without gasoline. Why has it folded up and died? Why has the population decreased so much in the last ten years? Why have people stopped having children? Give me reasons. Not sociological excuses. I . . . Mr. Hughes, all I'm saying is that you've managed to scrape through the majority of your years. You've stayed sane, or at least appear to have. Either way, it's to your credit, but I've got too many years to face and too little courage to put up with them. I'm too realistic to think they'll even be as good as the ones I've had so far."

I looked in her eyes for a trace of that frustrated adolescent I thought I'd find. But behind her cool, hard glare, she seemed more honest and sincere than anyone I'd met in years. She frightened the hell out of me.

"You really don't care about getting your time back, do you?"

"Tell me when I would ever want to live a second longer than necessary?" She laughed ironically. "If someone thinks my time tape is valuable to me, they're in for a rude shock. I wouldn't pay any more for its return than I would for last week's garbage." Allison watched me watching her for a few seconds. "But I haven't told you why I wanted to meet you, have I? It's simple. You're a detective, or at least willing to say you are. I've never met a detective before. You're a member of a dying profession. Just as we're all members of a dying species. One of the major characters in my new book is a detective. I thought it might be a good idea if I actually met one. Would you care if I made you a character in a book?"

"I could use the publicity."

"How long have you been a member of a dying profession?"

"Ten years, more or less."

"Do you enjoy the work?"

"It's better than working for the government like most other people."

"Before. What did you do?"

"I was a lawyer."

She nodded appreciatively. "A good one?"

"Some people thought so."

"In Manhattan?"

It was my turn to nod.

"Why did you give it up?"

"Personal reasons."

"You're married?"

I didn't answer for a moment. The floor next to us slid open and the empty table there sank into the opening. "Not any more."

"Divorce?"

"My wife slipped out the back door."

She shrugged neutrally. "I'm sorry. Did you have any children?"

"We did. My wife thought they would want to go with her."

Allison nodded slowly. She was too sensitive to probe further in that direction. Her smile lanced the serious mood she had inadvertently created. "You take your work seriously."

I looked at her young hands lying on the tabletop. They were smooth, so smooth they looked like kid gloves. "So do you."

"My writing, maybe. Not the other. I don't even take the writing as seriously as I once did. It used to be my refuge. The place I went to kill time. I've got a much better place now. It's no loss. I never wrote what might be mistaken for literature."

"People read it."

"Of course people read it." She stubbed her napkin into the puddle of broth that remained in her tray. The table next to us suddenly rose out of the floor, a bright Phoenix set for two. A couple in their mid-thirties seated themselves. They wore matching tunics that were split to the waist. One revealed a hairy chest. The other had contours instead of hair. Other than that, the diners were identical twins. Pseudo-cloning is an affectation of style I've never been fond of.

Both new diners grunted to Allison, and she responded in kind. For all the expression the three of them packed into their greeting, they could have been lobotomized.

Then Allison looked up at the massive wall clock over the food displays. "I've heard they never used to hang clocks in restaurants. People sat as long as they wanted without worrying about the time. Is that true?"

"It might be. I don't really remember."

"Today, everyone knows the time, but no one has any place to go."

"We manage to get around."

"I know. Around. And around. And around. The comical thing is, I do have some place to go right now. I'm helping my uncle write his memoirs this afternoon. He really is quite an interesting man. You should meet him sometime."

I remembered the note on Darling's desk calendar, and knew there was no need for Allison to hurry away. Of course, I didn't tell her that.

"Don't think I haven't enjoyed our conversation, Jack. I have. I'd like to talk some more about being a detective. Maybe we could get together later. After you solve this case. I'm sure I could learn a lot from you."

"And me you. I'm in the book."

"I don't have a phone book."

I scribbled my number on the back of my napkin and handed it to her. Allison looked at the number for a second, then wadded it up and threw it on her plate. The paper made a sharp indentation in the film of oil that had formed. Allison looked up at me. "I've been cursed with a photographic memory. All the more reason I need Mr. Wightman's services."

"Life is rough all around," I said, standing up with her to leave.

8

Allison Bashcock went east. I went west and, two blocks later, found a phone booth that hadn't been cannibalized. I dialed Joan Dark's number, but again got no answer. I wasn't in any particular hurry and needed to numb the bit of Allison Bashcock's pessimism that lingered in my mind, so I decided to walk up to Forty-second Street and investigate this office of Joan Dark's. It seemed the only way I had to get to her mother.

Even for a Saturday afternoon, the street was packed. At Thirty-eighth, shoppers were standing in a tight, boisterous knot around a shop window. Like a blind man in a steambath, I felt my way through the crowd to discover the cause of all the excitement. An enterprising merchant had set up his cart against the abandoned store. On its front window, he had scrawled "ONLY 20 SHOPPING DAYS LEFT TILL 2000." Creativity of that caliber was wasted huckstering shoddy South American boots.

At Forty-second Street, I remembered I had to call the morgue and get the report on Darling's autopsy.

I found one phone booth still working out of the bank of four that stood at the corner of Fifth and Forty-second. After only two rings, a husky male voice answered, "Midtown South."

"I'd like to talk to coroner's assistant Dietz."

"So would I, but she's out to lunch."

"When will she be back?"

"Couple hours. Can someone else help you?"

"I don't think so. I'm calling about an autopsy that was supposed to have been done on a man named Gregory Darling. You wouldn't know if they got to him yet, would you?"

"No, but hang on. I'll ask around."

He put the phone down, leaving me standing in the chilly phone booth. From where I was, I had a clear view of the crumbling hulk of the old Public Library. You don't usually think of buildings dying, but this one had, a long time ago. Only it had never received a burial befitting its former grandeur. The windows and doors had just been boarded over, and the grounds, building, and books left to the sympathy of time. I remember once the city had tried to use the hardscrabble park behind the library for a refugee tent city. But the huge flocks of poor all winged south for a winter that has lasted ten years.

Before they built the library, a city reservoir stood on this block, and after that, for a brief time, a crystal palace exhibition hall. What were they going to store here next? Pigeon artifacts?

Then the voice from the morgue retrieved me. "Hello? Darling's the gruesome cargo Slovinsky and Mangelli hauled in early this A.M.?"

"Right."

"Listen, you're supposed to talk to Sergeant Murtaugh."

"Who's that?"

"The detective who's been assigned to the case."

Little alarm bells started going off in my head, but, like a fool, I ignored them.

"All right, put me through."

"Murtaugh's out right now. Could you call back in an hour or so?"

"I suppose," I said with trepidation. I put the phone down and walked east between the ruined curbs of Forty-second Street and the vacant lots of buildings fallen to the promise of progress that had yet to arrive. Grand Central Terminal, the Lincoln Building, the Commodore Hotel, even the Chrysler Building, that gem of high-rising gems, had all been dismantled in favor of the complex of buildings that was going to, as the sign in the empty lot said, "Lead Manhattan into

the Brighter Tomorrow of the Third Millenium." The Park
Avenue overpass, which had once soared high over Forty-
second Street and now ended in mid-span, offered many a
prospective deep-ender the chance to take a flying leap at
the Pan Am building. Something about this long empty block
never failed to remind me of the septic jaw left after the
wisdom teeth have been yanked.

Three Forty-two East Forty-second seemed to be a healthy
incisor in that decrepit jaw. I could tell immediately it was
a high-rent sort of place. A white-haired lockmaster wearing
a gray dovetail uniform slouched next to an open elevator
that looked like more than a cheap way to get cold air from
floor to floor. The doorbell was out of order, however, and
I had to pound on the glass till I snapped the lockmaster out
of his reverie. He buzzed me through without even looking
in my direction. So much for expensive security.

I checked the building directory and saw Joan Dark's name
next to 1102. I started for the elevator but was informed by
the lockmaster that the next trip up wasn't for another twenty
minutes. He also told me that Joan Dark hadn't come in yet.
I asked if I could wait, and he pointed to a broad beige couch
at the opposite end of the mirrored lobby.

The latest copy of the *Times/News* had been crushed into
the corner of the couch. I smoothed out the wrinkles and sat
down to catch up with yesterday's news.

A temporary air seal in the upper hemisphere of the orbiting power station had collapsed, sucking three construction workers into open space. The picture of their bloated
bodies hanging majestically in the shimmering void of space
took up most of the front page. The caption under the picture reported only minor damage to the station itself. Completion of the project was still scheduled for next fall.

A Japanese scientist had absolutely proven that the
world's average temperature was rising significantly, disal-
lowing fears of a new ice age. He predicted glaciers now
threatening the tundras of the world would begin to recede,
shifting moister air currents back into their normal patterns.

This would also end the years of drought that were turning all the world's grain fields to dust. The report also noted that the rising waters of the ocean would facilitate the reemergence of cargo-carrying deep-water clipper ships.

The conversion of offshore oil wells into hydrogen-producing wind generators was being studied for practicality. According to the report, the additional hydrogen production might boost the nation's energy capacity by as much as ten percent.

The president announced another goodwill trip to the Mexican oilfields. He always seemed to be traveling where winter had no teeth.

The mayor of New York City announced the new piers were still almost completed, as they had nearly been for six years. If the Japanese scientist predicting rising ocean levels was right, by the time the new piers were finished, they'd only be good for servicing submarines.

Leafing back through the paper, I arrived at the obituaries on pages sixteen through eighteen. I was surprised not to see even a whisper about Darling. But on the second page, under "Suicides of the Day," I found the following listing:

> CREEK, Angelica. Formerly of
> western New York. Present
> address 322 E 61. 7:00 P.M.
> E 73 and Madison. Run and
> hit. BMBC MdtnS

Reading death notices today takes as much expertise as reading the stock listings once required. BMBC means "Body may be claimed"; MdtnS means "Midtown south." BMBC is a kind way of saying "no known relatives." The police keep the body for a week and then make methane with it in the city retorts. That's common knowledge. The fact is even advertised. It's supposed to discourage would-be deep-enders.

I'm not prone to tearing up other people's newspapers, but, for memory's sake, I wanted to keep that particular

article. I began ripping it carefully from the paper, but someone behind me coughed disapprovingly. I neither stopped
ripping nor looked up. "It was someone I knew. Death Notices . . . "

"All that life has been too blind to see."

I hadn't laid eyes on Joan Dark in over twenty years, not
since the afternoon of her parent's divorce trial. She was
fourteen or fifteen then; I was all of thirty. Before that day,
any memories I have of Joan are drawn from that collective
pool I've gathered about all children but my own. I recall her
only as a thin child, quiet and sexless, at least by the inflated
standards of a society which accepted as normal color pictures
of nude ten-year-old nymphets spread-eagled on the covers
of its weekly newsmagazines, or a society which truly believed
that eternal orgasm was a cure for the common cold.

The divorce had been particularly nasty, a never-ending
stream of accusations; the trial itself was just plain cruel. Lea
decimated Alex so severely in her divorce testimony that the
man left the courtroom in tears. One week later, he fled to
France to recuperate from the strain and shame of the trial.
I never saw Alex Dark again.

I remember Joan had sat all afternoon in the stifling courtroom quietly watching her parents' final attempts to destroy
each other. When the case had been concluded to Lady Justice's satisfaction and I stood to leave, I noticed that Joan was
enveloped by a dusty shaft of light filtering through the dirty
courtroom window. She must have sensed my attention, because she turned immediately and trapped my stare. Her
child's face, soft and untried, was eclipsed behind the full,
frightening blaze of her eyes. In that instant, a human being
forced herself into my consciousness. The effect on me was
electric, unsettling, as if an inanimate object, a table or a
chair, suddenly spoke. "Look at me," it said. "I am real."

"You don't remember me, do you?"
"Joan Dark."

She laughed softly. "I'm surprised."

"At?"

"That you remember me."

"Why? I've come to see you."

"Me?" She nodded but said nothing for a moment. Then she looked down at the torn newspaper in my lap. "Someone you knew well?"

I shook my head. "Someone I didn't know at all."

Joan didn't try to understand, and I didn't try to explain. I folded the item into my pocket.

"Well," she said. "You haven't changed much. You hair's longer and grayer. You seem to have lost some weight. Maybe found some muscle. You're wearing the same clothes. That suit must be twenty years out of style."

She was right, and I smiled. "At least. You have an exceptional memory. You weren't more than a child when I last saw you."

"Children have good memories, too," she said simply. She moved around the corner of the couch and stood in front of me. "And, have I changed?"

I had no basis for comparison. Before me stood a woman grown from a child I barely remembered. She was wearing a dark-gray tailored suit of that masculine design that is never really in or out of style. It accentuated the best of the figure of a woman in her mid-thirties, tall and full, but tight with the physical discipline that too seldom replaces the softness of adolescent pulchritude. Yet, her face was somehow fuller than that child's face I so dimly recalled. Her hair was styled long and easy, jet black sprayed through a floss of early gray. Her face had the rosy glow no camouflage can approximate. The only makeup she wore was dark liner to counterbalance the still-smoldering depth of her eyes. She was beautiful, not perhaps by the transient dicta of style, but certainly by the classic fiat of human appreciation.

"Have you changed? Not at all. You're as lovely as I remember you."

Joan smiled easily. "I'm surprised you remember me at all, let alone so flatteringly."

"I should say the same."

"I admit, I didn't really know you. Not until Paris. My father spoke of you often. He thought highly of you. And there were your pictures. And your letters. You were one of the few who didn't forget him as soon as he could. That was kind, and much appreciated."

"Kindness didn't enter into it. Your father was a fine man. And a friend. I admired him too much . . . " I didn't finish my thought.

Joan nodded silently and sat next to me on the couch. She moved with confidence, ease, and grace. "When I came back to New York, I intended to call and say thank-you. Somehow, I never got around to it. So many things had to be taken care of." She touched the tip of her nose with her fingertips, hiding her face for a moment. "Do you still practice law?"

"No. Not in ten years." There was a silence neither of us wanted to fill. Then I spoke again. "I'm a private investigator. That's why I've come to see you."

Joan stared at me with amused curiosity. "An investigator? I . . . pardon my surprise, but I would as soon have thought you a blacksmith or some equally obsolete profession."

"Quite all right. I'm used to the reaction."

"A real Sherlock. Well, Mr. Detective, what can I do for you?" She clapped her hands softly and smiled.

"I'd like to talk to your mother. I was told you were handling her affairs."

"How do you mean?" She smiled oddly and it took me a moment to figure out why.

"Her business affairs."

"My mother handles those herself. But, since she's been ill, she's made me a buffer zone between herself and those whom she doesn't choose to acknowledge."

"She's ill?"

Joan nodded. "Angina pectoris. An oxygen deficiency to her heart. Almost any effort exhausts her. In fact, she's taken to spending most of her time in a wheelchair."

I watched Joan as she spoke. There seemed little effort or emotion in her words. They were the words of a tour guide invoking the historical significance of this or that on her thousandth trip through a crumbling monument. "Why should you want to see my mother?"

"I've been hired by a man named Ivory Wightman who operates—"

"I'm familiar with Mr. Wightman and how he operates. My mother is one of his addicts." She spoke sharply.

"You don't approve of him?"

"Putting it mildly, I think the man is a criminal."

"Does your mother feel the same?"

"As I said, my mother handles her own affairs."

"Even over your disapproval?"

Joan laughed, almost bitterly. "My mother is old enough to be responsible for her own actions. It's not up to me to approve or disapprove. I do know she's given Mr. Wightman a great deal of money over the years."

"You called her an addict."

"Do you know a better word for someone so totally under the influence of an electronic toy her entire well-being is dependent upon it? My mother is an addict. What difference does the particular narcotic make? A rose by any other name."

"You don't believe Wightman's device does what he claims it can?"

"Store time on a magnetic tape? Do you believe that? I've got no reason to trust Mr. Wightman, and lots of reasons not to. But my mother has faith for ten doubters. She spends the majority of her days off in an electronic cloud. Somehow, I would feel better if she had fallen for some religious fanatic instead of your Mr. Wightman."

"He's not my Mr. Wightman. He only hired me for four days. But if you're sure your mother's being conned, why haven't you done something about it?"

Joan looked at me with an expression that was half smile

and half smirk. "What do you suggest? Contact the police? You know how much good that would do. I've pleaded with her but she continues to believe only what she chooses." Joan almost succeeded in masking the bitterness in her voice. "Tell me how you happen to be involved with a man of Mr. Wightman's caliber."

"He hired me. Someone has managed to steal several of those magnetic account tapes. My job is to find them." I added after a moment, "One of the missing tapes belongs to your mother."

Joan looked at me stiffly as my meaning sank in. For a flash, I saw something in her that reminded me of the little girl in that courtroom. But, whatever it was, it was gone too quickly to name. "My mother's tape," she said flatly. She touched her nose again with her finger, almost as if she had to reassure herself her nose hadn't vanished. "When she finds out, it may kill her." She massaged her brow with the same finger.

"I'm working to establish a motive for someone to go to all the trouble of stealing the tapes."

"Tape-napping?" she suggested.

"That's the obvious reason. But no ransom demand was received. I thought I'd find out if there was a reason only those particular tapes were taken. That's why I'd like to talk to your mother."

"It's out of the question."

"Surely, if she values her tape as much as you say, she'd be willing to see me."

"I've no doubt she'd be willing. I'm afraid the shock of hearing her tape is missing might do her serious damage."

"She doesn't have to know."

"She'd suspect something." Joan turned away from me and looked at the lockmaster, who was snoozing on a high stool next to the elevator entrance. When she looked back at me, her face was set into an angular stiffness, reminding me of Alex when he was deep in thought. The resemblance was uncanny. Joan didn't physically look much like her father, but many of the expressions she used, such as the twitch in the right corner of her mouth when she smiled, were his.

"But I suppose we'll have to risk it if there's any hope of getting her tape back. Perhaps you and your wife could come to dinner this evening? I can use the excuse that I met you on the street and invited you for old time's sake. My mother still loves to play the southern hostess."

"That would be all right, but I'll have to come alone."

"Your wife is busy?"

I shook my head without energy or emotion. "Alicia has been dead over ten years."

"I'm sorry. I didn't know." She spoke without embarassment or pity. "Then it will be just the three of us. That will work as well, I suppose." She held up her right hand. The fingers were long, slender, used to getting what they reached for. "Would eight be too early?"

"No, not at all."

"Fine. I'll phone Edward and tell him to expect you."

"Edward?"

"My mother's butler. Bodyguard. Cook. Edward has many functions. You know the address, don't you?"

I nodded.

"Well, then, until eight. I must go now. The elevator's scheduled to leave soon." Joan stood and smoothed her skirt. "This has been a pleasant surprise. I'm looking forward to this evening." She offered me her hand in the old-fashioned way, and I shook it. Then she smiled and turned away.

Both the lockmaster and I watched her disappear into the elevator. We watched the doors close and the pointer slowly mark her vertical progress. When she reached the ninth floor, we lost interest. He went back to his daydream. I went back to my apartment.

I found a message from Wightman on the electrosecretary. I called him back but got no answer. Then I called the morgue and got right through to Detective Murtaugh.

"Murtaugh."

The voice sounded as if it belonged to a squat man whose teeth were bad and feet flat, someone who had learned at birth that the only way to keep from getting pushed around was to push hard first. But then, I was probably jumping to unjustified conclusions. Most bureaucrats sounded like that.

"The name's Hughes. I'm calling about—"

"I know why you're calling."

"I called before but you were out to lunch."

"Lunch my ass. I was out rounding up some answers about this Darling corpse you dropped in my lap."

"Sorry about that. You figure out what killed him?"

Murtaugh didn't answer immediately, and when he did, I heard a subtle change in his voice. "Autopsy's done."

"What killed him?"

"What's your interest in Darling?"

"Simple curiosity. I'm the guy who found the body. I guess I just want to know what could do that to a man. You'll admit there's something thought-provoking about the body." I wasn't anxious to tell this cop Murtaugh my reason was to keep the police from inventing another suicide. "Did you talk to Slovinsky?"

"Yeah, and I'd like to talk to you, too. I think you'd better drop in for a visit."

"How about first thing in the morning?"

"How about right now?" I was liking Murtaugh's voice less and less. Too much shove in it. Too much venom.

"What's the rush? The man's dead. He's not going any-where."

"That's wrong. Seems someone wants him buried. This guy had friends. Tomorrow'll be one day too late."

"Listen, Murtaugh, if there's anything suspicious about Darling's body, why not hang on to him for a few more days?"

"No need. Autopsy's been done. We got as much from him as we're ever going to get."

"Then why bother me? All I wanted is to know what killed him. Just one simple answer."

"One simple answer is all anyone wants. Do I have to send

a car up for you?"

"No. I'll be down as soon as I can." Then I added a little acid to my voice. "You know, Detective Murtaugh, it's co-operative, understanding public officials like you who make life worth living."

His voice became cool, distant. "You know, Mr. Hughes, it's public officials like me who keep things from completely falling apart." After that, I hung up with a little more respect. The man, after all, was right.

9

I changed my clothes and was on my way out the door when the phone rang. It was Wightman.

"Good afternoon, Mr. Hughes. I'll be leaving town, but first I wanted to compliment you on your quick progress."

"What are you talking about? I've just started the ground-work."

"From what I just read in the afternoon paper, you've been doing a type of groundwork I never anticipated." The sar-casm in his voice had a dull, nasty edge to it. "You were hired to recover the tapes, not eradicate my depositors."

"I haven't seen the afternoon paper."

"Well, you should. Poor Mr. Darling. You're much more

efficient than I thought. And more direct than I gave you credit for."

"I didn't have anything to do with Darling's death."

"Mr. Hughes, I'm suggesting only that you should have a look at this afternoon's *Post/World*." He chuckled maliciously. "I'll leave matters in your capable hands. But please don't feel it necessary to make any more of my valued clients dead."

"You are coming back, aren't you?"

"Ha. Don't worry. I'll be back by Tuesday and you'll get what's coming to you. In my absence, feel free to contact my assistant."

I made sure I thanked him politely before I put the phone down.

I went straight to the nearest working newsbox I knew of, waited my turn in line, and inserted my plastic in the slot. The dispenser whined tinnily and, five seconds later, spit out a freshly printed copy of the *Post/World*.

The picture on the front page needed no headline to catch my eye. A photographer had somehow managed to capture in four colors the full, twisted horror of Darling's death. The life-sized face, still distorted by that grotesque, unceasing scream, would sell more papers than the world news it had pushed off page one. It was riveting, fearsome, unforgettable, except, of course, that most people would forget it an hour after seeing the picture. Only those who had a chance to contemplate the real thing would never get Darling's face out of their minds. The short paragraph squeezed in under the picture contained just enough of the ungarbled truth to qualify as nonfiction. I, for one, found the last few words on the page of particular interest. "The police have mentioned a private investigator, Jack Hughes, in connection with (turn to page eight)."

The only problem was that this particular copy of the paper lacked pages seven through eleven. I bought another and it had a page eight, but the ink was so smudged, it was illegible. I was luckier on the third try, but nowhere on page eight did

I find any mention of Gregory Darling. Nor anywhere else in the paper for that matter. I threw the kilo of newsprint into the nearest dumpster and headed downtown. These days, you never know if news is missing because of a printer's error or because the editors had more space to fill than facts to fill it with.

Everything about the morgue at the Midtown South police complex gives the sense of a building that has been badly overused. Trails worn into the faded beige linoleum mark the dull progress of scuffling heels and the wheels of countless gurneys. Once upon a time the building was a public school, but, in the early nineties, the city found itself with a dearth of pupils and a glut of corpses. Classroom partitions were ripped out, new walls built, a quick coat of institutional gray slapped on everything that didn't move, a larger incinerator installed, and a new high-rise stack erected to disperse the sweet aroma of burning flesh over the widest possible area.

But, still, you weren't in the building five minutes without noticing that everything, including you, was being coated by a thin, greasy film not salty enough to be sweet and not acid enough to be pollution. And everywhere bloomed the fetid stink of magnolia air freshener.

I interrupted the balding receptionist's game of solitaire to ask where I could find Detective Murtaugh. Without looking up, the man, who had a face terraced like a bombed-out rice paddy, pointed down a dark side hall. I could have found Murtaugh's office even if I had been blind. Halfway down the hall, I heard a horsey, intimidating laugh which told me I was headed in the right direction.

I had the direction right, but my supposition about Murtaugh's looks couldn't have been more wrong. He wasn't fat. He wasn't short. He probably didn't have flat feet. And, most importantly, he wasn't a he.

Detective Murtaugh was leaning back in her chair with both her feet up on the desk. She had short, steel-gray hair, dark Irish eyes, and, though she was probably only in her early forties, she looked hard and furious enough to have been a servant of Lady Justice for a thousand years. She permitted no trace of feminine softness to mar her appearance nor made any effort to mask her contempt when she spotted me standing in the darkness outside her office.

"You got business here, fellow?"

"My name's Hughes. I talked to you about an hour ago."

"Yeah. Hour and fourteen minutes to be exact. What took you?" Murtaugh rippled her high-arched eyebrows, and looked me over the way only a cop can, noting nothing in particular but leaving nothing unnoted. After a second, she snorted, "Come in and join the party."

I entered the office already feeling sorry for whomever Murtaugh had been berating so furiously. It was my poor friend Slovinsky, half shielded by the door and pressed as far back in his chair as the human skeleton permitted. He looked as serene as the receiving half of a knife-throwing act.

"All right, Slovinsky," Murtaugh said with almost syrupy politeness. "Beat it. I'll talk to you later."

Slovinsky meekly got to his feet and left the room without even acknowledging my presence. Only after Slovinsky closed the door behind himself, did Murtaugh speak again. "And you can take the seat of honor."

"I'm not sure I deserve it."

"Suit yourself. Stand if you want." She paused to brush at a fly on her arm. "Slovinsky has been telling me what happened last night. Interesting. He claims he and his partner, a rookie named Mangelli, found you at the home of the deceased. That's interesting." She implied more with the insinuating sneer in her voice than she said with her words.

"I called the report in."

"You had a reason for being at Darling's house last night?"

"I'm a private investigator."

Murtaugh nodded.

"Like I told Slovinsky yesterday, I had been to see Darling

earlier in the day. He asked me to come back last night. When I got there, he was dead. I called the police. They came. I don't see why that should be so difficult to understand."

Murtaugh didn't say a word but stared coldly at the newspaper that lay face down on her desk. I didn't have to see the front page to know it was the *Post/World*. "Slovinsky says Darling was under a heavy piece of glass." She tensed her right eye and looked where Slovinsky had been sitting, as if she expected the empty chair to confirm her statement.

"A coffee table. It worked with magnets."

"You think that's what killed him?"

"I was under the impression you knew what killed him."

Murtaugh ignored me and asked again, "You think that's what killed him?"

I shook my head.

"You're sure?"

"That glass is heavy, but not that heavy. Besides . . . you've seen the body."

"Yeah, I've seen the body. I've seen too much of the body. And, every time I open a paper for the next few weeks, I'll see it again." She shifted heavily in her chair, swinging her feet off her desk. Picking up a clipboard, she regarded it casually. "When do you claim you last saw Darling alive?"

"Yesterday afternoon a little past four."

"And when do you claim you discovered his body?"

Her tone had begun to annoy me. With every prod, I got the feeling she was compulsively testing me for soft spots, the way a child pokes wet cement. "Before we go any further with this conversation, Sergeant, let's get this one thing straight. I don't *claim* to have found him dead. I *did* find him dead. We wouldn't want there to be any misunderstandings about that point, would we?"

"No, Hughes, you get this one thing straight. I ask the questions. You answer them. Now, when did you find Darling's body?"

"After nine. Maybe half past. Maybe later."

"Exactly doesn't matter. Slovinsky and his partner didn't

get there till past twelve. What did you do for two and a half hours?"

"Waited for the police to arrive."

"For two hours? You didn't help yourself to any of the deceased's treasures? You just sat on your hands like a queen in a bus station? Or were you taking inventory?"

"Right the first time. I waited upstairs in his bedroom. Would you relish spending the better part of three hours in a dark house holding Darling's hand?"

Murtaugh didn't look as if she had the slightest idea what I was talking about. "What about later, after Slovinsky and Mangelli dropped you at home?"

"I tried to sleep. What else do you do in the middle of the night?"

"Go back to Darling's house and tear the place apart. It would have been a good opportunity for you. You knew nobody was home, and you'd already given yourself a good alibi with the police. Slovinsky told me the place looked neat enough when he got there."

"I didn't go back. After seeing Darling, I don't think I'd ever go back."

"Somebody did. Before I got up there this morning. The place was a shambles. Drawers and closets turned inside out. Furniture moved. Someone was looking for something."

"Darling had a maid."

Murtaugh picked up a pencil and waggled it slowly in my direction. "I know about the maid. I talked to her earlier this afternoon. She hadn't been back to the house, and she didn't know her boss was dead until I told her."

"You're certain?"

She nodded. "Certain enough. I think you better sit down now, Mr. Hughes."

This time, I took her up on her offer. "Sure, I looked around a little before Slovinsky got there, but I didn't tear anything apart. And I didn't steal any of Darling's goodies either. I'm not that stupid."

"No," she allowed. "You probably aren't that stupid."

"A thief?"

She shook her head. "Now, that would be convenient. But too many valuables were left untouched. Someone was looking for something in particular. Whoever it was looked a long time before he found it."

"What makes you think he found what he was looking for?"

"I hoped you might help me with that, Hughes."

"Hope springs eternal, but I left with Slovinsky and haven't been back. All I know about Darling is what I saw."

"What did you see, Hughes?"

"Darling's body. That was enough. You saw it, didn't you?"

"I saw it, but not the way you did. Or the way that photographer from the *Post/World* saw him. By the time I got in this morning, Darling looked like any other stiff." She thought of something and made a note on her clipboard. "When you found Darling, he was under this piece of glass, right?"

I nodded.

"You didn't do anything to help him?"

I looked at Murtaugh coldly a moment before I answered. "No, I didn't do anything. The man was dead. I didn't have to give him the kiss of life to know that."

"Well said," she sneered.

"Besides, the police always want first crack at bodies, don't they?"

"Only in murder cases. Do you think Darling was murdered, Hughes?"

I slid back in the chair. I had warmed most of the seat, but where I hadn't felt like ice against my trousers. "It wouldn't be hard to convince me."

Murtaugh made another note on her clipboard. While she wrote, she asked, "How well did you know Darling?"

"I met him yesterday for the first time."

She didn't stop writing. "Another coincidence? Yesterday? The day he was murdered?"

"Darling was involved in a case I'm working on. I was

asking him some questions, we were interrupted, and he asked me to come back after nine. But I'm repeating myself."

"You haven't said who hired you or what you're doing."

"Neither has anything to do with Darling's death."

Murtaugh stared at me in feigned disbelief. She was busy chewing something, probably her tongue. "Are you going to give me a hard time?"

I shook my head slowly. "On the contrary. I'm anxious to cooperate as much as I can, but unless Darling's death has anything to do with my case, I owe my client anonymity. There are laws to protect the relationship between an investigator and a client."

"There were laws to protect whales," she said without warmth.

"Funny, Murtaugh, you don't look like a conservationist."

She sniffed and went back to her clipboard. "If Darling's death has nothing to do with this case of yours, why were you so hot to have an autopsy performed?"

I hesitated, not anxious to tell her my reason was that I didn't want Darling's death listed as another suicide. There was little doubt in my mind he had been murdered. I wished I was as sure he didn't die because of his time account. Since I hadn't come equipped with better reasons, I told Murtaugh the truth. She took it better than I expected.

"I'll accept that. I'll even believe you're a concerned citizen and not a private operator looking to make a lifetime job out of a once-in-a-lifetime opportunity. Not that there's anything wrong with that. We all have to make a living." Then she did a little trick with her voice, and, suddenly, it had an edge. "But I also know this Darling business is going to wind up a bigger ass pain than either of us needs."

"Why are you so interested in Darling?"

"Because you got Slovinsky to request an autopsy. So, instead of dropping the corpse off downstairs for normal processing, he put it on ice while he went to fill out the necessary forms. That was a mistake, because a *Post/World* prowl boy was hanging around the ice trays looking for pretty pictures to sell newspapers. He spotted Darling's pretty face and spread it on the front page. We all have to make a living. A lot of people saw that picture. A few of them were important. So you see, if you hadn't complicated matters, all we would have heard of Darling was a nice paragraph in the slab reviews. Don't you feel just a little guiltier now?"

I shook my head.

"Well, maybe you can tell me who is so interested in the wreck of a used-up actor. Maybe you can tell me why someone was hot to have him buried instead of turned into gas. Maybe you can tell me why someone lit a fire under the mayor's ass."

"A relative?"

"I checked in Atlanta where Darling was born. The only known relative of his is a sister no one's seen for forty years."

"How about some bored power broker looking to stir up a little excitement?"

"Maybe, but we usually like to keep our fires small around here, Hughes. That way the only people who get burned are already dead. When I get orders to put a fire out, I don't ask questions."

"So you need a blanket to smother the flames. I appreciate your problems, I really do. But isn't that what you get paid for?"

Murtaugh didn't like that. I know, because she got mean. "And I appreciate your problem. Maybe better than you. I don't have to look far for Darling's killer. Not far at all."

It took me a split second to understand. In that second, I nearly panicked, but I caught myself just in time and shook my head as coolly as I could. "You won't pin Darling's death on me. The autopsy. Darling was dead when I got there, and I've got solid witnesses for the hours before that if I need them."

Murtaugh grinned, and showed me twin rows of very white teeth. "The autopsy fixed the moment of death at about three A.M." She turned a page on her clipboard. "Three fifteen and nine seconds, to be exact."

"Then the autopsy is wrong. Or rigged. Slovinsky checked the body with an encephalometer. Darling was dead. No brain activity at all. And that was around midnight."

Murtaugh shook her head like a patient mother watching her child splashing his stewed prunes. It was the first vaguely feminine expression she had shown me. "Portable encephs aren't worth a damn unless you've had special training. Slovinsky hasn't, and anyway, he doesn't have the brains to tell a good shit from a close shave. The batteries in his unit were installed backward. Darling died from suffocation at three fifteen."

I stood up and leaned over her desk. "That's crap. Darling was dead when your boys hauled his body away."

"Darling was alive until the three of you loaded him into a plastic body bag and killed him. The coroner's report shows a period of severe trauma, a coma of some sort, prior to death, but the actual cessation of life occurred at fifteen minutes and nine seconds past three. And that undeniable fact is why you're going to cooperate, Hughes. You're going to tell me why you were talking with Darling, and I'm going to be the judge of how relevant it is. You haven't got any choice, unless you want to be held as an accessory to murder."

I shook my head. "The best you'd get is manslaughter."

"What are you? A legal expert?"

"I used to practice law."

"You should have practiced harder." She laid the clipboard in a drawer of her desk.

"You couldn't build a case against me without bringing two cops into it."

"What makes you think that bothers me one bit? There are ten recruits just waiting to yank the badge off Slovinsky's shirt."

"You're bluffing. When you start making waves in the department, the union will go crazy. We both know that, so don't bother trying to scare me into a confession. I'm not saying I can't be scared, but it'll take a better bluff than this one. Darling's death doesn't have anything to do with my

case. I'll help you as much as I can, but I won't have a clod
like Slovinsky on my heels every step I take."

Murtaugh used a few seconds to consider my tirade. "I'll
accept that, Hughes. For the moment." She stood up so she
faced me across the desk. She was shorter that I would have
guessed. "That doesn't get you off the hook, but I'll let you
wiggle a while longer. Provided you're more cooperative.
You and Darling were interrupted yesterday afternoon. By
who?"

"I don't know," I half lied. "A woman, but I didn't get a
chance to see her. Darling was too anxious to get rid of me."

Murtaugh rubbed a stained finger across her dry lips and
sat back down. "Darling still screwing around at his age?"
She smirked, though this time it might have been motivated
as much by admiration as sarcasm.

"That's probably what kept him looking young."

"That and twenty doctors. He had so much plastic in his
face, it probably got soft in the summer." Then, within the
space of a second, Murtaugh's face closed up again. "The
woman's name was Jeanette."

I tried to look surprised by the revelation, and, in fact, I
was, though not for the reason Murtaugh assumed. "How
do you know that?"

She pulled open a drawer and extracted a square manilla
envelope. From the envelope, she took a piece of folded
paper. "We found this in Darling's pants pocket. How'd you
miss it?"

It was the missing page from Darling's desk calendar.
Printed on it in red ink was the message the impression of
which I had had trouble reading. The initials I couldn't make
out weren't really initials. They clearly spelled out the name
Jeanette. The last name was just the letter "D." "Jeanette D.
brings time."

I refolded the paper and laid it carefully on the edge of
Murtaugh's desk. "So, we're looking for someone named Jeanette D."

"Wrong, Hughes. I'm looking for someone named Jeanette, or have you forgotten already?" She smiled a grin that was pure Irish Satan. "Darling's death has nothing to do with the case you're on. We're not going to get in each other's way, are we?"

"I stand corrected. You're looking for someone named Jeanette, and I hope you find her."

"When we took Darling apart, we found a couple of things you might be interested in. This we had to pry out of his left hand." She reached in the envelope and produced a square object which she slid across the desk. "Any idea what it is?"

I didn't have to pick up the transducer to answer Murtaugh's question. But I did anyway, and studied it with interest before I handed it back to her. "Sorry," I lied sincerely.

She took the transducer between her thumb and forefinger and examined it with disdain, as if it were a wad of hair she had just pulled from the bathtub drain. Then she shrugged and dropped the transducer back into the envelope. "How about this little item? We took it out of Darling's head."

She casually flipped something to me and I caught it in my palm. It was a disk the size of a poker chip. Silver scalpel marks showed through the mottled brown patina. I examined it a moment1before returning it, unable to shake the feeling I was handing her a dead man's soul. "Sorry, I guess I won't be as much help as you thought."

"You'll have your day, Hughes. Don't worry."

Neither of us said anything for some seconds. Then, to fill a silence that was growing dangerous, I asked, "You don't really know what killed him, do you?"

She looked at me curiously. "I said he suffocated."

"Yeah, but what induced that trauma you mentioned? Drugs? And what kept him alive for almost three hours in an airtight bag?

She shook her head. "I don't know. His blood was clean except for a trace of alcohol. The trauma was neurological. Something shot his nervous system to pieces. I thought maybe the electromagnetic coffee table till I found these gizmos." She began to drum on the edge of the clipboard.

"Maybe one of them kept him alive that long."

"Good luck figuring it out."

"I've handled tougher cases than this."

"We both have." I didn't know about her but I was lying through my teeth. "Can I go? I've got an important appointment tonight."

Her tongue started to play with the hint of a mustache on her upper lip. "Don't leave the city."

"Where would I go? And how would I get there?"

She smiled, and, for the first time, I got the feeling it was because she thought I had said something funny.

I was almost out the door before I remembered something I wanted to ask. "Say, Sergeant Murtaugh, where do I ask about BMBCs?"

"Try the front desk."

"Thanks."

"Hughes, is there something else I should know? You got another body involved in this?"

"No," I said shaking my head. "This body is a nobody. That's why she's downstairs. I just want to pay my last respects."

I tried not to think about what Murtaugh had told me. Nor about how I had been sitting calmly in Darling's bedroom while he lay pressed in living horror downstairs. Nor about how I might well be the cause of his death. Nor about how he had looked at me when Chick raised the table. And especially not about why I was suddenly so positive Darling was short-circuited by a transducer.

The note meant a little more to me than it did Murtaugh, but it was only a matter of time before she discovered what the other two items were. That would land her right in the middle of my income. Then, to make everything a bit brighter, I suspected both Murtaugh and I would be looking for the same person. Once Murtaugh figured out what the transducer was, it wouldn't be long until she discovered it wasn't Darling's.

I asked the attendant guarding the seedy room in the basement about Angelica Creek. He flipped lethargically through a dog-eared rolodex for a few minutes.

"Crick?"

"No, Creek."

He turned back a few cards. "The body was claimed this morning by a brother. After the relationship was verified, the body was released in his custody."

That was all I wanted to know. I said good-bye to Angela Creek and left the room feeling not quite so rotten. It was enough to know that someone else cared enough about Angelica the mad cyclist, to claim her body. That made the whole mess seem not quite so senseless. Who knows, maybe Angelica Creek had a perfectly good reason to want to ram a bus.

10

If the transducer Murtaugh had didn't belong to Darling, the most obvious assumption was that it belonged to his visitor. The note said she'd be bringing time. Jeanette isn't an uncommon name, but Jeanette D's are a bit rarer, and I could think of only one who might have known what a transducer was. Not that I let myself think for a moment that Darling's Jeanette D. and Wightman's Jeanette

D. might be one and the same. Real life is somehow usually more subtle.

Still, I had an hour and a half before I was due at the Dark's, twice as long as I needed to get there. Since the Dark house on Riverside Drive was only a few blocks west of Wightman's, I had time to stop off and ask Jeanette Dobbson a question or two. Just to make sure.

The uptown train was right on schedule. I boarded the last car and sat down before I noticed the colorful drapery blocking off the rear half of the car. You don't see many long-riders these days. Of course, back in the mid-eighties when apartments were fantastically expensive and the subway fares eliminated, long-riding was a common practice. Entire families moved into the subways, claimed a car, and set up house. After the initial outrage, the transportation authority began seeing advantages to having permanant residents on the subways: crime and vandalism decreased, sanitary conditions and the general appearance improved. As long-riders took care of their neighborhoods, the subway system became a more pleasant place to be. What killed the practice of long-riding was the slow glut of free housing. When the elevators and electricity began failing with disturbing regularity, disgusted tenants abandoned the upper stories of buildings, and anyone could have a lovely penthouse for little more than the trouble it took to reach it. The few familes that stayed on the trains did so because they enjoyed the life, supporting themselves by the traveling public.

As the car began to move, a great brown leonine head topped by a tossled afromane parted the heavy drapes. The man nodded his head in perfect rhythm to the moving car, and although he was nearly two meters tall, he defused any fear of him I might have had with his huge, infectious smile. He seated himself across from me with all the familiar ease one might use welcoming a visitor in one's home.

"Riding far today, brother?" The man's voice was quiet though it resonated above the din of the train. As he spoke, he swayed forward and back, automatically countering the uneven roll of the car.

"No, I change at Forty-second Street."

He smiled and nodded sympathetically. "Too bad. My woman makes wonderful soup. Uses real vegetables. We'd be pleased to have you join us for dinner. Good food. Good company. Both hard to find on a cold night."

"Sounds first class, but I do have to get uptown."

"Uptown. Downtown. Upstairs. Downstairs. Heaven. Hell. All the same." He patted his knees and got to his feet. "Well, that's too bad. But remember us, brother." He smiled and started moving back toward home. He was almost there when a thought struck me.

"Does your wife tell fortunes?"

When he turned around, he wore a broad, ironic smirk. "Fortunes? No, sir. I don' know anyone who still does them. To tell fortunes, you got to have a customer who cares about the future." He spun around with surprising agility and disappeared through the drapes.

This time, I didn't have to fight my way into Wightman's office. The door opened a second after I pushed the bell, and Jeanette Dobbson greeted me so heartily, I almost believed she meant it.

"Ivory told me you might be stopping by." Trigger stood back to let me pass. She was wearing a yellow dressing gown that matched her wet hair. "Two minutes sooner and you would have caught me in the shower." She smiled with a coy expression a man could interpret in a dozen different ways.

"I've got a few questions."

"I heard about Gregory Darling," she said with the proper note of sadness in her voice. "It's a shame. He was such a nice man. One of our oldest customers. I remember how disturbed he was when he discovered his tape was missing. But he was still polite. Now he's dead. That picture was so awful. Did you kill him?"

Her tone was so offhand, the question couldn't have sounded less threatening. "No. There was a woman with Darling when he died. The police think she killed him." I tried to pack insinuation in my voice. "Her name was Jeanette D."

My meaning went right over her head, and I had to stare at her till she caught on.

"Well, you don't think it was me, do you? Mr. Darling was a sweet man. Once he was even famous. I suppose any woman would have been flattered by his attention, but Ivory forbids me to see any of the customers." Then, as an afterthought, she added, "And I was here all afternoon yesterday. You know that."

"The police don't."

"You'll tell them, won't you." And that settled that. She turned quickly and looked at the clock mounted on the desk console. "It's getting late. Can I get dressed while we talk?" Trigger disappeared through a doorway in the rear wall. While I sat on the edge of the desk listening to the sounds of a woman dressing, the seconds pranced by like bathing beauties, each fuller with lusty insinuation than the last. "Mr. Hughes, why should the police even think I'm that Jeanette? Mr. Darling must have known a thousand women. He had a reputation as a studsman. Why should the police think this woman had anything to do with the bank?"

"They discovered a transducer on Darling's body. They still don't know what it is, but they will soon. Then they'll bring their suspicions here. The transducer didn't belong to Darling. Will they be able to trace its owner?"

"Well, it isn't me because I don't have a transducer."

I toyed with the rheostat mounted on the side of the desk, making the room lighter and darker by degrees. It was something of a luxury to be able to burn electricity like that. "Can they trace the owner of a transducer through the bank? Are there any serial numbers or other means of identification?"

Jeanette appeared in the doorway, and I turned the lights

up as bright as the rheostat would permit. In place of her sexless bathrobe, she now wore a tan velvet body stocking that was split from her chin to a tantalizing few centimeters below her navel. All that kept the two halves of her costume from losing touch with each other was a translucent weave of white threads spanning the straining chasm. She took a half turn and stared at me.

"How do I look?"

"Like a candidate for pneumonia if you go out like that." She grinned broadly. "I'll wear a snowsuit."

"You haven't answered my question. Can the police trace a transducer's owner using the transducer itself?"

Jeanette thought a moment. "No, I don't think we could identify a transducer unless its owner brought it in. There aren't any identification numbers on transducers and they can't be activated unless the owner is actually holding one. I mean, we couldn't even activate our console without a set of matching fingerprints."

"By chance, would any other depositors be named Jeanette?"

She stopped for a moment, her right leg half in a furry snowsuit. "Until recently, we had two. Mrs. Siqua's first name was Jeanette. But she's out of the question."

"Why?"

She regarded a cuticle on her right hand with displeasure. "She snuffed herself. Swallowed a can of Roach-away two months ago. That leaves only Jeanette Dumbrey."

"What's she look like?"

"You know, sort of average. Maybe middle-aged. Maybe not. It's hard to tell. She always wears a lot of camouflage. And sequined sunglasses. One thing is funny, though. That red wig. I always thought that was weird. Why would someone who wears such expensive clothing bother with such a cheap red wig? Ivory says many of our customers wear disguises. It seems silly to me, but the customer is always right, I guess."

"I have the same problem. Does this Jeanette Dumbrey seem the sort of woman Darling might have been attracted to?"

"Mr. Darling never seemed picky to me. I know he'd pinch me every chance he could. He didn't seem himself unless he had a woman next to him."

"Is Jeanette Dumbrey a large depositor?"

"Not large, but frequent. A real in-and-outer, if you know what I mean."

"I don't."

"She makes a deposit one week and yanks it out the next. Most of our customers keep much more than they use. I mean, keeping time is the point of this bank."

"When was her last visit? Do you keep track of things like that?"

Trigger nodded. "All the visits are recorded by the computer, but I remember her latest. It was early yesterday afternoon."

"After Darling discovered his tape missing and after the inventory of the vaults." A thought struck me. "I'd like a list of all the visits each victim made in the last six months. Can you do that? I'd also like a list of Jeanette Dumbrey's visits."

She nodded. "But can it wait till tomorrow? I'll be late. To see my girl friend," she added with obvious guilt.

"Sure, but can you get me Jeanette Dumbrey's address right away?"

Jeanette walked to the desk and, after fingering through a file case, pulled out a card and handed it to me. "Here's her registration card."

It listed Jeanette Dumbrey's current address as 11 West Thirty-fourth Street, apartment 1506. No phone number was given. It also listed her date and place of birth as January 6, 1912, Paris, France. I turned the card over and looked at the snapshot on the back.

Trigger was right about one thing. The woman in the picture was so camouflaged, it would have been hard to describe her accurately without also describing a hundred other women. One thing, however, was certain. She was no nearer eighty than I was. Camouflage can do a lot, but even it has its limits.

"According to this information, Jeanette Dumbrey is eighty-eight. She doesn't look that old."

Trigger shrugged. "Probably isn't, but we're not supposed to ask the customers too many questions. What difference does it make how old she is? I'd feel stupid asking another woman her age. And Jeanette Dumbrey must be one of our oldest customers. She even knew Jacques Delacroix."

"Who's that?"

"Ivory's original partner. I don't know how they knew each other. Jacques died just before Ivory and I met. He was some French guy. I think he invented the transducer, but I'm not too sure."

"When a woman lies about her age, it's usually to make herself younger."

"I suppose." Trigger looked away from me. When I realized she was staring hopefully at the door, I knew it was time to go. While she went to get her snowsuit, I pulled the photograph of Jeanette Dumbrey off the file card and stuck it in my pocket. Then I put the file card back into the holder.

When Trigger closed the office door behind us, she pressed her palm against the nameplate. The red light over the door winked off, and I heard the suck of hydraulic seals locking into place. Wightman was right about one thing. A person would have a hard time breaking into his office.

11

It's odd how differently people react to the encroachment of age.

Gregory Darling, for example. I barely knew the man, and yet his horror of growing old had been obvious even to me. The pain and expense he had put himself to preserving that mustachioed youth were testament to both his fear and his failure.

Lea Dark was another matter. Even rooted to a wheelchair, she didn't look or act as if so much as a week, let alone twenty years, had passed since we had last been in each other's company. She still exuded iron confidence and received my visit with the same hard-edged, southern graciousness she reserved for "social inconveniences."

The source of Lea's agelessness was no secret. Simply, she maintained herself in a world in which everything was measured against one standard, Lea Dark. That standard never changed; everything else did. In Lea Dark's world, the realities of life, her disease, her confinement, her age, even her morality were minor annoyances, temporary setbacks, or mere "social inconveniences."

Lea was always a strikingly beautiful woman. Sixty years of living hadn't altered that. Her hair had lost all its auburn luster, her face was slightly thinner, but she had retained the white-hot symmetry of the portrait of her, which dominated the dining room. Many years ago, an artist had captured in oil that steely fire in a new bride's eyes. He had painted that fire as aristocratic hauteur, but, in the bright light of hindsight, I could see it was only pure selfishness. Nothing separated that bride from the woman who sat across from me impassively dissecting the chicken breast on her plate, nothing but forty years. Both women dreamed the same dreams, cursed the same curses, and neither had ever wasted a warm thought on anyone but Lea Dark.

Joan had prepared her mother for my arrival with a simple story. We had met by chance, and Joan had invited me to dinner for old time's sake. In this fairy tale, I was still practicing law. Lea accepted the lie without a question, probably because the truth wouldn't have mattered to her anyway.

Lea was, in one sense, a consummate hostess. Not once did she permit our conversation to turn to the past, a topic that might have been unpleasant for me or uninteresting for her. Instead, all through our meal, the three of us chatted idly and almost amicably. Only after the dessert plates had been cleared did Joan even attempt to steer the conversation to anything of substance. She casually mentioned Lea's angina, and immediately the old woman bristled. It was clear that the serenity which had been the one of the meal was, like Lea's beauty, only skin deep.

I tried to leaven the suddenly tense atmosphere. "You seem well adjusted to your infirmity, Lea."

She glared at me, and I honestly think for a few seconds, she didn't understand what I meant by infirmity. "It's been cured," she said. "Even though I'm not able to get around quite as freely as I'd prefer. Would you care for some coffee, Mr. Hughes?"

"Thank you," I said, helping myself to the steaming pot. The smell was glorious. The taste was better. "Brewed," I commented appreciatively. "It's so rare."

"Not only brewed, Mr. Hughes," Lea observed dryly "Brewed from real coffee beans. A close friend of mine . . . "

Joan spoke quickly to stop another one of her mother's rambles. "My mother mistakenly thinks she's recovered enough to stop her rehabilitation. We have one entire room filled with exercise devices she never even touches."

The glacial stare Lea gave her daughter was one she had developed over the years. Joan ignored her totally, and instead turned to me, opening her mouth to speak.

But Lea was faster. "My daughter has never learned to doubt the opinions of charlatans and quacks. Put a white coat on a gibbon and my daughter would follow him as if he were God. She is, you see, an impassioned believer in obsolete virtues, hard work, perfection through suffering, an omnipotent good will, and last, but not least, fervent faith in some mystical Rightness. She should have been a stewardess. Mr. Hughes, every fiber of my body and soul resists entering that chamber of tortures she and her quack advisors have prepared for me. Because I'm wise enough to prefer the path of least resistance, my daughter considers me a moral reprobate."

Joan followed Lea's inadvertent lead quickly. "Why don't you tell Jack about your path of least resistance, mother. See if he doesn't think it's the most ludicrous scheme he's ever heard." Joan's voice stayed calm, level, and quite civilized, which only made her acid tone bite deeper.

"Mr. Hughes," Lea said, hardly glancing at her daughter. "All the doctors, even the quack my daughter employs, tell me my heart will never recover regardless what exercises I subject myself to. For reasons I don't fully understand, a transplant is impossible. My heart will always limit my acitivities. I'm told at best I will only be able to stave off death a few years while the slow, lethal weight of gravity pulls me into the ground. My daughter wishes me to subject myself to a daily ritual which leaves me too exhausted for other activity. Doesn't it make sense to reserve my strength and time until I am able to escape that ponderous weight entirely?"

I said yes and watched while my answer percolated down through the tension. Joan, I assumed, was leading Lea so we could talk about the time deposit without her being suspicious. But there was more urgency in Joan's voice than called for. War was being waged between the two women. I didn't know what the particular motive was, but the first shots had been fired long before I arrived for that dinner.

"Tell Jack about your plan, mother," Joan prodded.

Lea regarded me without charity. "It's simple. Rather than wasting away on earth, I intend to escape to a more favorable climate. The orbiting space colony will be completed. Since gravity there will be only half its earthly strength, I'm told my heart will provide me the strength to function normally for many more years."

Her revelation not only surprised me, it appalled me. The thought of this old woman bouncing around in a space suit was more than ridiculous. It was the plan of a lunatic. But I knew better than to let her see my feelings. "Life on Orbicol will be spartan," I said with a solemn face.

"Spartan perhaps, but better than continuing this shadow existence here."

Joan, watching for my reaction to her mother, said nothing for a few moments. I also hesitated, trying to find the proper tone for my answer. I realized how easily I could alienate both women. "It sounds like an ingenious plan, but are you sure it can be done? Apart from the rigors of the trip itself, there will probably be strict passenger selection. People our age . . . "

Lea cut me off. "I've made all the necessary arrangements."

I could see no gain in continuing. "Then I wish you success, Lea." Behind my coffee cup, I threw a wink only Joan saw, just to reassure each woman that I was on her side.

But Joan wasn't about to let the matter rest. "Tell Jack about your little nest egg, mother. I'm sure he'll find that interesting too."

Even considering the tension that hung over the table, I wasn't prepared for the bolt of pure animosity Lea aimed at her daughter. But Joan didn't even blink. "Tell Jack the real reason you refuse to do your exercises. Tell him how you prefer to waste your time in a semi-conscious stupor."

Lea had no answer for a few seconds. In that time something again reminded me that the similarities between Alex and Joan I had observed that afternoon were all mannerisms, the physical quirks of a parent copied by a child. Joan physically resembled neither of her parents, but now she was showing the edge of a vein of pure vindictiveness. It was a trait I had never seen in Alex, but one which ran deep in Lea. I wondered how much more of her temperament Lea had willed her only child.

Then Lea broke the silence. "My daughter refuses to believe in the wonders of technology, Mr. Hughes. Who can blame her? She lacks the historical perspective we have. For her, the world has always been static at best, crumbling at worst. We, on the other hand, have lived through one of the greatest periods of technological development mankind has ever seen. And we've lived through its decline. So we have some perspective; my daughter sees in only one dimension.

"For several years now, I have been a depositor in a most unique bank. I won't bore you with details, but I have been able to take moments out of my life to save for future use. In this way, I've managed to store a good deal of my time. Instead of wasting my life on idiot exercises, I have been garnering moments for when I can again be a whole person. I shall use them when I reach space."

"It sounds too good to be true," I said, not without interest.

"I can see doubt in your eyes, Mr. Hughes, but I assure you the process does work."

"It's not doubt you see, Lea. It's envy. I was about to ask you the name of your banker."

Lea stared at me, suddenly suspicious of my concern. "I hardly see what good that information would do you. The service is far from free, and you are obviously far from rich."

The silence which followed was just too risky to fill. Only after a few moments did Joan add, "I should say the service is far from free. My mother has poured—"

That tore it. Lea cut her off in midsentence. "My daughter is under the mistaken impression that, because she has access to my financial records, she has the right to comment on how I spend my money. I find her concern tiring." Lea turned her head and regarded the smooth skin of her shoulder. "In fact, I find this whole conversation tiring. So I'll leave the two of you. Do stay, Mr. Hughes. And help yourself to as much coffee as you can possibly guzzle. No one will charge you for a second cup, and you are obviously enraptured by it. My daughter will, I'm sure, entertain you. I've recently discovered she has a facility for entertaining men which, if I must say, borders on the obsessive."

Lea spun her wheelchair and had nearly completed her exit before Joan could parry. "If that's true, mother, it's because I've had such an excellent example."

Lea stopped at the door, looked over her shoulder, shook her head slowly and frowned, as if at a particularly obnoxious smell. Then she left. Hers was just the right answer.

A few moments later, glancing at the portrait over the table, Joan suggested we move to the living room.

12

If Joan had suggested the move for comfort's sake, she miscalculated grossly. The living room was a sterile, oppressively modern room some interior decorator had tried to warm with the addition of dark, angular chromette furniture, the kind that makes sitting an act of contrition. To round out the effect, everything that could have been was covered with ice-blue fabric. A pair of bright electric lights might have made the room more decorous, but

I assumed because of the blackout, four kerosene lamps were burning instead. As a result, a pale jaundiced glow high-lighted all the wrong places, making the room seem a bit like a furniture-store display window at night. If human beings ever used the room only an archaeologist would have been able to tell.

I sat on the couch while Joan attended to a cabinet filled with bottles. "I'm afraid we haven't much left in the way of liqueur. A little Napoleon brandy, some cognac, a few hash mints. There's plenty of coffee."

"Where do you get the beans? I didn't know they were still for sale. I thought the blight was worldwide."

"As far as I know, it was." Joan turned toward me with a sardonic smile. "You can't buy coffee beans anywhere. But we have a cellar-full packed in airtight barrels. My father dabbled in coffee futures when coffee still had a future. As it turned out, a bad investment turned good. He purchased a lifetime supply. In fact, the supply will probably outlast all of us. Would you like another cup?"

"Not right now. I've forgotten how strong real coffee can be. Cognac will be fine."

She returned with two snifters. Joan had completely re-gained her composure, but something about it seemed the-atrical. It reminded me of the public face Gregory Darling wore over his private character.

"Jack, has my mother changed much? You do have a cer-tain perspective I lack. It's been so long since you've seen her, but you must have known a side of her I never did."

I swirled my brandy around the walls of the snifter, looking for an answer. "On the contrary, I'm surprised how little your mother has changed. Of course, when I knew her, she was only a little older than you are now. I know almost noth-ing of her life before that. There was a rumor that your father had met her at law school in Georgia; that she had been a waitress or drink slinger. I know they had so little in common people wondered why he married her.

Joan nodded. "Did she say anything to help your investigation?"

"Only that nonsense about the space station," I said, taking a sip of the brandy. "But she left before I could ask her any of the things I'd have liked to."

"Then maybe I can help you. Who are the five victims?"

Perhaps I was still tense, or maybe too observant, but something about Joan's eagerness to please seemed artificial. "I don't think I ought to make too much public knowledge. Wightman would like to keep his depositors as much of a secret as possible."

"Of course," she said, crossing her legs, "But I thought if Mother didn't help you with your investigation, maybe I could. I know most of her friends."

It sounded logical, but still I changed the subject. "Your mother is the third depositor I've talked to. Each has had a different reason for being one of Wightman's customers."

"You've noticed that too, have you? He's a persuasive salesman. Every customer gets an individualized sales pitch. Why are you working for him?"

"There isn't much call for private investigators these days."

"If that's true, why did you quit the law?"

"I don't think this is the time or place to go into it."

"Why not? If I'm interested . . . " She stopped and looked at me with a tiny blossom of understanding. "But, of course, if you'd prefer not to discuss it."

"As it is, I spend too much of my time dissecting the past. It does no good; nothing changes."

Joan brushed a few stray wisps of her dark hair back into the smooth flow that crossed her forehead. "But that's precisely the problem. Talking to yourself never brings real understanding. That was the lesson of the eighties. Yet everyone keeps talking to himself and no one else. The world . . . "

"Yes, I know. A friendly ear for every problem. A cure for what ails you. Crap. That was the hard lesson of the seventies." I finished my brandy in a swallow.

Joan sat quietly cradling her glass like a chalice. "I know you're not trying to be funny. But life would be so much more pleasant if people didn't close themselves off. Everyone's so damn constipated. . . ." She looked at her untasted drink and laid it on the arm of her chair as if it were a broken toy. "Can I get you some more brandy?"

"No thanks. I've been balancing a too long day on top of a sleepless night. Soon, even that blessed caffeine isn't going to keep me from keeling over."

We sat there with nothing for our hands to do. Then, after a minute, I thought of something I wanted to know, something that had nothing to do with Wightman or his bank. "At the end. Did the alcohol. . . ?"

Joan understood immediately and shook her head slowly. "No, my father held up well until just a few weeks before he died. I don't think of those weeks anymore. For too long, they were a filter that clouded all my memories of him. Only recently did I learn to put it in its proper perspective. Now I see alcohol was only the painful way my father chose to kill himself. He was one of the first deep-enders. He only started a little earlier, before anyone found a label for the lemming phenomenon. He anticipated the Apathera and knew he preferred not to change. But, by the time he died . . ." Joan didn't actually stop talking but she turned her head and her voice dropped below the level of audibility. I saw no need to ask her to repeat herself.

"I'll have that second brandy after all." I stood up, found the liquor cabinet, and poured myself two fingers from the bottle which proudly wore a silver pourer with the initials "A.H.D." engraved on the neck. Maybe that's the best we should expect from this hotel; to check out as a sterling drunk. If we hang around here in the lobby too long, we'll all end up sucking out bar rags for a profession.

I was lost in my thoughts and had my back to her when she said, "My personal history can't possibly be helping your investigation."

I walked back to the couch not quite as suspicious as when

I had left it. "Did your mother know Gregory Darling?"

Joan tightened her shoulders and pursed her lips, appraising my question. "The actor? Didn't he just die?"

"Last night about this time. Has your mother heard about his death?"

While she thought, the tip of her tongue crept across her upper lip. It completed two slow laps before she answered. "I honestly don't know if she knew him or not. She's never mentioned him to me. But it's possible. My mother seems to have known just about everyone at one time or another."

"Has she heard about his death?"

"I don't think so. She doesn't read the papers. If she did, our story about you being a lawyer wouldn't have worked. But why do you want to know if she's heard about his death?"

"Just a thought. I'd still like to talk to her, and I thought maybe I could frighten her back to the discussion table."

"I don't think that's a good idea. My mother wouldn't take the news well." Joan uncrossed her legs, jarring the coffee table in the process. "I don't remember reading the cause of Mr. Darling's death. It didn't have anything to do with his time account, did it?" she asked with sudden concern. "It's one thing for my mother to be taken in by a con man's fiction about a time account. It's another matter if her expensive fantasies are dangerous."

"The police listed the cause of Darling's death as suffocation."

"Suffocation?" Just a stray flicker of puzzlement shot throught her eyes. "Suffocation. How did you get involved?"

"I had an appointment with Darling last night to talk about his time account. I got there a little late. He was dead. So the police naturally think I was somehow responsible."

"But you didn't actually get to talk to him. How frustrating that must be. I see why you're so anxious to talk to my mother." She shook her head in sympathy, loosing a few strands of hair from behind her ear. "How did he suffocate?"

"The police don't really know."

"The police?"

"Yes, you know. Those folks in blue uniforms you see everywhere but where you need them. A hundred suspicious deaths every week never get investigated. Darling is one of the luckier ones. It's a lottery of some sort, I think." I polished off my second brandy in one toss. It had been so long since I had had good liquor, I had forgotten how to sip something that didn't taste like drain reamer. I balanced the empty snifter on the arm of the couch and tried to beat back the picture of Darling that was forming in my mind.

So instead, I looked at Joan. She was prying behind the edge of her upper teeth with her thumbnail, lost in thoughts of her own. When she realized I was watching her, she licked her dry lips and smiled self-consciously. "Sorry, I was thinking about my mother. I couldn't forgive myself if . . ." She hesitated, and I had the distinct impression she was trying to sort out her feelings. "I couldn't forgive myself if this time recount turned out to be dangerous. I've permitted it to go on too long already."

"I wouldn't worry about your mother if I were you. She'll survive. After we're all long gone. And, in spite of our best efforts."

"Just what do you mean by that?" Joan's voice was heaped with angry indignation. "My mother is essentially a fine person."

"Like hell. Let's be honest. Your mother is a cruel, calculating bitch. She tortured your father and God knows how many other people unfortunate enough to be standing between her and her private vision of immortality." I wasn't sure what I was trying to accomplish with my outburst, but I knew it felt good.

"My mother has had a hard life. It wasn't easy. . . ."

"Through no fault of her own. I don't mean to insult you, Joan. You're to be credited with living with her as long as you have." I watched her quietly tracing the lines in her palm with her right index finger. Then she looked up at me.

Her eyes were dry, but they shined unnaturally in the dull glow of the lanterns. "Thank you, Mr. Hughes. But I can't see how your opinion will get you any further along in your case." There was bitterness in her voice.

"I don't suppose it will. But it had to be said."

"Why? Perhaps you'd get more satisfaction if you told my mother in person how you feel about her." She looked at me and smiled wearily. "But I wouldn't advise it unless you've got your bomb shelter all picked out. Now, if you've finished with my mother, I'd rather let the subject drop."

We were done with that topic, but we didn't have another one quite ready to throw in the breach. I spent the silence deciding if I should treat myself to a third drink. The thought of a long trip home to a cold apartment that hadn't seen a drop of good liquor in longer than I could remember getting without being maudlin settled the issue. I hoisted myself off the couch and tried to ignore the fact that I almost lurched toward the liquor cabinet. "Can I get you another?" I asked, not really caring if she wanted one or not.

"Not for me. And I think you've had enough too."

That stopped me in my tracks. I turned around. "I'm sorry. I didn't think I was that drunk."

"I didn't say you were," she said stiffly. "But I'd prefer not watching you try to reach Nirvana. You'll forgive me my eccentricities, but I've seen enough drunkenness to last me several lifetimes."

I stood there rooted in the middle of the floor like a garden weed. Then, dumbly, I nodded. "I suppose this is a good place for me to say good night."

Joan tightened her lips. "You may stay if you wish. We have several extra bedrooms, and I'd rather not have to worry about your going home in your condition."

"What condition is that? How do I look?"

"Like a man who has miles to go before he sleeps." She smiled warmly, and suddenly I felt foolish.

"Thanks for the offer, but I have a cat to take care of," I lied. "If I leave him alone too long, he harasses the goldfish just to spite me. I don't really care what he does, but it doesn't make the fish too happy."

Joan stood and smoothed the front of her dress. "Well, I'll drive you over in the Volts."

"You've got a Volts?"

"Yes. And batteries to run it. It really won't be any trouble."

I didn't try to be a fool and protest. I waited in the hallway while she got my coat. When she handed it to me, she smiled.

"What's funny?"

"It's been a long time since I've seen a coat with so much character."

"It's been a long time since they made coats out of textured nylon. But it's warmer than the airbags they stamp out these days, and a lot better made." I sealed the velcro strip which had replaced the zipper which had replaced the original buttons. "This coat will last another twenty years."

Her Volts wasn't anything fancy. Just a pale-blue two-seater with twenty horses and a set of high-gain, double-standard batteries that would go for two days on a full charge. Nothing special. Voltswagon had turned them out by the thousands, and, ten years ago, you could buy one for a song. But the song turned sour, because, without a garage and a plug with some juice in it, Voltswagons were as useless as Detroit specials were when the last puddles of gasoline dried up. During the early brownouts, Voltswagon owners began to desert their lifeless vehicles wherever they ran out of power. In the blackout years, dead Voltswagons littered the highways like locust husks after a plague. These days, just paying taxes on a vehicle that worked was a luxury; powering it was an extravagance.

Joan unlocked the car door, and I slid into the passenger seat. The interior of the car was frigid, and our breath immediately coated the front window with translucent ice ferns. Joan pressed the retract button, and the car detached itself from the umbilicus of the house batteries. After she punched out the five-letter combination, the electric motor began to hum warmly. While the car woke up, Joan cleared the crystalline frost flora from the front window. Neither of us spoke, reserving our heat to fight the chill.

We had backed out from under the steps and were halfway up the block before I asked if she wanted me to scrape the rear window.

"No, there are wire defrosters in the glass. Give them a chance to work; otherwise you'll smear it. Besides, there isn't much traffic."

There wasn't any at all. We went another block before Joan asked, "What was it like?"

"What was what like?"

"Finding Gregory Darling. I should think it was horrible. His face. In the paper. . . ."

We were passing three men attempting to pry the frozen top off a garbage dumpster, though I couldn't tell if they intended to put something in or to take something out. One of the men was perched on top of the dumpster, leaning with all his weight on a metal rod he had jacked up under the lid. The other two men hung from the far end of the rod where the leverage was better. They were bouncing the heavy rod up and down, and watching their gloveless hands gripping the icy metal made my fingers ache. Over the hum of the Volts, I could just make out a sharp voice yelling against the wind. "We almost got her that time, Armando." I couldn't tell which of the three men had spoken. As we moved out of the circle of the streetlight we shared with them, both the dumpster and the three men were frozen into a stiff tableau, storm-tossed fishermen and their catch.

I looked at Joan, but her eyes were riveted on the street in front of us.

"Darling's face was something I'm going to spend the rest of my life forgetting."

Joan evidently understood, because she didn't mention him for the rest of the trip.

Once we got across the park, I directed her south on Park Avenue. "You know," she said, "I've always wondered why they call this Park Avenue. It doesn't go within three blocks of the park."

I didn't have an answer for her and, for once, didn't try to make one up. When she pulled to a stop in front of my building, I got out of the car.

"There isn't much sociability in my apartment, but the walk up will warm you."

"What floor?" she grinned.

"Only four below mine."

"And no elevator?"

"That's right."

"Well," she said, glancing back up Park Avenue. "I think I'd better be getting home. The cold really drains these batteries quickly. They're too old, and it's impossible to get replacements. But I'll be glad to make the climb another time. Just say when."

"You don't need an invitation. Despite my boorishness, I did enjoy this evening more than any in a long time."

She cocked her head slightly to the right, almost as if she were waiting for a kiss. She flaired her nostrils slightly. "Why, thank you, Jack. The feeling is mutual." A slight shiver raced through her; it was probably caused by the cold, but I let myself think otherwise. "In a way, it's ironic, our meeting again after all these years."

"And under these circumstances," I added as I let the car door close. Joan waved through the window and pulled the car around with a sharp electric roar. Turning too sharply, she nearly scraped the dumpster, which stuck out in the street.

I had two messages waiting for me when I got upstairs. One was from Detective Murtaugh, informing me Darling was going to be buried in Queen's Cemetery at 10:00 Monday morning. The other was from Senator Sieg's electrosecretary. The Senator was back in town and would wait for my call. That's one of the joys of being a private investigator. You always get such exciting messages.

I reset my recorder and walked through the office to the bathroom, dropping my clothes as I went. There was a little warm water left in the solar heater, and I used some of it to wet the wrinkles of exhaustion on my face. Then I crawled into bed, blew out the light, and switched on the radio.

A panel of experts was talking about the prospects of something they called the "electrical renaissance." Listening to mindless chatter is usually the perfect soporific. The dull, uniformly baritone drone of the speakers lulled me into a dream. I was barely conscious when the newsman reported the death of Carlo Mountain.

13

The news took a moment to sift through the layers of weariness, but once it did, my reaction was dramatic. I fumbled on the light, almost burning myself with the match, and sat for a few minutes quietly contemplating my bald, bony, bruise-mottled knees. Then I began to swear softly and at myself.

The bulletin of Mountain's death was sketchy, even by radio standards, which are lower than those of the newspaper industry. An unnamed member of his staff discovered Mountain's body in his apartment complex on Saturday evening shortly after nine. Apparently nine was the hour to find bodies. No cause of death was given, but the radio station's informed source did spend a few minutes listing the number of people who stood to gain by Mountain's untimely demise, as if the death of anyone eighty years old could be untimely. My name, however, was mentioned nowhere on that list.

The report ended with a brief encapsulization of Mountain's career, which told me nothing I didn't already know. I tried to keep from jumping to the obvious conclusion. There had been no mention of grotesque facial contortions or post-mortal activities. Mountain was an old man, and, after all, old men die every day of natural causes. Hell, young men die every day of natural causes. One thing this world has never run short of is natural causes.

Only a pessimistic detective would suspect that Mountain's death had anything to do with his time deposit. But that's also what I was still telling myself about Darling's death. The thought didn't calm me. My mind jogged long laps around the case. In fact, by the time I crossed the finish line into dreamland, I had run a marathon.

I can still remember when they called Sunday the day of rest. Once upon a long ago people got up slowly, fooled around a little in bed, talked to the kids for the first time in a week, read the paper, and emptied six cups of fresh coffee. On Sundays a long, long time ago, we went to church and didn't feel guilty even if we wasted the whole day. But that was before we traded in weekend quiet on two more days of everything open and everyone moving. By the time we realized exactly what we had lost, that all we were getting was one eternal sludge of never-ending weeks loosly packed with identical days, it was too late to cancel the deal.

Sunday, December twelfth, 1999, however, began for me in a most atypical way, with an early morning visit from a woman. This particular woman, unfortunately, wasn't there to reknit a brow savaged by another night of jagged slumber. I knew that even before I found my robe. Angels of mercy don't pound on the front door. They don't have to. You can hear their breath in your dreams.

"Sergeant Murtaugh, how nice of you to drop by. But I got your message about Darling. No need for the personal delivery."

I wouldn't say Murtaugh knocked me over as she entered the room, but she wasn't particularly ladylike about it either. Had I been a second slower moving my face, I would have had my upper lip split by the door.

"Can it, Hughes," she growled. "I don't have time to waste delivering funeral notices, and I didn't climb all these steps to listen to someone mumble in his sleep." She planted herself in the middle of my office and looked around, appraising everything with a calloused eye. Any resemblance between Murtaugh and the killer whale on the top of a totem pole was purely a product of my imagination.

"What time is it? And what do you want?"

Murtaugh poked caressly at the switch on her wrist appliance, and its soulless voice announced, "Eight twenty-seven twenty."

She looked at me menacingly. "Got that? Or should I turn up the volume?"

I shook my head.

"Got any coffee cubes?"

Without thinking, I nodded. It was a reflex. After all, you're always supposed to be honest with a cop.

"Make them," she commanded. "I've got only a few minutes and don't want you to miss any of them."

I turned and shuffled in my bare feet toward the kitchen across a floor that would freeze water. Murtaugh skated after me. "You live here alone?"

I answered without turning around. For some reason my answer amused her. "Amazing," she said. "That one person could create this much mess."

I'm not usually long on stoicism in the morning, so I didn't have to pretend to be mean when I glanced back at her. "Cop, you're full of shit. This place is immaculate. God knows I spend enough time around here with nothing to do but clean."

"I see how neatly you lined tea cups on the floor?"

"You didn't come here to insult me. You could have done that over the phone. Get to the point." Then I finished my walk into the kitchen and filled the pot with hot water straight from the solar tap. Murtaugh sat at the table. I had extra coffee cups under the sink and filled one with water. Plopping in a coffee cube, I slid the cup across the table to Murtaugh.

"Hughes, you sure have class. Know how long it's been since I've seen a Mickey Mouse mug? You don't have to drag the antiques out to impress me."

"Murtaugh, you got your coffee. If you have something to say, say it. Otherwise pardon me if I pitch you out and go back to sleep. We still have such things as civil rights, you know."

She stiffened, though not disagreeably, and raked her fingers through her gray shock of hair. For a moment, she watched the coffee cube fizzing in the cup. Then she looked up at me. The bags under her heavy lidded eyes had settled into dark rings, and she suddenly looked weary, even for a cop.

"Hughes, I've been up all night with the coronor taking apart Carlo Mountain. Know the man? Mountain, I mean."

"Not personally." Then I added, "He was rich, wasn't he?"

She sniffed and nodded. "He had fat pockets." For the next few seconds, the only sound in the room was the slow, rolling wheeze of her breath. Then she continued, "There are plenty of people anxious to get their fingers into those fat pockets, but before any one of them can help himself, Mountain's death has to be certified. Regulation." She chewed on her opinion of regulations for a second and then rinsed it down with a swallow of coffee. "Now normally that sort of thing doesn't take more than half an hour. Hour at the outside. Quick coronograph, a few cuts, and it's over. And you can be sure there were enough vultures to make sure we didn't take any longer than necessary."

"Find something interesting?" I hesitated a moment and

completed my thought. "Something interesting enough to get you to walk up these five flights?"

Murtaugh grimaced at her cup. "Got anything to cut this acid? I've got a stomach, not a cast-iron tank."

"Could have fooled me." I reached into the table drawer and slid the pack of Creamettes over to her. She dropped six into her cup with a daintiness that belied the veins standing out on her wrist.

"Mountain died a natural death. His heart quit. The guy had a history of heart trouble. No undue trauma suspected. The lady who found him says he was watching an old video-movie, *The Sorrow and the City*, one of Darling's best films. When the movie ended, Mountain was dead. But there wasn't anything suspicious about his death. Just another case of natural causes."

"So why bother me? I never even met the man."

She shook her head wearily and mopped it with her sleeve. "I said yesterday I didn't like complications. Things are usually smooth and simple for a reason. But these important stiffs get special attention, and their coronographs are examined closely. If there's anything strange, the death certificate can't be filed. You ever seen a coronograph?"

I shook my head.

"Everything about the body is recorded against medical records. Every flaw, every blemish, from the hair right down to the soles of the feet, anything that doesn't jive sticks out like a sore thumb." Murtaugh reached into her breast pocket and hauled something out. She laid it on the table between us, and I tried to keep any stray expressions hidden because I knew she was watching me carefully. "The flaw in the ointment," she announced.

The silver of the transducing disk was flecked with brown. Short lateral scratches laced the surface, as if someone had been engraving with a pin, or a scalpel.

I looked Murtaugh in the eye. "You showed me that yesterday. I couldn't identify it then. I still can't."

"Wrong, Hughes. Three times in one breath." She toyed

casually with the flat disk, flipping it over slowly with her finger. "One. This isn't the same disk I showed you last night. We cut this number out of Mountain's head. It stood out on the coronograph like bird shit on your sleeve. Two, you knew last night what it was. Three, you still know but don't want to cooperate. You're a liar. And you make lousy coffee."

I started to protest, but she stopped me. "Don't worry, though. I'll find out what these things are today, as well as that other gizmo we found on Darling's body. You could help me, but you won't. That means extra work for me. And extra trouble. I thought we had an agreement. You save me some trouble now, and I could save you some later on."

"I've heard that before." I am a lousy liar, but that didn't stop me from trying. "I know you don't believe this, but nothing has happened since last night to change anything I told you."

Murtaugh took it better than I expected, which is not to say she took it well. "All right, Hughes. I tried to be nice. I let you go last night. Murder suspects don't usually get such gentle treatment. Now it's time to go down to my office and do some serious talking. You'd better bring a toothbrush." She poked her wrist appliance and spoke into it. "Slovinsky! Come on up. We're having company for breakfast." She shook her wrist to clear the circuit. "Slovinsky's not pleased about getting hauled out of bed either. He's in a mean mood. Think's you've caused him a lot of trouble lately. I'd have to agree." She pulled a wristicuff from her pocket and went through the motion of arming it. It was a new model, designed not to restrain the criminal but to kill him if he got too far from his controller. The poison it used to do the job was rumored to be especially painful, and not many people tried to escape these days. I let Murtaugh finish her act before I said anything.

"Well, I guess I'd better get dressed. It's the middle of winter, and this robe wasn't meant for the cold. I know how chilly you keep it down in the crypts. Mind rinsing out that cup, though? I hate coming home to dirty dishes."

I walked into the bedroom, picking up my clothes along the way. I could feel Murtaugh's eyes following me down the hall, and she stood in the doorway while I dressed. I had only started when there was a sharp bang at the door.

"That's Slovinsky," she said. "He must have sprinted." She went to let him in. I was glad for the privacy. Having people watch me dress or undress has always made me uncomfortable. It must be something about the transition. Being naked never bothered me.

I pulled on my boots and walked out into the office. Murtaugh was leaning casually against the door.

"Where's Mr. Stooge?"

Murtaugh flicked her head twice quickly as if she were clearing water from her ears. "I told Slovinsky to wait outside. He'll be there if I need him. He needed to catch his breath." For the first time since I met her, Murtaugh failed to look tough. "Hughes, it doesn't have to be this way. You're not going to do either of us any good in jail."

"I won't argue with that."

"Then why force me to pin a murder on you?"

"You said Mountain died a natural death."

She smacked her lips wearily. "You know who I'm talking about. Darling's case doesn't get closed with his casket, and you're still the prime suspect. You and that jerk outside. He knows what a jam he's in. Why do you think he sprinted up the steps? I just have too many things to do to find another jerk to stand in for you."

"What about your mysterious Jeanette?"

"Why should I bother? You have any idea how many Jeanettes there are in this city?"

"And you're only looking for one."

"Yeah." She flicked at a speck on the table next to the door. For a moment, I thought the speck was dust, but it crawled down the wall. Murtaugh stamped at it indignantly with her foot. "Even the little ones are impossible to kill. Nice roach ranch you got here."

"Yeah." Both of us watched the speck bore into the crack

between the floor and the wall.

"I'll make a deal with you, Murtaugh. Lay off me for two more days and I'll turn over absolutely everything I come up with to you then. For the first time in months, I've got a job with money coming in. I don't want to blow it. My case doesn't have anything to do with these two deaths. I promise that much. But having you hound me isn't making either of our jobs easier, and, as you say, you have plenty of other things to do. You give me forty-eight hours, and I'll give you everything on a gold record."

"I don't see gold in it for anyone but you, Hughes. I take the risk, and you leave town. Then what have I got? If I take you down right now, I have at least one death solved. A check in the hand, as they say, is worth two in the mail."

"That won't solve the mystery of those silver gizmos. Sure, you can take me down now, but I don't think I'll be too cooperative. I can hang on for at least two days, and they won't be easy. Not for me. Not for you. On the other hand, I'm offering you a chance to sit back and have the whole neat bundle dropped in your lap on Tuesday. What have you got to lose? It's a cinch I'm not going to leave town." I displayed the office with a dramatic flourish. "How could I leave all this?"

"That's fine for you, but what am I going to tell those vultures circling Mountain's pockets? Do you think they'll wait two days? With inflation the way it is, Mountain's fortune gets a few percentage points smaller every day."

"You'll think of an excuse. The police are good at that."

She watched me closely while she thought. "All right. Forty-eight hours, Hughes. And no excuses or delays. I won't waste another minute on the Darling case. It's you or whoever you come up with to take the rap."

I offered her my right hand as I closed the door with my left. "Detective Murtaugh, it's a pleasure doing business with you."

She just stared at my hand. "Nothing personal, Hughes,

I don't shake hands with doomed men." Then she walked out.

I used the first of those forty-eight hours to piece back together the remainder of the night's sleep Murtaugh had shattered. About ten, when I got up for the second time, I celebrated my freedom by fixing a proper Sunday breakfast consisting of a hot cup of coffee, two slices of toast, and a pair of poachers. I washed the evidence of my feast and put all the dishes away, returning the Mickey Mouse mug to the cabinet, next to the Superman glasses.

It was eleven before I let myself think about the case, relishing the false sense of innocence the truce with Murtaugh gave me. But, enough was enough. I ran Jeanette Dumbrey's name through the data console and got nothing but blank paper. Then, putting my feet up on the desk, I dialed the number Senator Sieg's electrosecretary had left on my recorder. I got an immediate connection with a woman officious enough to be the senatorial spouse. She instructed me to wait, and, after a minute, she was replaced by a broad baritone reeking of political dignity.

"This is Senator Sieg."

"Vic? This is Jack Hughes."

"Dreyfus, how the hell are you?" The Senator's voice went through a quick change that left it sounding like something that might belong to a human being. "I was amazed when I got back from Washington and got your message. When did you get back in town?"

"I never left."

There was a pause. "But I heard that you left M. D. and D. I checked around a couple of years ago, but you weren't working anywhere. I figured you'd moved to the sunbelt."

"I just quit practicing."

"You quit practicing?"

"In your own way, so have you. You've made quite a name for yourself, Victor."

"I keep busy," he said with the smug stink of false modesty. "Have to keep the wolf and bad ratings away from the door, right?"

"That's right, Vic."

"Listen, Dreyf, was there any particular reason for calling?" I couldn't quite tell whether the kink in his voice was hesitancy or impatience.

"As a matter of fact, there is. I've been doing investigative work for—"

"Investigative work? What do you mean?" There was a noticeable decrease in the friendliness quotient of his voice.

"You know. Detective work. Private eye. Bogarting."

"How the hell did you get messed up with something like that?"

"It's a long story I'll gladly tell you sometime, but right now there are a couple of things I'd rather find out. Maybe we could get together this afternoon. I had another appointment, but it's been cancelled."

"Jack, you know I'd love to. But I've been out of town for three weeks. Inspecting the progress of the fungus control experiments in Mexico. I promised to spend the day with the family."

"I'd be glad to come up there."

"No, I don't think that would be wise."

"How about tomorrow?"

"Gee, Dreyf, the whole day is filled with appointments. You know, a politician's life is never his own. Maybe in a few weeks."

"This isn't a personal call. It won't wait that long. You're a depositer in Ivory Wightman's bank, aren't you?" It wasn't an accusation, but it wasn't exactly a question either.

He greeted my words with a silence as chilly as last year's lover. "The bastard swore to me all accounts were secret. I should have known better than to trust him. I wouldn't think you'd sink low enough to . . ."

"Listen, Senator Sieg. This has nothing to do with blackmail. At least not yet. Your secret is still intact. Even the police don't know about Wightman's setup. But that didn't stop someone from breaking into his vault and stealing five account tapes. Yours was one. I think it would be a good idea for you to help me find it before someone does think about blackmailing you. How much would you pay to get your tape back? I'm only asking for a little of your time."

"I wouldn't pay anything. I don't think I've saved five minutes the whole time I've had an account. So you see, I'm the wrong depositor to ask."

"That's what Carlo Mountain thought. He's dead."

"Carlo Mountain dead?" Sieg sounded genuinely surprised. "When the hell did that happen?"

"Last night." It wasn't hard to sound ominous.

"Maybe I can make some time tomorrow morning," he said hesitantly.

"No good. In the morning I have to attend the funeral of a friend."

"Anyone I know?"

"Gregory Darling. He was a depositor too."

"Maybe I can squeeze you in tomorrow afternoon. About two?"

"That's fine."

"By the way, Dreyf," he said, looking for a friendly note to part on. "How are Alicia, Annie, and your little boy?"

"They're dead, Vic. For ten years."

"Oh, God," he said, sounding as sincere as a hairdresser. "I'm sorry to hear that."

"I'll see you tomorrow, Vic."

I put down the phone and removed my feet from the desk. Neither fame nor fortune nor fifteen years had changed Victor Sieg one bit.

14

There was something naggingly familiar about Jeanette Dumbrey's address, but I wasn't clever enough to figure out what until I climbed out of the subway at Thirty-fourth Street.

I had forgotten the lower floors of the old Empire State Building had been turned into apartments. After all the squatters had been cleared from the upper stories following the riots at the Stair Sprint Championships in 1993, the building had been boarded up. Only recently has it been reclaimed. It has survived the years of disuse well; its high facades are intact, rows of still-lifeless windows glistening in the sunshine. It remains a proud monument to all the lofty dreams that made Manhattan what it is today.

The lobby of the building was surprisingly clean, considering most of the usable floor space was occupied by the various narrow stalls of a farmers' market. Shoppers bustled through the rows picking fruit and vegetables from the pushcarts and shanty stands. The room had the atmosphere of a circus and smelled a little that way, too. It took me some minutes to find anyone who even knew where the entrance to the upper floors was hidden. The passageway, set apart from the pandemonium by a thick glass partition, was guarded by a sloe-eyed, dark-haired lad of about twenty. His sidekick, a Doberman the size of a small ox, owned a set of teeth that said "Keep Out" in a language anyone can understand. Most cautiously, I poked my head around the edge of the partition and succeeded only in attracting the attention of the dog. The kid, busy hanging up heavy clouds of that old sweet smoke, was too preoccupied to bother about intruders. When I started to ooze around the glass, the dog's xenophobic reaction yanked the kid back from wherever he had been floating. Almost casually, the pimple-faced wimp back-handed the foaming storm of claw and tooth across the snout. "Stuff yourself, Hitler." As quick as a nickel cab ride, Hitler melted into a puddle of cuddly fur which burrowed into his master's lap. So cute. A boy and his dog.

"He always do what you tell him?" I asked, cautiously taking another step forward even though I saw Hitler's eyes following me all the way. If the kid heard me, he didn't react at all.

"I asked if he always listens to you."

The kid looked down and gave the dog a playful tug on the muzzle. "Yeah." Then he looked up at me. "Unless you had a bitch in heat. You want something?"

"I'd like to see somebody."

"I'm somebody and you see me."

"Somebody upstairs."

"Lots of people would like that. Read the sign." "No Pedalers Allowed!!!!" it said.

When I asked him if he had written the sign, he nodded.

"No one gets by unless they know the password. You know the password?"

I shook my head. "I just said I wanted to see somebody."

The complexity of my logic didn't impress him. "Somebody up there wants to see you, then you'd know the password."

"She doesn't know I'm coming."

He looked at me blankly. "Maybe she don't want to see you."

"Maybe, but we'll never know unless you call up and find out."

The kid looked at me as if that was the most asinine suggestion he'd ever heard. "We ain't got no phone. Why do you think we got a password? You don't know the password, you don't go upstairs."

"Can I take a guess?"

That threw him. He rolled his eyes in their pea-shaped

sockets and said, "What do I look like, Rumblestilsky?"

"I just thought maybe the password might be, say, a hundred dollars."

He needed some time to catch on, but slowly the bright light of greed cast a long shadow over his flat face. He rubbed his burnt-out nose and sneered. "No, but it might be two hundred. Paper. No plastic."

I nodded, reached into my pocket, and fished out four fifties, which I dangled in front of me. The kid covered the distance in two strides. He reached out to grab the bills, but I caught his hand. "First you tell me a couple things."

He glanced back over his shoulder at Hitler, who was regarding me with suspicion.

"If that dog so much as moves, I forget the password. Understand?"

He looked at me with an expression of profound confusion, but he shook his head up and down slowly.

"About the woman who lives in 1506. . ."

His eyes opened wide, but not as wide as his mouth. "You sure about that number? No lady lives in 1506. There ain't no 1506 in the buildings. No numbers go over 600. Who told you 1506?"

"She did."

His grin was slightly moronic. "Mister, you got mistooken." He pointed his blunt chin at me and said, "Who you got to see?"

"Jeanette Dumbrey." I spelled out the name but got the impression the letters made no sense to him.

"Dumbrey? Dumpray?" He tried pronouncing the name a few different ways, but none of them worked. "Nobody with a name like that lives here."

"Has anyone with that name ever lived here?"

"I don't know about ever, but not in the last four years. Either she gave you a dud name or a dud address. Maybe both. What's she look like?"

I handed him the photograph I had taken from the file at Wightman's. He just sucked his lower lip and shook his head. "You was mistooken by a real skag."

"How sure are you that she doesn't live here?"

"Surer than you are she does."

I started to slowly retreat back into the lobby. "I guess I was mistooken."

But the kid grabbed my wrist. "Don't forget the password. I got two hundred coming."

"For what? The two hundred was for letting me go upstairs."

"Who's stopping you?"

"There's no need for me to go up now."

"That's not my worry. Two hundred." It wasn't the hold he had on my wrist that kept me from slapping him silly. It was the hold he had over Hitler. The dog had gotten to his feet and was eyeing me as if I were a kilo of prime rib.

"I didn't get what I wanted, but I did get what I needed. Here's a hundred." I stuck two bills in his hand. He looked at the fifties, licked his lips, and shoved them under his belt.

"Pleasure doing business with you, mister," he said as I backed out of the room. A hundred dollars wasn't much. There are two things in this city that are still cheap. Information is one. A Thanksgiving Special at Augustino's is the other.

As I walked along Thirty-second street toward the Hudson, I tried to digest this new turn of events. I could think of a dozen reasons I might to keep my real address from Wightman if I were a depositor, but only half those reasons were legal. So what if Jeanette Dumbrey wanted to keep her privacy? I still had no evidence but a questionable set of initials and a batch of hopes to link Jeanette Dumbrey to the theft of the tapes. Finding someone in this city isn't that difficult. Usually, it's much harder to stay hidden. The advantage definitely lies on the side of the invader of privacy rather than the invadee. On the other hand, a full scale investigation does take time, and suddenly I didn't have much of that to waste. Before I got too involved looking for Jeanette

Dumbrey, I wanted to make as sure as I could she'd be was worth the effort.

I caught an uptown train to Seventy-ninth street and was still half a block from Wightman's office when I spotted the robin's-egg-blue Voltswagon parked on the street in front of his building.

I stopped in a doorway to figure out why Joan Dark might be visiting Wightman. All the reasons I came up with sounded no more than plausible, so I decided to wait where I was until she left.

I waited half an hour before Wightman's door opened. It was a Dark woman all right, but not the one I was waiting for. Lea Dark, looking properly agitated, came storming out of the building. Trigger held the door open while Lea was busy delivering a tirade that looked as if it would have made a stone blush. But Wightman's assistant stood her ground, smiling like a sponge bunny and absorbing every word of Lea's abuse. Trigger looked concerned, helpful, but not in the least cowed by the formidable old woman. Even at that distance, the gall of Lea's words was so bitter that I watched for a few minutes before I realized the old woman was using up a lot of energy for someone with a debilitating heart problem. She stood there, toe to toe with Trigger, without a hint of a wheelchair or a butler's supporting arm.

It took Lea a surprisingly long time to realize her strongest words were just bouncing off Trigger's equanimity. Then, using as much energy to control her temper as she had used venting it, Lea shot her class jaw into the air, turned on her heel, and was in the Voltswagon so quickly, she was a block away before my subconscious pointed out an interesting detail. Lea's dark-gray fur coat, the one with the natural swath of black across the back, looked very familiar.

It didn't take me another second to realize why.

15

For a few minutes, I didn't move, trying both to relish this latest revelation and to keep my imagination from running with it off into the sunset. This unexpected link between Lea Dark and Gregory Darling fascinated me, but there was too much empty air between seeing her in a coat similar to the one I had seen at Darling's and proving her guilty of a punishable crime.

I leaned on Wightman's buzzer until Trigger opened the door. Surprisingly, she didn't exhibit the slightest scar from the barrage Lea had just leveled at her. Trigger smiled serenely, exactly as she had smiled each time she opened the door for me and, I suspected, everyone else in the world with the exception of Wightman himself.

"I hope last night was more enjoyable than your most recent visitor," I said when I had finished smiling.

Trigger looked at me blankly. "Much more enjoyable, but how did you know?"

"I didn't about last night, but I did catch the last act on the doorstep a few minutes ago."

"Mrs. Dark wasn't happy," Trigger acknowledged.

"Putting it mildly. Is she always so energetic?"

"Energetic?"

"Active. She's supposed to be a sick woman."

"If she's sick, I never knew it. At least not physically sick. Mental is another thing. Mrs. Dark always acts like she was a queen or someone special like that." Trigger's blank expression was totally uncompromised by any understanding of the old woman's motives.

"Does she always come alone?"

"Sometimes she brings this tall, quiet man with her. She calls him Edward."

"That's her butler."

"What's a butler? Is it like a battler?"

"No," I chuckled. "A butler is a servant. Someone you hire to do things for you that you don't want to do yourself."

For some reason that amused her.

"Was Mrs. Dark here to make a deposit?"

Trigger shook her head energetically. "She wanted me to give her another transducer. She claims hers isn't working right."

"She wanted another transducer? Is that usual?"

Her eyes opened wide and she shook her head. "Everyone gets only one transducer. I said if hers wasn't working right, she should give it to us and we'd repair it. When I told her we couldn't give her another one, she started to get nasty."

"What did she say when you told her that her tape was missing?"

"Strange, but she never asked for it. So I didn't tell her." Trigger smiled guiltily. "There didn't seem to be any reason to. It would have only made her madder."

"Absolutely right." I strolled over and parked myself in one of the plush chairs. "Did you make up those lists I asked for?"

"I was just finishing when Mrs. Dark arrived. Should I add her visit to the list?"

"That won't be necessary. I won't forget it."

Trigger reached into the desk and handed me two sheets of paper. Both were neatly covered in the large block letters of a child's script. One list showed the dates each of the five victims had visited the bank during the last six months. The other gave the dates of Jeanette Dumbrey's visits for the same period.

"Jeanette Dumbrey seems to be a more frequent visitor that any of the depositors on this other list."

"She's a real in-and-outer. She'll never save much time."

"And this is interesting," I said. "She's been in here a day or two after each of the final visits of the five victims. Her last visit was early Friday afternoon. Did she make a deposit or a withdrawal?"

"I made stars next to the deposits."

No star marked Jeanette Dumbrey's last visit. I laid the lists down. "I visited the address on Jeanette Dumbrey's file card. The lockmaster never heard of her."

The news didn't surprise Trigger. She shrugged. "The clients fill out their own cards. We never check if they're lying. As long as they pay their bills, it doesn't make any difference what they tell us."

"Even if they use false names?"

She shrugged a second time.

"I'll bet Jeanette Dumbrey always pays her bill on time."

"Right on time."

"With plastic?" I asked hopefully, knowing the federal credit reserves are more particular about things like correct names and addresses.

"No, she always pays in cash."

"That's odd."

"I know. Why would anyone want to use cash? It's so old-fashioned. And dirty. Plastic is much more convenient."

"Last night, you said you didn't know how old Jeanette Dumbrey is. Take a guess."

"I don't know," she shrugged. "She's middle-aged."

"What's middle-aged?"

Trigger waved her right hand in the air, trying to snag an answer that wouldn't offend me. "You know. Thirty-five. Forty. In there somewhere."

"And she's a conservative dresser who wears a red wig and sunglasses?"

"That's right."

"How tall is she? Anything strange about her? Does she walk funnily? Anything distinguishing at all."

"She's about my height. A meter forty. Average build. She wears a lot of camouflage, especially darkener. I can usually tell a lot about a woman by the way she uses camouflage."

"What about her?"

"Nothing special. She's rich, but all our clients are rich. Do you think she's the thief?"

"Maybe. I'd like to be surer, though, before I waste too much time looking for her. Can I see her account tape?"

Trigger looked shocked by the suggestion. "That's impossible. A depositor's account is private."

"I wouldn't ask if I didn't have a good reason. You remember my theory about how the theft was carried out?"

"Yes, and I also remember we decided even if a thief could get into another person's compartment, he'd still have to present his own tape for processing. There wouldn't be time to get two."

"Yes, but if the thief brought in her own tape when she came, she could get her victim's tape from the compartment, and still process her own at the desk."

It was a struggle, but Trigger slowly followed my logic. She even went a bit further on her own. "That means the thief's compartment would be empty. And that means Miss Dumbrey couldn't be the thief because her tape isn't missing."

She was gold-star correct, but the detective manuals all tell you to take nothing for granted. "I'd still like to check. Your boss said you'd help me any way you could."

She regarded me warily. "I suppose so, but I don't like the idea."

"I'll take full responsibility. Trust me." There is no way in the world to make those two words sound sincere, but Trigger nodded, reached behind her desk, and pressed the combination of switches and buttons that opened the vault. Then, standing so I couldn't see, she punched out a long sequence on the securidial. A moment passed and all the compartment doors popped open with tiny hisses like the last gasps of so many dying balloons. I followed her into the vault.

"You can see well enough from there," she said when I had reached the middle of the vault. "Don't get close to any of the compartments. That's Miss Dumbrey's. The third from the right on the top row."

The red sheen of a tape cassette was clearly visible. "I thought you said only five tapes were missing," I said after a moment's inspection of the wall.

Trigger glared at me with a look of growing horror. "What do you mean?"

"That whole row is empty."

She exhaled slowly. "Those are all unassigned compartments. Of course they're empty."

I shrugged sheepishly and walked back to the desk. Trigger closed the vault and followed me. "I hope you're satisfied," she said with a certain amount of sarcasm. "Your theory is all mush."

"Maybe. Maybe not. Miss Dumbrey was in here the other day. She could have replaced her tape then."

"But her compartment would have been empty for the inventory."

I nodded and looked over the two lists again. "If Darling discovered his tape was missing on Thursday. The last victim in here before that was . . . Lea Dark, four days earlier. Jeanette Dumbrey made a deposit the day after that. She could have taken Lea's tape then."

"But, according to your theory, she couldn't have both stolen a tape and replaced hers on the same day. And, even when she was in here the day before yesterday, she had no reason to think any one had discovered the theft. No one but you knew the tapes were missing."

"Darling knew. He could have told anyone." But Trigger was right and I knew it. My case against Jeanette Dumbrey was evaporating back into the air from which it had been conjured. "We don't have much on Jeanette Dumbrey except a similarity of name, a possible acquaintence with Gregory Darling, and the fact she gave you a false address. I can't rule her out entirely, but there are other leads to check before I waste the time trying to find her. We still have five good suspects."

"Five? Not the victims?"

"Why not? Until I establish a motive or discover some solid

evidence, any one of them could, according to my theory, be the guilty party."

"But not one of the victims."

"Let's look at the lists." I laid both pages out next to each other on the desk. "It couldn't be Mountain. He hasn't been in here for months. Neither was Victor Sieg, so he's out too. Allison Bashcock was here two weeks ago, but Darling and Lea Dark have been in since then. I doubt Darling was the thief. Why would he have blown the whistle if he was? If we assume he's not guilty, that makes Allison Bashcock innocent. She would have had to take his tape on her last visit, and Darling would have said something before the day before yesterday. We have to assume his tape was taken since Allison Bashcock's most recent visit. That eliminates everyone."

"Everyone but Lea Dark."

"Everyone but Lea Dark," I agreed. "She was the last of the so-called victims to be in here before Darling discovered that his tape was missing."

"She must have taken his tape." Jeanette's jury was out for only an instant before it returned its guilty verdict. "I'm glad Mrs. Dark is the thief. I never liked her."

"Whoa. We don't have any proof. I'm sure even your boss would think twice before accusing one of his best customers. Evidence. Until we get some of that, we've got nothing but unsupported theory."

"Where do you get evidence?"

"You can make it up, of course. But we won't get away with that. Not against Lea Dark. I think I know where to look. Hang around the right tree long enough, and an apple or two will hit you in the head."

I winked at her, but she didn't have the slightest idea of what I was talking about.

Neither, come to think of it, did I.

When I left Jeanette Dobbson, she was busy thinking up evidence to use against Lea Dark. I tried to explain to her that evidence can't be created out of nothing. Either it's there or it isn't. Finding it, cultivating it, takes dilligence, intelligence, and creative insight. You can't construct it out of thin air. Or at least I couldn't. Creating evidence out of error didn't seem to worry Murtaugh.

Since the day was warm and relatively sunny, I decided to walk back across the park to my place. A light breeze trailed at my heels, bringing with it the warm, piquant aroma of New Jersey. The hot roast-beef sandwich smell reminded me of spring the way any warm breeze does in the middle of winter.

Sunshine still brings out the citizens. I spotted a few dozen sunbathers lying on banks of winter debris trying to find a winter tan for their faces. That's an encouraging sign. At least that many people are possessed by a vanity strong enough to overcome their obdurate lethargy.

Heading south, I emerged from the park at Fifty-ninth and Fifth. A fair chunk of Sunday commerce surged along the broad concourse. When you're hungry to acquire goods and have the money to fan that hunger, Fifty-seventh Street is still the place to go. I'm told business here goes up to the ninth story, though I would think that many steps would dull the sharpest urges to spend.

Passing the government center on Madison, I ran into a gaggle of my fellow citizens standing in front of a plate-glass window. A triview screen two meters across had been set up, and its crystal-clear image created the illusion of silver-clad construction workers bouncing around in a gravityless void on the other side of the glass, even though the sign over the triviewer advertised a live broadcast from Orbicol.

A slight, nervous man with a tic in his right eye and a gray cadaverous mole that crested his chin like a nipple, moved in close on my right. He was mumbling something like "Can't believe it" under his breath, and the smell of sweaty feet clung to him like a cheap date. Then, directing his remark at no one in particular, he said, "Look like guppies in a goddamned bowl, don't they?"

"A little," I answered without thinking.

"A little," he hissed, turning toward me, his bad eye doing a little dance. "A little! You know, mister, the day I was born, the first man took a walk on the moon. I should know what I'm talking about."

I nodded, still more interested in the distant maneuvering of the space jockey with the cutting iron than the histrionics of the man with the waltzing eye who stood next to me.

But he continued. "I took my first breath on earth the same day man took his first breath on the moon. And you know what?" He leaned into me conspiratorily and giggled inanely under his breath. "I couldn't care less. They say this is a direct broadcast, a live transmission straight from Orbit Alpha. All these people here, I call them the sheep of Earth. They think they're looking right into the gun barrel of the universe, staring into eternity's eyeball. They ain't. That geek with the cutting iron. The one with the blue slash across his helmet. That's me. I was master welder up there for six months. Three weeks ago I came downside for a month's vacation. Been the longest damn month of my life. That other guy, the one holding the I-strut. His name's Digger Gear, from Texas somewhere. Right now, though, he's dead. Got sucked through a collapsing airlock the other day. So I ask you, if he's dead, how can they call this a live transmission? That's what I'd like to know."

I backed away a few centimeters and tried to ignore the man. He looked far older than the thirty-one years he claimed. I've heard that space work ages a man quickly, but he could have as easily been lying his head off. Space grandeur is still a common enough delusion. Everyone's looking for a way out, and space is a better dream than most.

My doubt must have been obvious because he leaned closer to me. If he had come any nearer, we could have worn the same coat.

"You think I'm spacebrained, don't you?" He snorted with disgust. "Well, what you think doesn't make any difference to me. You wouldn't know a welder's whistle from a pig fart. All you earthies are just going to dry up some day and blow

away. Like dead leaves. Like dog shit in the summer." He
shuddered and, having delivered his message, moved away
a bit. I kept watching the screen just long enough to make
my exit look like an escape from boredom rather than an
escape from fear. No telling what little thing might send
another deep-ender over the edge.

The front door of my building was wide open, and the
dark lobby was freezing as I passed through, pausing only
long enough to push the elevator button. I'll say one thing
for fifth-floor living. It keeps your heart young and your
knees happy. I wasn't even breathing hard as I reached the
top. In fact, I was halfway down the hall, whistling as I went,
before I noticed the visitor leaning on the door of my apartment.

16

"This is a surprise!"
    "Jack, I hope you don't mind, but I invited
myself for dinner." A red-faced Joan Dark took two steps to
meet me and laid a brown paper bag in my hands. I looked
at the bag and shrugged.
    "Coffee and cognac," she explained. "The cognac's nothing
special, but the beans are ground for sun brewing. Have you

ever had sun-brewed coffee?"

"I don't think so."

"You let the coffee soak in cold water overnight and the sun warm it in the morning. I think you'll enjoy it."

"You shouldn't have," I said, making no move to return her gift. "Have you been waiting long?"

"Not nearly long enough to recover from the climb. How do you manage?"

"You get used to it. I only go out when necessary and don't bring back anything heavy. There's a completely furnished apartment on this floor that anyone could have for the asking. The couple that used to live there left everything rather than carry it all down the steps." I unlocked the door. "But don't get the idea it's all misery. Living this high has some real advantages. It's the warmest floor in the building. And the safest. Heat rises, but burglars don't."

Joan chuckled and followed me through the open door. I hung up our coats in the bedroom, put the bag of pleasures on the table in the kitchen, and went out to join Joan in the office. When I entered the room, she was sitting on the couch by the window warming herself in the last whispers of afternoon sunshine. The combination of her cream-colored blouse with its high lacy collar and silver piping against the pastel bleach of sunlight cast her profile with the regal diffusiveness of a pre-Raphaelite madonna.

When she realized I was watching her, she turned toward me. "It's cozy here. This room gets a lot of sun."

"It's the only direct heat it does get. Luckily, the insulglass manages to hang on to most of it."

Joan nodded absently and turned back toward the sun, her face in three-quarter profile. I walked over and sat on the edge of the desk. "I hope you're not a fussy eater. I'm not geared for company, and the cupboard is almost bare. You've got a choice of pseudo-beef burgers with mushroom plasma for gravy or fish sticks with onions."

"You make both choices sound so appetizing I can't decide. Which do you recommend?"

"Fish sticks always remind me of blotters, so I guess I'd go with the beef. I could uncork some wax beans. I've got one bag of '95 left. That was a particularily good year for wax beans."

"I didn't know that."

"Oh, yes, you'll find them pleasant, full-bodied. They're from the south slope of the valley."

"That makes a difference?"

"Oh, I should say it does. The growing season is longer on the south slope. There the beans ripen slowly to their full maturity and develop their characteristic tang."

"Pray tell, where is this bucolic vale?"

"That I don't know. Someplace populated by tiny green humanoids, I assume from the label."

"Are the beans really four years old?"

"Almost five. I've been saving them for a special occasion. Aging mellows wax beans."

"Mellows and yellows." She stood and hugged herself, smoothing the wings of her blouse. "My visit qualifies as a special occasion?"

"Such lovely company making that climb qualifies as a miracle."

"Then let's be daring and have those beans. Is there something I can do to help?"

"Not at all. Heat and eat. A meal in a minute or your money back. Good thing, too. With the price of gas, the preparation of a meal costs as much as the food itself."

Joan followed me into the kitchen and watched while I retrieved the pseudo-beef patties from the window box. I turned down the foil lid so the patties could air brown, and got the beans from the lifeless refrigerator that served as a pantry. I opened the pouch, added some warm water from the solar tap, peeled off the label, and set the beans and the patties in the ovenette. "Now, any time we're ready to eat." Bringing two tumblers with me, I sat across from her at the table. I opened the bottle of cognac and poured a few fingers in each glass.

"I'd offer you something else if I had it."

"I'd have brought something else if I'd known. Cheers."

We clicked glasses and smiled at each other. "Thanks for bringing this. It's tasty."

"It was the least I could do. After all, I did invite myself."

"That's not true. I extended a carte blanche invitation last night."

"You're wondering why I came?"

"I know it wasn't for the food."

She grinned. "No, it wasn't." She turned serious, and her fist started to buff uneven circles on the dull formica tabletop. "Did you know Carlo Mountain died last night?"

"I heard about it on the news."

"Carlo was a friend of my mother's and a customer of Ivory Wightman's. Do you think his death had anything to do with his time account?" She gazed over my shoulder at the wallpaper, which time had faded to the color of library paste.

"How did you know about Mountain's time account?"

Joan looked back at me and cocked her head a notch to the left. "He's had dinner at our house many times. He and my mother are old friends, and I think he may have been the one who first introduced my mother to Wightman's bank." Panic began to spread across her face. "Jack, do you think that . . . ?"

"The police say Mountain died of natural causes. A heart attack. They don't know, however, that he was one of the five depositers who had his tape stolen. With Darling, that makes two of those five who've died since Friday. That might be a coincidence. It might not."

I sometimes have a knack for snatching defeat from the jaws of the mouth. I had intended to calm her, and ended up scaring her. She forgot all about polishing my table and stared at me. "Jack, do you really think that . . ." I could see her fighting back her worst fears. "Maybe your visit last night got me thinking or maybe it was the news of Carlo's death, but I know I have to do something to help my mother." Joan faltered for a moment, as if she were a child looking for the resolve to own up to her first mortal sin. "Lately, she's been acting very strangely. She's always been a bit. . . odd, but, in the last few months . . . It's nothing you could put your finger on. More an attitude she's developed. An aura of invincibility."

"Invincibility? Go on." I was most interested in Joan's diagnosis, but not for the reason she thought.

"After our talk last night, I realized my mother should know her tape is missing. She'll find out soon enough anyway, and at least, if I tell her, I can prepare her for the shock. This morning, after breakfast, I went to her room. Jack, I didn't even bring up the subject of the tapes before I had the oddest feeling she already knew. I didn't even get a chance to tell her about her tape. As soon as I mentioned the time deposit, she practically threw me out."

I was surprised to see I had finished my drink before Joan had touched hers. I poured another glass and made a silent promise not to drink it. "Have you got another for instance?"

"I feel silly telling you all this, but I don't know who else to turn to."

"Don't feel silly."

She watched me for a moment. Her concern and vexation were more than obvious. Fine wrinkles marked the corners of her eyes, and furrows lined her forehead. "Another thing. Edward. He's been with us for years. We're lucky. Good help is nonexistent these days."

"For that matter, so is bad."

Joan smiled disconcertedly. "My mother has always been so appreciative of Edward, but, in the last few months, she's begun to harass him so much on several occasions he's complained to me. I tried to speak with her about him, but she just smiles and denies ever being cruel." She started her buffing again, and I took that as a cue for me to allow myself a sip of the cognac. "That's not everything. Sometimes, in the space of an hour, her mood will swing from wild exuberance to morose sulking. More and more, she spends her time plugged into that transducer. You should see her. She'll sit rocking for hours on end, barely conscious of anything around her. She'll scowl like a petulant child one moment and break into gales of hysterical laughter the next. And, she's started going half-dressed around the house, not even wearing camouflage. If there's one thing my mother has always been conscious of, it's her appearance. She'd never let anyone see her without her camouflage, not even my father."

"It sounds as if she's getting senile. It happens to a lot of us."

"At first, I thought that too. But I checked with her doctors, and all four of them agreed that, except for her heart, she's in fine condition. When I heard that Gregory Darling died . . . And now Carlo. . . ." She put her elbows on the table and propped up her heads with her hands. "Could their deaths have anything to do with this cult of time?"

"Joan, I don't know anything about either the physical or psychological effects of Wightman's gizmo. Hell, I'm not sure it does anything at all, but every depositor I've talked to has sworn by it. Wightman claims it's neither dangerous nor addictive, but Henry Ford said the same thing about the automobile. I'd be lying if I told you I knew your mother's condition wasn't related to her use of the transducer. Look at it this way. Three hundred years ago, someone with a device like a transducer would have been burned as a witch. The human animal has always been a little slow to accept the dangers of his own technology. Or, for that matter, even understand what that technology did. Who knows what impact a process like time transuction might have on a steady user. Even if it doesn't do anything physical. Scientists can often cure patients with sugar pills as long as those patients actually believe they're getting potent medicine. What can you do about your mother? You admit she rules her own life."

"I could have her declared mentally incompetent."

"Not a chance. You won't find a judge or lawyer willing to listen to you. They'll all have better things to do, or at least that's what they'll say. The real reason is, of course, they're afraid. Since the legal malpractice laws were established no one would risk the possibility of a countersuit by someone with your mother's clout. For every expert you could produce to certify her incompetence, she'll produce three to certify yours."

"But if this transducer is destroying her. . . ."

"Not good enough. If self-destruction was a criterion of incompetence, we'd all be lying on the floor with our elbows strapped to our sides and our hands laced together behind our backs."

That opinion didn't satisfy her one bit, so I tried another. "Look, you've lived with her this long. Maybe she's just getting old. Or maybe she's finally caving in. In either case, there's nothing you can do to stop her. Believe me."

She shook her head violently. "I'd rather see my mother dead than watch her become a sniveling, half-human lump of dough like the rest of the world." The sudden bitterness in her voice stung. It eclipsed any emotion which had preceded it. The usually soft lines of her mouth became rigid. "Jack, I'm sorry. Of course I don't want anything to happen to her. But I don't think I can bear to watch her deteriorate." After a second, she added, "Any more than she already has."

"You're not, I take it, a fan of present world conditions."

She sniffed. "How could I be? I'm old enough to remember life as it once was. How could anyone be a fan of this hollowness?"

"A lot of people have made peace with it."

"Too many people, I'd say. They sit around like logs rotting in a forest."

"When was the last time you saw logs rotting in a forest? For that matter, when was the last time you saw a forest?"

She ignored my attempt at humor. "And you're telling me to give up on my mother."

"Just one minute, Ms. Dark. It's not a question of telling you to give up. It's a question of facing reality. Either you figure out a way to live through the day, or you don't."

"Those are the choices?"

"Those are the choices. Too many good people have gotten themselves bent in half believing in others."

She chuckled snidely. "I used to tell myself it was just me getting older, more conservative, that the world wasn't really going to hell." She wiped a speck out of her eye. "But I was wrong. It has already gone to hell. We passed through purgatory when no one was looking. I don't see how things could get any worse. There's optimistic pessimism for you. Can you tell me what would be worse than this living death?"

"No," I said honestly. I think I surprised both of us. To celebrate, I filled my glass. All that fine liquor in it seemed to have evaporated when I wasn't looking.

For an uneasy moment, we sat at the table, staring into each other's eyes. My admission hung ominously between us like a nest of hornets. It was beginning to sound as if Joan and Allison Bashcock subscribed to the same magazines. Then I stood up.

"Shall I start dinner?"

Joan nodded absently.

I turned on the gas and struck a match. I stood quietly until the timer sounded a few minutes later. As I was taking the food from the oven, Joan, her voice full of cool strength, broke the silence.

"Jack, I want to ask something personal."

I dumped the patties onto the plates and began to ladle on pasty gravy to hide them. "What?"

My back was still toward her, but I could hear her taking one deep breath before she spoke. "Why did you quit the law?"

I didn't turn around. "I had reasons."

"Was your wife's suicide one of them?"

"Joan, do you want me to spill the beans, or would you rather help yourself?" She didn't answer me, so I spooned a portion of the reconstituted tubes on to each plate. I carried both plates to the table and laid one of them in front of her.

"The beef is a little overdone. I'm treating you like a Greek goddess, bringing you a burnt offering."

She looked at me but said nothing.

"Tell me something, Joan. Why are you so curious?"

Her eyes seemed dewy. It would have been easy to think I saw tenderness in them, but her lips were set tight in the tense frame of a frown. "I want to know what made you give up a successful practice."

"A lot of people did the same thing, if you'll remember. We blamed it on the Apathera."

"That may be true, but everybody had a private reason. What was yours?"

"What makes you think I was so successful?"

"And what makes you so evasive? My father said you were one of the most promising young lawyers he'd ever seen."

"So, I was just one more promise that wasn't kept."

"That's the sort of thing a failure would say."

"I'm not afraid of being called a failure."

"But you weren't a failure," she protested. "You left McCracken, Dark, and Dimeswell after they offered you a full partnership. Your name could have replaced my father's on the door."

"They felt sorry for me."

She finally finished her first drink. She put down her glass and sneered at me. "Did you ever know a law firm to act out of compassion? My mother told me Alicia killed herself a week after they made you the offer, so, even if they were acting out of compassion, what was their motive? All I want to know is if Alicia's suicide was the reason you turned down their offer and quit. It's a simple question."

"I wish I had a simple answer. I'd be lying if I said yes and I'd be lying if I said no. That leaves a solid maybe. Will that do?"

I managed to sneak a forkful of food to my lips before she asked her next question.

"Do you blame yourself?"

"For quitting?" I asked too casually.

She shook her head. "You know what I mean."

"Alicia was never what you would call a stable person. Trivial things, things most people could ignore, knocked her for a loop. One psycho-quack I consulted diagnosed her condition as spiritual hemophilia, the complete inability to heal, to forget, to forgive. Maybe, if she had lived in a less exasperating time. . . ."

"She was another victim of the Apathera," Joan said with a hard, almost cruel edge.

"I certainly didn't help her. I was too busy solving my clients problems to help her solve her own. Or maybe I avoided . . ." I laid down my fork, the patty on my plate suddenly seeming as tempting as a sponge soaked in old oil. "Maybe, during those last few months, I expected her to try something. Maybe I expected to come home one night and find her . . . Maybe I was looking forward to relief from the strain of trying to save what I was incapable of saving. Sometimes I got the feeling she had filled her life with things she never intended to dust. I was one of them. Joan, this is pointless. There's no way I could tell you my true feelings. In these years, I've tried all of them on at one time or another. I don't know any more which were tailored for me, and which came off the rack. All I do know is that one night, I came home, the gas was on, and it was too late to kiss my family good night."

"Could you have prevented it?"

"I said before that when someone's ready to cave in, there's nothing anyone can do. Maybe if I had payed more attention, maybe if I hadn't been so busy ignoring the situation, maybe I could have kept her from killing the kids too. But only maybe."

"So, to open your private eyes, you killed your career, and became a cheap detective."

"Not all at once." I resented the harshness in her voice, resented its mocking lilt. I resented her concern. There was no reason for me to explain anything to this woman. But I couldn't leave it at that. "I was tired of the continual drain of the law. Tired of fighting against a general collapse no one else seemed to care about. I was chasing my own tail. So I stopped."

"Just like that."

I nodded slowly. "Just like that. Of course, at first I called it a leave of absence, but I knew I'd never go back."

Joan dissected a wedge of patty and laid it on her tongue, chewing the pseudo-meat with agonizing deliberation. When she had swallowed it, she said, "So, you've resigned from life, liberty, and the pursuit of happiness."

"If that's how you want to see it," I countered quickly. "For me, those sacred goals seemed pointless, cheap mythical illusions created to keep the world running. Only the running is important. The only other member of our family to survive Alicia's deep-end run was a calico cat named Bilbo. Old Bilbo and I had a little game we'd play to while away the empty hours. I'd take a hand mirror and play a spot of light across the floor. Bilbo would chase himself silly trying to catch up with it. The faster I played that light, the faster, more frantically Bilbo would dance after it. But I had to keep the light moving. If I let it lay still, Bilbo immediately lost interest. Without so much as a sniff at the spot of light he'd been chasing, he'd go off and lay in the corner. You see, Bilbo knew what the game was all about. He knew what was illusion and what was reality. He knew better than to confuse the two. What fun is it if you know you're chasing an illusion?"

"Clever cat. So you've gone to lie in the corner to wait for someone to move the mirror. That does sound cozy." She forked in another wedge of patty. "Why aren't you eating, Jack? You did say you preferred these things to fish sticks."

"Listen, lady, I don't need your sarcasm."

"What do you need?"

"Not your pity, either."

"Pity? Why should I pity you? You have everything worked out. A life, a home, a satisfying career. You've made your corner, and now you intend to lie in it."

"What the hell are you after?"

Joan finished the last of her meal, laid aside her fork, and shrugged. "I thought I came here to save my mother from herself. Maybe I see I want to save what's left of Jack Hughes from himself."

"Don't go to any trouble." I poured another drink.

"Oh, but it's worth the trouble. They used to say a good man was hard to find. It hasn't gotten any easier."

"They also said a hard man was good to find." I got up and fed my dinner to the sink. "So don't get yourself too excited. Or take my refusal too personally."

Joan also stood up, taking her time, obviously as surprised by my sudden crudity as I was. "Perish the thought," she said with hurt in her voice. "If I made a habit of taking other people's problems personally, I'd have been in line for a quick ticket for a long nap years ago. Don't worry about me. It's you who needs the worry. I think it's time I went. Where's my coat?"

"In the bedroom. I'll get it."

"Don't bother. I can find it myself."

I waited silently at the front door until she had buttoned up. When she was done, I opened the door.

"Joan, I apologize for slapping your wrist. It wasn't called for. It's been too long since anyone was interested enough to be kind."

She put her finger softly to my lips. "No apologies necessary. I know how it feels to be the one left behind. Just don't convince yourself that's how it has to be. If that happens, you may as well join Alicia."

Of course I've told myself the same thing a hundred times over the years, but I never really trust anything I say when I'm feeling that miserable. Somehow, coming from an innocent bystander, that truth seemed much more believable. It was easy to see how on target she was. If I could be that crude and defensive to someone as right as Joan, I was clearly closer to that final truth than I ever suspected, even at four A.M. of my worst, sleepless night.

"You're right. I am acting like an idiot. But it's an old habit. They die hard. Old Bilbo's been dead for five years, and I still remind myself to put him out every night."

"Habits like those are only protection against pain. Routine you can lose yourself in."

"Or protection against emptiness. Or fear of the back door. Joan, is there something I can do to make up for that remark about a hard man?"

A slow smile broke out across her face. "You could offer me a cup of that coffee I brought."

"But it won't be ready . . ." And then I understood. "I'll put the beans in to soak." It was my turn to smile.

I laid each garment gently on the chair as she handed it to me. While I've never enjoyed undressing, undressing someone else has always been sublime.

"I'm afraid I forget how it's done," I said.

"How what's done?" And she took my hand and we tiptoed into bed like two samaritans on their way to a good deed.

I had lied to Joan. I hadn't forgotten how people make love. I had only forgotten why. All my old moves were there when I needed them. All the reactions were right. The soft caresses, the slow scratches, the luxurious stretching, the high arching of backs, the frantic thrusts, the hardness, the heat, the soft words all followed in their logical order. They were the easy part of the routine, the part I had recreated in my mind with a hundred partners as I lay alone in bed year after endless year. Masturbation requires only the rawest of materials, disembodied externals, a face to fixate on, a quick pan across the bed to set the mental stage, and a disjointed image flashed again and again from every imaginable angle. It's so easy to produce the motions because the emotions are so simple, so one-dimensional.

So, in the beginning, to that cameraman crouching inside my head, I looked and sounded like an expert.

Not until later did the cameraman get into the act, eliminating the void between the actor and the action. Only later, after we had caught our breath, did the cameraman cease to be. Then, as I was sliding down into that deep, unthreatened, and unthreatening sleep of true exhaustion, I thought I heard an angel of mercy breathing in my ear.

17

I never heard her leave, but in the morning, all that was left to prove the night wasn't just another dream was a note on my desk:

> Jack,
> You were so asleep. I must go. Talk to you P.M.
> Enjoy breakfast.
>
> Joan

Not much evidence, but I'm good at taking a little a long way.

Joan was right about another thing. The coffee she brought was, without a doubt, the finest I had tasted in years. The label on the pouch was printed in a language I couldn't read but assumed was Arabic. The coffee itself was dark, strong, full-bodied, and mellow, all the things advertisers love to call the plaster pills they peddle these days.

I used three cups of the stuff as a crowbar to pry me far

enough out of sleep to function, but not so far to let me ask myself too many questions about the night before. It was a delicate balance.

I managed to avoid looking outside until well past eight. Had he looked for a thousand years, Darling couldn't have picked a gloomier day to get buried. Marbled clouds, thick with the threat of snow, were foaming over the city-scape. All Queens Cemetery is at least one subway, one bus, and, since I was bikeless, one cab ride from my apartment. With good connections, at least an hour's trip; bad could cost me an eternity.

Luck, however, was still with me. The subway and bus connections meshed neatly, and when I got off the bus at the end of the line, I found a cab without much looking. Borough cabs are always tricky. The drivers are invariably private operators who've memorized a few safe routes and refuse to stray far from them. When I asked the one I found if he went anywhere near All Queens, he nodded somberly. The handsome, Scandanavian-looking cabby, whose name, curiously enough, was Hassan, maneuvered his dented battery-op with the skill of a master surgeon through the snowdrifts and craters of Northern Boulevard at fifty klicks an hour. I watched the speedometer with trepidation the whole way. It's been a long time since I've been moved through daylight that quickly. I was shaking when, twenty minutes later, Hassan slowed enough to let me out at All Queens. I handed him my plastic, and he marked off fifty dollars. I threw him in an extra ten as a tip for sparing my life.

"I come this way a lot," were the first words out of Hassan's mouth. Then he spotted three new fares waving to him from another entrance to the cemetery. "Got to keep moving if you want to make expenses," were his last words.

All Queens is an enormous place built originally on landfill adjacent to La Guardia airport, if build is what you call making a cemetery. The logic was, I suppose, that even the noise of jets wouldn't wake the dead. When the airport closed down, the cemetery expanded along the old runways toward the main terminal. It was a convenient arrangement, with plenty of parking and unplowed acreage. By the time all the open ground was filled, the parking spaces had become unnecessary. So the asphalt was rolled back and the bodies rolled in. Now, the immense field looked like a clear-cut forest except that, instead of stumps, there grew white markers. It isn't common knowledge, but at the core of each of those gravestones is a worn-out tire. They dip them in concrete, stamp on a few words, and sell them for marble. They also cost a fortune. I know. I've had occasion to buy a few.

I found Darling's gravesite posted on the schedule board and started hiking out along celestial runway number 4D, a thinning ribbon of crumpled asphalt which happens to be the site of one of the worst air disasters in history. One winter day, thirteen years ago, a jumbo jetload of evacuees arriving from Knoxville collided in midair with a transport packed with soldiers and high explosives heading for the Gulf campaign. Easterly winds rained atomized flesh on Long Island the following spring, and our lawns looked like putting greens all that summer.

It took me fifteen minutes to reach the gravesite, and, as I neared it, I was surprised how many other people had made the same trek. The funeral wasn't elaborate, but, by modern standards where three people constitute a quorum and ten a crowd, Darling had packed them in. Maybe forty people huddled in tight knots of three and four around a narrow slit in the frozen earth. The grave had been gouged out by an ancient diesel trenching machine which now served as a windbreak for about half the group. Everyone was so bundled against the gale off the bay I couldn't make out even one familiar or, for that matter, unfamiliar face. I didn't think Darling had been overly religious, at least not in the churchy sense, but a woman who was obviously a priest stood at the head of the swaddled casket struggling to make herself heard over the inconsiderate wind.

A fair portion of the crowd was in the ninety-nine percent tax bracket, judging from the silver minks and Voltswagon limos in attendance. I stood next to a large woman wearing an ancient, silver fox snowsuit, which made her look like a fur-covered cookie jar. Only a small disk of her powdered face was exposed to the elements, and the coffin was already half lowered into the grave before I recognized her. She wore fifteen years and weighed twenty kilos more than the last pictures of her I had seen, but she was definitely Blanche Tarbridge, the gossip columnist who once proudly called herself "The Eyes and Ears of Hollywood." As the sanguine priest stiffly tossed the first frozen clods of former airport on Darling, I noticed a tear in the cloudy "Eye of Hollywood."

The old woman noticed my attention and whispered something so softly I had to lean in from the wind to hear her. Even then, I only caught the tail of what she said.

" . . . ever had," she repeated.

"I beg your pardon."

She looked at me curiously and almost shouted, "I said that Gregory Darling was the best fuck I ever had."

Even in that stiff wind, I was close enough to smell the moth balls and musk that clung to her ancient fur. The dark lines of camouflage she wore to disguise the treadmarks of age stood out in garish relief against the pale, capillary red of freezing flesh. Blanche regarded my stifled mirth with casual dignity. "He could make a woman sing with gratitude. Did you know him well?"

"Not that well. I only met him the other day."

"Then you never knew Gregory in his prime." She looked into the grave. "What a shame. For you." Her lips set, and I watched her nostrils flutter with each short breath she took. "We were almost married many years ago. It wouldn't have lasted. Gregory Darling was a wind only time could tame." She sanctified her glance toward the grave with a shiver that showed even through the layers of her clothes. "All that is history now. Dry, dead history," she sighed.

The mourners had begun, one by one, tossing lumps of dirt on the casket. As the rotation reached us, Blanche reached into the pocket of her snowsuit. Saying something only the wind and Darling could hear, she threw what she had taken from her pocket into the pit. I only had a glimpse before the object bounced off the casket and rolled off the far end.

That glimpse was enough. Blanche had thrown in an apple, a huge, Golden Delicious apple, the kind that costs twenty dollars a bite. After her performance, I felt cheap tossing a frozen clod on a man I helped kill. But, as they say, thought counts, not price.

I didn't tell Blanche that. Instead, I said, "You just threw in an apple."

"I know that. Gregory was a sucker for symbols."

"I don't understand."

"I see no reason you should. And I don't believe I know who you are."

"My name is Hughes."

A light of understanding clicked on in her eyes. "Jack Hughes? The detective?"

I nodded.

"That explains why you've made this long journey for someone you met so recently. The newspapers have linked you rather closely with Gregory's death."

"I wouldn't believe everything I read in the papers."

She sent me a sly grin. "Mr. Hughes, I assure you that I would be the last person to make that mistake."

"Touché! I forget your former profession, Miss Tarbridge."

She nodded appreciatively. "If you remember me, Mr. Hughes, you're a man with a good memory. You asked why I threw Gregory an apple, but to understand you would have had to know him in his prime. He was the biggest stud in Hollywood, a place which has seen its share of cocksmen. That poor boy from Atlanta was voted 'Stocking Stuffer of the Year' six times running in *Screen Scream's* national poll.

A remarkable achievement. How could I let them incinerate a man like that?"

"You're responsible for this funeral?" I asked.

"In a manner of speaking. So are you, in another manner. Yes, I arranged for Gregory to be buried here. We long ago promised each other we'd spend eternity side by side. I have no desire to lay all that time next to a bottle of ashes."

"You knew each other well?"

Blanche snickered huskily. "You could say we've had a close relationship over the years. We've been friends, confidants, and lovers in every way except that we never quarreled. It's lucky we didn't marry. I haven't stayed as close with any of my former husbands."

"But why the apple?"

Blanche smiled wickedly and her eyes twinkled with the memory she conjured. "Gregory went planting in so many orchards, I called him Johnny Appleseed."

Darling lived under a far greater burden than I had imagined. A cold sheet of snow suddenly blew past us, and, to banish the chill, I clamped my hands tightly together. A woman across the grave from me nodded approvingly. I think she thought I was praying.

"You wouldn't happen to know of a woman Darling has been seeing lately?" I asked. "Her first name might be Jeanette. Her last name might begin with a 'D.' "

My question amused Blanche. "Mr. Hughes, if I tried to keep track of all of Gregory's women, I would have needed another secretary. I don't know the real name any particular woman he's seen recently, Jeanette or otherwise. In my experience, I've learned discretion is the better part of self-protection. What makes you so certain her name is Jeanette? That sounds very like another of Gregory's *noms d'amour.*"

"The police found a note on his body. It mentioned a Jeanette D."

Blanche stuck her lower lip out far enough for me to read her answer on it. "That means nothing. Gregory was a romantic in the truest sense. He often gave his lovers other names. He claimed it helped to elevate a woman above her normal cares, helped to open her to new passions. He may have been right." A broad grin spread across her well red cheeks. "He called me Marguerite of the Camellias. Gregory always had a passion for anything French. Jeanette would certainly fit in that category. So you see, this woman's name could as easily have been Gladys as Jeanette."

The snow was falling with a vengeance and some of the sunshine mourners began to desert the grave for their vehicles. As one particularily frigid gust tore through the crowd, several people to our right turned to avoid it. One of them caught my eye, and I raised my hand to acknowledge her look.

"Allison Bashcock, the writer," I explained casually to Blanche.

"I'm well aware of who she is, Mr. Hughes. And of what she does." A forced monotone in Blanche's voice approximated the drone of the wind.

"She's also Darling's niece," I continued.

"Niece?" That bit of news tickled the "Nose of Hollywood" immensely. "Where did you obtain that snippet of misinformation?"

I looked at Blanche in surprise. "Straight from the horse's mouth. We met the other day."

"Yes. I wonder if she still tells everyone that, or only a select audience? I would have thought she'd outgrown that particular lie. Mr. Hughes, Gregory never married and, as far as I know, he has no siblings. So how could he have a niece?" Blanche rolled her eyes in slow amusement. "I must say that I hadn't realized Allison's capacity for euphemism. She usually affects that polish of sophisticated honesty, but I'm afraid she misinformed you."

"She definitely told me Darling was her uncle."

"I assure you that's not true. Allison Bashcock is one of Darling's Little Apples, as we used to call them. And you don't have to look closely to see this particular apple hasn't

fallen far from the tree. Gregory may not have been close
to all his children, but Allison never suffered for a lack of
attention from her father. That man was always proud of his
own children. Only circumstance and an occasional jealous
husband kept him from acknowledging a child of his creation." Blanche regarded me carefully for a moment. "You
aren't, by any chance, related to him, are you?"

I laughed. "I don't think my mother ever had that honor,
as often as she may have wished for it. Besides, I'm older
than I look."

"Who isn't?" Blanche cocked her head and showed me a
fine set of porcelain teeth. "And don't be so sure. Gregory's
career was as long as it was glorious. He was a generous
man."

"I'd like to ask you some more questions about him."

"Maybe later, Mr. Hughes. But not here and not now. We
come to bury Caesar, not to raise him."

How could I get around logic so artfully stated.

The trenching machine had almost finished the job of
covering Darling, and the few mourners who still stood silent
vigil watched while the chalky white marker was rolled into
place. I looked at the group that remained with a new curiosity. Why had each of them come, and why had these few
stayed to the very end? They couldn't all be former lovers
or members of the apple corps.

When the priest finally closed up shop, I escorted Blanche
back across the frozen ground toward the cars parked along
what was left of the runway. Allison Bashcock stood in front
of us, her arm linked with an intense-looking man wearing
a bright red parka which, with his long, thin legs, made him
look like a cherry popsicle. As we approached, I was aware
of Blanche's frown. When we were two meters away, Allison
stepped forward and greeted me tersely. "Well, hello, Mr.
Hughes. I'm surprised to see you found the nerve to come."
Blanche tugged on my arm and we stepped to the side. Allison blocked our way. "I see you've met my mother."

Blanche's frown widened slightly. She glared at her daughter and the popsicle on her arm. "Mr. Hughes has been entertaining me, Allison. He's not too impatient to listen to an old woman, nor does he take himself so seriously that he refuses to speak at all."

Allison assumed that vaguely bored, obviously tolerant expression petulant children reserve for dottering grandparents. "My mother doesn't appreciate Rinaldo. Rinaldo, this is Jack Hughes, the man who killed my father." Her tone would have cut steel.

The popsicle nodded.

"Rinaldo," Blanche explained sarcastically, "is a devout nonverbalist. He thinks words and languages in general are useless, so he never uses them. My daughter thinks he's profound. I think he's an asshole. And so is she if she believes every word printed in the gutter press."

Allison didn't react to her mother's scorn, but Rinaldo grimaced and stuck out his tongue. Then he hoisted his right hand in a parody of a salute that resembled a startled subway rider reaching for a strap.

Blanche sneered again. "Eloquent little fart, isn't he?"

"Mother! I won't have you picking on Rinaldo. He was kind enough to bring us out here this morning and deserves some respect and gratitude for that at least. Nonverbalism is a legitimate symbolic protest to the alienating dynamics of modern life. Nonverbalists are our only hope for breaking down the artificial barriers between people which the Apathera created."

"How she figured that all out, I'll never know." Blanche poked me in the side with her padded elbow. "Darling daughter, why doesn't Rinaldo just hold his breath until his socks inflate? That would be a much more meaningful protest."

Allison ignored her mother, or at least she tried to. She couldn't stop a little smile sneaking out between her tight lips. So, instead, she turned her attention back to me.

"If Mr. Hughes didn't have anything to do with Gregory's death, why didn't he spare me the necessity of going to

Ninety-third Street and seeing the shambles of my father's life? He obviously knew at lunch on Saturday. I remember the smug expression on his face when we talked about Gregory."

"Allison, I didn't kill your father." It wasn't a lie, not exactly anyway. "But the police needed a convenient name to dam a flood of questions. They chose mine. Maybe I would have told you if you had been more honest with me. Why did you tell me Darling was your uncle?"

She stared into my face a moment, looking for something that wasn't there. Then she dropped her eyes. "I don't know. Maybe it's because I do like to think of him as a kind uncle. My mother always kept me well supplied with pseudo-fathers, but none ever hung around long enough to create the illusion of family. Gregory, however, was always there. He certainly didn't fit the image I had of fathers."

"My part in your father's death was purely circumstantial. I met him Friday afternoon, we talked, were interrupted, and I was asked to return later that evening. He was dead when I got there. I called the police. Would I have done that if I had killed him?"

Allison shook her head slowly. "You were one of the last people to see him alive. Did he seem disturbed to you?"

"He didn't seem like someone getting ready to die, if that's what you mean."

Allison looked at her mother for support. Blanche smiled warmly. Then the young woman turned to her silent lover. The dark man stood watching me, his head nodding slightly, his black eyes full of sadness.

Blanche put an arm around her daughter. "Did you drive out, Mr. Hughes?"

"No, Hassan brought me, but he left already."

Blanche nodded. "There's room in Rinaldo's car. You may ride back to town with us if you'd like."

"That would be most kind." I followed the three of them to a green GM wagon with a huge dent on the hood. Rinaldo opened the left door for the two women, and I crawled into the right front seat next to him. A bitter chill permeated the vehicle, and the plastic seat covers grabbed at my clothing. I hoped Rinaldo had a set of good batteries. I've been in cars that have died sitting half an hour in places warmer than All Queens Cemetery. But Rinaldo confidently punched out the starting sequence, and the electric motor clicked on immediately. Once we were moving, he switched on the heater and the car began to warm. Which was more than the conversation did.

Nobody spoke as we joined the procession of cars creeping slowly toward the cemetery entrance. It was a dull, depressing sight, the dim headlights struggling in vain for a foothold on the blank wall of gloom, the passengers silently trying to escape uneasy memories of a man they had just buried.

After a few minutes of silence, Allison leaned forward. "I suppose it's just as well you did come. I was going to call you this morning anyway. Carlo Mountain is dead. The other day you told me he was one of the five who had their tapes stolen. That makes two of those five who are dead. Should I start packing for that long trip, too?" She spoke casually but failed to hide the concern in her voice. "I'll put it another way," she said before I could answer. "Is this thing going to kill me?" She pulled her transducer from her coat pocket.

"After our conversation the other day, I got the impression that didn't matter to you."

Allison said nothing, but looked into her mother's warm eyes.

"The police found nothing at all suspicious about Carlo Mountain's death," I said after a moment.

"I already know that."

"How?" I said, turning around to look at her.

"Last night after I heard about Mountain, I got frightened, and called the police. I talked to a detective named Murtaugh. I saw the picture of my father taken before the camouflage experts got to him.

"The other morning, I said I wasn't concerned about getting my tape back. That's true, but if the expression on my father's face is any indication of the pain he went through dying, and if his death was caused by the transducer, I'm having mine removed in the morning."

Allison settled back in her seat and stared out the frosty window. We were bumping across the narrow pontoon bridge that the army corps of engineers had hastily thrown up when the Triborough Bridge collapsed. The jagged skyline of Manhattan peaked to our left, and the moldering desolation of the South Bronx steamed on our right. It wasn't a scene to inspire one's confidence in the future.

So, now Murtaugh knew all about Wightman's bank. I wasn't sure how that affected our truce, but I knew it effectively removed any hold I had over her. I couldn't blame Allison for leaking the information to the police. All things being equal, I might have done the same thing. There are only so many places to turn when you find yourself in trouble. Few people realize that confiding in the government's crime-prevention monopoly won't make anything better.

Blanche looked at her daughter with concern. "Mr. Hughes," she asked after a moment, "did that thing in Gregory's brain kill him?"

"Something in Gregory's brain killed him. It would be easy to think it was the transducer. Wightman claims the transducer has a built-in safeguard against misuse, but I don't think there's ever been a gadget made in the last thousand years that couldn't kill in one way or another. I once heard of a woman who commited suicide with a disposable diaper."

Blanche nodded. "I understand. Gregory always wanted me to open a time account, but I'm not about to let someone cut a hole in my head for any reason. I wish he had never told Allison about those transducers. She was a much more attentive person before she had her operation."

"Why didn't you stop her?"

"My daughter asked me for my opinion. I gave it. What she did then was her own business." Blanche had no bitterness in her voice. It was a simple statement of facts. "It happens I voice some opinions more loudly than others. I'm not at all shy, for example, about telling anyone how I feel about motormouth up there. But I've never tried to run my daughter's life. I've had enough joy running my own, thank you."

I watched the two of them, the large, lusty mother and the lush, frightened daughter, and a strange thought popped into my head and out of my mouth before I could think. "Allison, did your father ever demonstrate any affection for you? Other than what might be proper for a father? Or an uncle?"

I don't know which of the woman was more offended by the question, but Blanche was the first to react vocally. "Mr. Hughes! Gregory Darling may have had a flair for seduction and perhaps even a kinky quirk or two, but I assure you he would never have gone rooting around in his own backyard. If anything, the thought would have horrified him. In his own way, he was a profoundly moral man. And his code of personal ethics was absolutely rigid."

"That may be, but more than one profoundly moral man has surprised people when all has been said and done. Your daughter is a very attractive woman, Blanche. Why don't we let her answer herself. Did Gregory ever make a pass at you, Allison?"

She shook her head. "You're really sick. Gregory would have killed himself before he let anything like that happen."

"A lot of men have said the same thing. But, all right. It was only a thought."

No one spoke for a few troubled moments as Rinaldo silently negotiated the car down the rutted track of Second Avenue. Burned-out shells of the great housing projects line both sides of the street like the ragged sentinels of a retreating army. Fittingly, Rinaldo was a superbly cautious driver, slowing at each corner even though he owned the right of way. One can never tell when a deep-ender looking for a partner might come barrelling out of a side street.

"Allison," I asked as we were crossing Ninetieth Street,

"Have you ever experienced any unpleasant effects of the transducer? Anything that might, say, cause pain?"

"What sort of pain?"

"I don't know. Headache. Nausea. Loss of memory. Any physical side effect at all."

She thought a moment. "No, the experience is always warm and tingling, relaxing, like masturbating in a hot tub. You can't misuse the transducer. I won't work any way but the right one." Then she recalled something. "Wait. Once, just after I had my transducer operation, I was impatient to see if the time transfusion worked. I didn't have enough time in my own transducer to put any into my life, so I tried to use some of Gregory's. I took his transducer and . . ."

"It's not possible to activate another person's transducer," I said quickly.

"I didn't know that then. But I do know as soon as I touched the transfuse sensor, my head started to burn. I felt like I was losing control of my body. It couldn't have lasted more than a second because I took my finger off the sensor instinctively, like you do when you touch something hot. That's what it felt like. Someone putting a hot iron inside my brain. It frightened me. When I told Gregory what had happened, he came down hard on me. It was one of the only times he ever acted like a father."

I made a mental note for Wightman to answer when I saw him next.

In the moments of quiet that followed, my mind wandered around the fresh revelations of this case. Wightman claimed one person couldn't possibly activate another's transducer. Allison claimed, in effect, she had done just that. Who was telling the truth? And what about Murtaugh? I took the fact that she hadn't been standing at my door this morning as an indication our truce was still on. I couldn't see any reason to assume otherwise. Then I thought about Joan and last night. I made another note to try and call her as soon as I could.

Suddenly, I realized Rinaldo was staring at me. Without

thinking, I answered, "The old U.N. complex." Only I didn't actually say it, I just thought it. Neither of us had opened our mouth; the question and answer had just appeared in my mind. I gaped at Rinaldo who continued driving as if nothing odd had happened. I turned toward Allison. She was grinning.

"Was that nonverbalism?" I asked, more shaken by the experience than I cared to admit.

Allison nodded. "You probably let your thought barriers down long enough for him to get a word in. Rinaldo really is quite talented. Nonverbalism works best if one's thinking of love, I'm told. I know going to bed with Rinaldo is a real experience. Nonverbalism is a glorious thing. There's no reason to be terrified of it. It's a natural body function."

Blanche poked her face between her daughter and me. "So is taking a shit, my dear. So is talking a shit."

18

They dropped me off at Forty-fifth and Second Avenue and I walked the remaining block to the oasis of buildings that comprise the old U.N. complex, the arena in which several of the more high-minded failures of our time have been played out. The late, great International University lasted only a quarter as long as its more political predecessor here, but the graffiti-covered, bomb-scarred walls along First Avenue are memorials to the spirit of international cooperation that fostered both experiments.

Senator Sieg's Manhattan offices occupy the entire second floor of the main building, even though his staff of five could have fit comfortably in an elevator. But prime offices are more abundant than elevators these days. The huge entrance lobby was dominated by a massive wooden desk bearing a glittering bronze plaque. The plaque indicated someone named "Parsons" occupied the desk but gave no hint of either Parsons's sex or present location. I walked the perimeter of the desk just to make sure the missing Parsons person wasn't hiding somewhere behind it.

Halfway down the hall behind the desk, a man wearing tattered white overalls was busy spraying paint on the walls.

"You Parsons?" I asked, noticing the paint in the can was a color the manufacturers called Milky Avocado.

The man shook his head heavily. "I'm the painter. Parsons went out to find some lunch."

"Is Senator Sieg in?" Then I added, "I've got an appointment."

The man obligingly stepped down off the chair he was standing on and disappeared down the hall, leaving tracks of Milky Avacado in his wake. When he returned a minute later, he asked, "Your name Dreyfus?"

"If the Senator wishes."

"You can wait in his office. Down there. Sieg's in the can at the moment." I nodded my thanks, slid past the painter, and followed his footprints to an office so large I knew it was the right place even though there was no name on the door. The desk in this office was so wide, it was a long-distance phone call from one side to the other. Floor to ceiling thermoglass panels revealed a rich man's view of the East River and a distant swirl of gray and black that was Queens. I sat in the second of seven chairs facing the desk and waited for the Senator to arrive. My wait wasn't long.

"Well, Dreyfus, how the hell are you?"

Except for the perfectly placed silver highlights along his temples, Vic Sieg hadn't aged at all since we had last shaken hands in a courtroom. His face was as firm and as unlined, and the knife edge of his nose had even been hammered straight. The improvement wasn't something a person would notice unless he had heard Vic gripe for years how his rippled nose accentuated what he called his "Semitic heritage." And yet, he was the only person who still called me Dreyfus, a nickname everyone else forgot as soon as we graduated from law school. The arm Vic offered me was a fine filigree of sinew and vein, and his firm handshake suggested confidence as much as it did strength. The smooth ease with which he moved betrayed the predatory grace of a well-tennised body.

I tried not to sound old or tired. "Well enough, Vic. And you?"

"Keeping busy. Just keeping busy." He released my hand and started the trek around his desk. "You'll have to pardon our appearance. You wouldn't believe what a holy shambles this place was when we moved in. The university decorators seemed to have had an ungodly preference for dismal shades of brown." He flashed me a full deck of shining teeth. "We've been keeping ourselves busy. Busier than polecats covering shit." He winked at me conspiratorially. "Busier than a farmer mending fences."

I didn't say anything, and neither did he until he got to his chair. He rested both hands on its leather-covered back and looked me right in the eye. "Well, tell me, Dreyfus. Private investigating? How the hell did that happen?"

"I'm just lucky, I guess." I spoke louder than necessary, half afraid my voice wouldn't span the distance separating us. "It gives me a lot of free time."

"That's just fine, Dreyf. I envy you, in fact. You couldn't begin to imagine what a migraine a hundred and eighty million bosses can be. I wish Congress could just pass some legislation and stick five extra hours in every day. Maybe then I'd have the time to see everyone with something urgent to tell me." After a noticeable pause, he added. "Of course,

I'm never too busy for an old friend like you. What can I do you for?"

"I've just been to the funeral of Gregory Darling."

"The old actor? Say, wasn't that a tragedy? Poor old fellow."

"He was a depositor in Wightman's bank and was one of the five who had a tape stolen. Mountain was another."

"Carlo was a powerful man." Vic was trying hard to look concerned, but his voice lacked any real edge of interest. His eyes wandered to the unopened pile of letters in front of him. "So you think I'm in some kind of danger, Dreyf?"

"I couldn't say. Two men are dead, but their deaths aren't necessarily related. Both were past seventy and working on borrowed time. My real concern isn't with their deaths. Wightman hired me to recover the stolen account tapes." I could see I wasn't making much of an impression on the Senator, so I thought a scare tactic might add the needed touch. "Of course, we can't rule out the prospect that our thief had something against all five victims. Do you know anyone who might want to harm you?"

Vic propped his head on his hand and massaged his chin thoughtfully. "I'm given a fair shot at the White House next year. I didn't get to this point without stepping on a few toes. Hell, I suppose there are still some people who shit their drawers at the prospect of a Jewish President. I can't keep track of all the people who might have something out for me. But that's why we have a Secret Service. I've never met Darling," he said after one of those pregnant pauses. "Seen his films, of course. Always thought he lacked any depth. Just another pretty face."

"Some people liked his acting."

"I suppose there's a tongue for every taste."

He looked at me quietly. Behind him, a snowsquall was quietly erasing the last traces of Queens.

"How well did you know Carlo Mountain?"

"I don't have to tell you, I hope, that it's important for me to keep my time account a secret. I regret having gotten involved with Wightman in the first place. The man's unreliable. Carlo introduced him to me. I made a mistake and bought what the big spade was selling. It's not worth blowing my reputation on him, though. More than one presidential hopeful has been destroyed by media whiplash. Presidents must be exemplary. Time accounts sound too much like a special privilege." Then he added dryly, "Or worse, moral weakness. That's a bad quality in politics these days. Actually, Dreyf, I'd appreciate it if you include me out of your investigation."

"You're not serious about that, Vic. The learned electorate no longer concerns itself with the moral rectitude of its candidates."

His stiff smile never faltered. "Maybe it does. Maybe it doesn't. I'm not going to be the politician who tests those waters. I'm a Jew and a Republican. I've already got enough going against me."

"I'll try and keep you out of the papers, but I can't make any promises. Did you know Mountain?"

"My relationship with Carlo Mountain is public information. Carlo and I often did business together. I've done work for him, and he's always been a strong supporter of mine." He looked down his nose at me. For someone who had acquired a sharp nose relatively late in life, Vic wielded his as if it had always been there. "You mentioned five names. Who are the others?"

"One is Allison Bashcock."

Vic looked me in the eye and shrugged. "Should I know her?"

"She's a novelist. Writes the sort of book women love to read in the bathtub. And she writes copy for Melray Johnson."

Vic looked only slightly concerned. "Melray Johnson handles my public relations, but I don't recall ever meeting the woman."

"Number five is Lea Dark." I watched his face closely, but not a flicker of surprise ruffled its polished surface. "You remember Lea, of course, Alex's ex-wife."

Vic sniffed. "Of course I know Lea. She's been a constant supporter of mine. When Alex left McCracken Dimes, Lea turned over all her legal work to me. That's public knowledge too." And then Vic leaned forward and winked, taking me into his confidence even though we were separated by a desk as wide as a broken promise. "Lately, and this is strictly off the record, Lea's been a royal pain in the ass."

I said nothing but nodded understandingly.

"I'm chairman of the joint Congressional committee over-seeing construction of the orbiting station. Somewhere Lea got the idea that if she doesn't move to Orbicol, she's going to die. She's been badgering me for months to have her name added to the draft rolls. I've told her a dozen times it's out of the question, but she hasn't gotten the idea."

"Lea's a persistent woman."

"Lea's a deep-south bitch. She's gone so far as finding several doctors willing to perjure themselves by saying she's physically capable of making the journey. She's not, of course, but that's not the problem. Simply, she's too old. Orbicol's not going to be a picnic, and we have to make sure we can get hard work out of everybody we put up there. I won't deny we've had problems getting enough volunteers to colonize the place. Christ, these days it's impossible to get people off their butts for anything less urgent than a bonfire in the toilet. The thought of spending a few years in a holding pattern over Ecuador doesn't seem to appeal to our coun-trymen, particularily those under thirty. We seem to have bred the taste for adventure out of our children."

"Just like we've bred the taste for children out of ourselves. Perhaps it might not be a bad idea to send us old folks up there, Vic. There certainly are more of us than there are of them. I read that the population now isn't that much larger than it was at the turn of the last century, and the majority of us are over forty. So, if Lea's hot to go, why not send her?"

Vic looked at me as if I understood nothing. "For one thing, it's against the law. We're going to introduce a draft of citizens eligible to man the colony. Similar to the old Selective Service Lottery. Make a big deal out of the honor of serving your country and all that. Eligible means thirty and under. It's their future we're trying to insure. Under the circumstances, it would require a presidential exemption to get that old lady up there. President Jonas certainly won't do anything for her. The idea is ridiculous, Dreyf. I don't know who put it into her head in the first place. No politician is going to risk a case of media whiplash by boosting that old bitch into orbit. It's our job to smooth passions while we make everyone think we're kissing ass. A politician who does the opposite doesn't last long."

"I don't see Lea giving up so simply."

Vic smiled at me confidently. "Dreyf, what can she do? Her hour in the sun is past. She's lost whatever political clout she may have once had. Sure, she's still got money, and sure, she's always been very generous to me in the past. Next month, when I announce my campaign, she'll be among the first to pledge her support. But she can't exert any pressure, at least not the kind that gets me to risk my political future on a ridiculous whim of hers. She knows how thin her ice is with me. That's why she kept badgering Mountain to talk some sense into me."

"How does Lea know Mountain?"

"Really, Dreyf," he smirked. "You're supposed to be the investigator. Carlo and Lea go way back. I wouldn't be surprised if they've rumpled a sheet or two in the past, though you'll never get them to admit that. Lea always had this strange attraction for men with charisma."

"And money. I knew they were friends, but I didn't know Mountain had any influence with you."

"As far as Orbicol is concerned, Mountain has a lot of influence. Or should I put that in the past? Mountain Industries is the major contractor for Orbicol. That project is top priority in Washington, and Carlo Mountain packed real punch there anyway."

"Enough punch to get a Presidential exemption for Lea?"

He pursed his lips and nodded. "But he'd have used up

a lot of favors. Valuable favors. Besides, he thought the idea was as ridiculous as I did. He wouldn't have wasted any megabegs on Lea. In fact, he asked me to help get her off his back. I guess he doesn't have to worry about her anymore." Vic realized the irony in his words and grinned. "And neither do you. Lea Dark may think she's going to be reborn on Orbicol, but, fellow, she ain't going anywhere. You don't think I'd let someone with Lea's spirit up there, do you? Hell, with her sense of destiny, she'd probably try to take the place over and blackmail the earth." He kept grinning as if it were a joke.

But then his smile faded. He began to remember the mound of unopened mail, and I could see the meter that regulated my time with the Senator ticking out.

"Have you done much time saving with Wightman, Vic?"

"Much time?" he asked, shaking his head. "Hardly any at all. I opened the account looking to save up some time to use on the campaign trail, but it's not so simple. Running the transducer takes too much out of you, and a Senator needs his wits about him every moment of the day. There's always a fire somewhere that needs to be put out. Once in a great while during some sub-committee meetings, I admit I steal a few of the taxpayer's minutes. A blank expression or two goes unnoticed there." He enjoyed his own wit until something more hilarious occurred to him.

"Have you heard the latest about Eustus Dickerson, the senior Senator from the great state of Ohio, the one who's still trying to end the Apathera by legislation? Now he wants to make laziness a federal crime."

"That's been done before."

Vic ignored me. With the tips of his fingers, he began to describe the circumference of an imaginary globe. "Well, I agree something has to be done, but doesn't that piece of foolishness tell you something about the state of your government? The country is in a bad way. But we need more than more legal jargon. We need energy." With a clap of his hands, he crushed the globe. "We have to get to the root of the problem. When did the Apathera begin? Eighty-six, the year of the gas rebellion. When we sent troops into Louisiana to get the gas flowing, how were we to know the gumbos would blow their own fields sky high?" He continued, ticking his proofs off one by one on his fingers. "Then the national electricity grid began to collapse. After those meltdowns, the nuclear power stations had to be taken out of service. Then the quake split off most of the hydrodams west of the Rockies. The worst winter in a hundred years, and the country froze its ass off. We never recovered. Look around you. You'll see a nation starved for energy. There's our real problem. And I'm not just talking about human energy. I mean electron volts."

"And not election votes?" I was going to tell him that the problem wasn't so simple, that the human causes went back a lot further than fifteen years. But I had hardly opened my mouth before he dismissed me with a wave of his hand and continued his campaign litany.

"A shot of good, old-fashioned raw power at a price any man can afford. That'll shock some life back into the system. We're finally getting close to passing a national energy bill, and raw energy is what we're going to get. In three weeks, Orbicol will go into operation, or at least the solar generating section will. We're also turning all the offshore oil rigs still standing into wind-powered electrolysis stations, and that means hydrogen to turn the country's wheels. And Orbicol to power its plants. We've got plans for Orbicol Two, Three, and Four on production schedule. They'll be finished in a quarter of this one's construction time. We've already got the men and equipment in orbit. We'll rip the raw materials out of the moon and produce the finished products right in space, faster, cheaper, and better than we could on earth. The third millenium is nearing. The future, Dreyf, has never been closer."

He spoke without bombast, exuding the calm, steady confidence of the political visionary. Melray Johnson had coached him well. "I'm also chairman of the national millenium celebration. Believe me, we're going to generate some real excitment this New Year's Eve. Remember what the Fourth of July used to be? We're going to have parades, festivals, fireworks, souvenirs, all the things that once made a citizen's blood boil. Our traditions need tending; our roots are dying for water. On New Year's Eve at midnight, the President and I will be standing on a platform being built right now on the front lawn of the White House. In the first minute of the next thousand years, I'll throw a switch, and the first volts will beam down from the solar generating plant on Orbicol and flow into this country's lifelines. And guess what we're going to do with that power? Do you know that some children in this country have never seen a Christmas tree all lit up? Well, this year, we're going to illuminate an entire forest of Pennsylvania evergreens. Hell, they'll be able to see the light in space. That display will consume as much power as Albuquerque does in a week, but it won't even dent the power-producing potential of Orbicol. Within the next year, all those things that made this country great, from blast furnaces to hair dryers, will be humming again. It'll be a glorious moment for mankind. The coming of a new era. No, make that epoch. Era's still got bad connotations."

"Why do you get to throw the switch and not old man Jonas?"

Vic winked slyly. "Because the old fool's petrified of electricity. Afraid the microwaves will short out his pacemaker, I suppose. Doesn't that tell you something? Standing there, at the end of the dark decade, the energyless era, at the very threshold of the industrial renaissance, and the leader of our country is frightened of electricity."

"But you're not."

"You bet your sweet ass I'm not." Vic stood and walked slowly to the window. With his hands clasped tightly behind his back, he began to rock slowly on his heels. I noticed he was wearing rubber-soled shoes. Because of the snow that shrouded the entire vista, I couldn't see what he saw. He turned back to me and grinned dramatically across the vast expanse of desk. "Would you like to hear the campaign slogan we've come up with?" With his nimble hands, he created an imaginary video screen around his head. " 'Back to Eden.' How's that grab you?"

"It's better than 'Victory With Victor.' "

"That's not bad either. When I throw that switch, I'll be turning on the lights all over the country. And I'm not talking about your low-watt, twelve-volt, have-to-turn-them-off-when-you-leave-the-room lights. I mean light. Bright light. Bright enough to illuminate the future. After January 1, wherever people see a light bulb burning, they'll remember the man who threw the switch. We'll get this country back on its feet. We'll drive the pessimists and doubters and soft hearts back to Mexico where they belong."

"Might as well send them too. Most of the country's work force has already migrated." I could see my sarcasm wasn't winning me any friends in high places. I hated to interrupt his vision, but I couldn't help asking, "Are you sure Orbicol will be operational in three weeks? Only the other day, I read the completion date had been set back another year."

Vic nodded and smiled. "Media planning. Public relations. We had to make it seem things were going poorly. Then, after a superhuman effort, we drive, drive, drive across the goal line. The colony's doing just fine. At least the generating station is. Hell, if we wanted to, we could have started sending power a year ago."

Now it was my turn to do some staring. "But, if the county is as starved for energy as you say, why the hell did you wait?"

Vic raised his hand and took a breath as if it pained him. "You can lead a horse to water, so to speak. You can kick an eagle in the ass, but you can't make him fly."

"I see."

"I don't think you do. You know how the public thinks. If we had just let this electricity trickle back without any fanfare, it wouldn't have done much good. We have to change the national skepticism. Create a spectacle. Inspire the collective imagination. Hype a new self-image for the country. Get them to rev their engines. Force them to feel their hunger. We won't get a better chance if we wait a thousand years." He nodded to assure me his word was gospel, and then he sat back in this throne.

"I understand. Without that celebration, Victor Sieg won't be remembered as the father of the third millenium."

He regarded me coolly. "That's just the brand of cynicism we can do without. You've become a troublemaker, Dreyf. It pains me." He looked away from me. "You'd better go. I have other people to see."

Without speaking, I got up and walked toward the door. When I reached it, I looked back to where the Senator sat. "Keeping the country waiting for that lifeline is a shit thing to do."

"When I throw that lifeline, you'll understand why we had to wait. When your lights finally go on, you'll know the future has arrived. Oh, and Dreyf, I advise you not to repeat anything I've said. I'll deny ever seeing you, and you'll never work again. Do you understand?"

"Don't worry about me, Senator. I'll probably freeze to death in a stalled elevator. See you at the polls next fall. Maybe this time enough people will be able to afford to travel to the nearest voting place. Maybe the county will get up a quorum for this election." I let the door punctuate my exit.

The painter had finished the hallway and was starting on the reception lobby. As I walked by, I glanced at the paint can. This new shade of brown was called Rusty Nail.

Parsons still hadn't returned.

19

I knew my time was running out, but, for the first time since Friday, I honestly felt I was solving the case. Despite his ramblings, Vic Sieg had given me what I was looking for. If Lea Dark was as determined to bull her way up to Orbicol as she seemed, I didn't doubt she'd take any action she thought necessary, including stealing time tapes. Both Sieg and Carlo Mountain were, for different reasons, vulnerable through their time accounts, or so it might seem to Lea, an expert at figuring out where people were most vulnerable. Of course, I still needed a reason to include Allison Bashcock and Gregory Darling on her hit list, but I knew I'd find one if I kept at it.

The results were even better than I hoped for.

I went back to my office and asked the data console for the complete histories of both Gregory Darling and Lea Dark. That's the beautiful thing about data consoles. They have all the answers, all you have to do is ask the right questions. Inside an hour, I had my motive. The strange thing is, I was already aware of most of the necessary facts. It took the data console to fit the pieces together.

I was busy congratulating myself when the phone rang.

"Hughes? I've been trying to reach you all day." Wightman had more than a hint of annoyance in his voice.

"I didn't expect you back in town so soon."

"I didn't expect it myself. I didn't return for my health. Where have you been?"

"Darling's funeral."

"I have to see you immediately." Wightman didn't sound as if he gave a Hoover damn about Darling's funeral.

"Sure, in a couple of hours. I've got some things I want to tell you. I think I may have your case solved. But I have a thing or two more to check out."

"No need to go to that trouble, Mr. Hughes. In essence, what I want to say is that the case is closed. Can I put it another way? Your services are no longer needed. You're fired."

The words took a second to form themselves into a cogent thought in my mind. "Wightman, I'll be there as soon as I can. We'll talk about this in person." I made no attempt to disguise the anger in my voice.

"There's nothing to talk about."

"I'm sure we'll find something."

I was in the subway fifteen minutes later and it wasn't quite five when I got to Columbus Circle, where I had to change to an uptown train.

For fifteen minutes, I stood waiting with no train in sight. As usual, the schedule wasn't worth its wiring. My head was so crammed with things to tell Wightman, I hardly noticed a well-used tramp sitting on the bench behind me. Not until I heard him mumbling under his breath did I bother to turn around.

His tattered, army-issue greatcoat blended with the graying stubble of a radiation-scarred beard. Even though he was struggling to break into a sardine can, his gaunt legs were crossed in almost childlike repose. He pried the chipped end of a knife blade under the can as he sang quietly to himself in a hypnotic tone halfway between a mumble and a mantra. Under the sheen of brown, oily grime, the bent twig of a man could have been any age or race, but he certainly looked like he had been around. When he realized I was staring at him, he said, in a strangely refined voice, "You wouldn't happen to have a can key, would you?"

"I'm afraid I don't."

A set of spit-shined teeth glistened through the pearl scruff of his beard. "No matter. I've been here since noon, and no

one else has had a key either." He grinned sardonically. "I
may starve." He worked the knife around another turn.
"That would be ironic. Me, with all my billions of dollars,
starving to death. Well, as I've always said, 'Man doesn't live
on bread alone.' Not enough protein. And all that green ink.
But, how thoughtless of me. I haven't introduced myself. Bet
you can't guess my name."

"You're right."

"A guess doesn't cost you anything but time, and chances
are you have more of that than you want. Besides, you're not
going anywhere. Power's down; won't be another train for
a while. Tides must be turning."

I wasn't in a mood to play games, but then, I saw no convenient way to escape either. Always listen to the man with
a knife, my mother once told me. "How many guesses do I
get?"

"How many do you want?"

"None."

His warm smile never faltered. "Having a bad day? Well,
I can understand that." He laid his sardines aside and offered
me a dirty hand that was short one finger and half a thumb.

"Name's Carlo Mountain."

I stared at the man, at his bulbous nose, at the scarred
knobs on his threadbare knees, at the filthy, yellow cotton
socks which poked a few centimenters over the tops of his
urine-bleached combat boots. "You're not Carlo Mountain,"
I said incredulously. Then, unnecessarily, I added, "Mountain's dead."

He stuck the tip of his tongue out and watered his lips
with glee. "Of course I'm dead. How else could a bum like
me be Carlo Mountain?"

"I don't follow."

"Somehow, you don't look as if you did. It's quite simple.
Carlo Mountain died yesterday, so who minds if I use his
name for a little while? Won't do anyone any harm, and it
might do me some good. Always some high life left in a

secondhand name after the original owner butt-ends it. So I smoke the last few puffs, as it were. You've got to admit it makes life a hell of a lot more interesting." He scratched his chin with the filthy stub of his thumb. "Last week, for example, I was Norman Toothby and Simone DellaBennia. The week before that . . ."

"Who are you when you're being yourself?"

"You mean originally?"

"Yeah."

"No one in particular. You could call me no man. He picked up his sardines and scratched thoughtfully at the can. Then he peeked past me into the dark uptown track and shook his head. "You know, I honestly don't remember who I was. It's been so long since I've had the same name three days running. But, whoever I was, I must be dead." He continued to stare past me, still smiling unthreateningly. "Yeah, or so sucked dry I was useless. I'm good at getting the last puff out of a name." He stabbed once again at the surface of the can. The knife blade slipped off the metal and almost skewered his knee. "Wish I was as good at opening cans."

"Keep that up and you won't be anyone very much longer. There hasn't been a drop of tetanus vaccine in New York City for months. If you give yourself a dose, you'll have to rough it." I sat next to him on the bench and took the can and the knife from him. Using the heel of my shoe as a hammer, I drove the blade through the metal and, working the handle back and forth, gradually peeled enough of the lid back to let him fish out the oily contents. I handed back his meal. "Those edges are sharp."

He held up two pitted fingers in a victory sign. "Thanks for the favor, mister. It's awfully modern of you. I would never have though of doing that." There was no sarcasm in his voice.

"Sure you would."

Carlo Mountain Jr. sat back on the bench and whistled low. "No. I've never been mechanically inclined. Talent like that is rare. These days not one man in fifty could break into a can of sardines like that. I should know. I was in the army. Mind if I ask you your name? I'll keep an eye open. It would be fun to be you for a few days, even if you're no one famous."

I gave him my hand and smiled. "Jack Hughes, Mr. Mountain. But I'm not planning on vacating the premises for a while yet."

He winked at me. "No trouble at all. A person doesn't have to die to move out. Listen, if you'd like to switch, let me know. I'll show you how it's done." Then he waved an imaginary cigar at me with his thumb and forefinger. "Maybe I can even get you a good deal on a trade-in. Wholesale prices. Low overhead. And you have a lifetime to pay. Sign on the dotted line before midnight Sunday, and you even get a free bonus gift at absolutely no additional cost." He smiled again. "No, seriously, dozens of good names go to waste every day. More than I could possibly use myself. Yesterday was a slow day, for example, but I had my choice of Carlo Mountain and Betty Bixby. The day before that, I could have been Gregory Darling. This is a great time for personality recycling."

"You can be a woman?"

"Of course! Walk a mile in thy shoes, is what I always say. What's in a name? You could be Betty Bixby for starters if you want. She's still fresh."

I shrugged. "I don't even know who Betty Bixby is."

"Was," he corrected. "As far as I know, no one picked up her option. Got to grab them while they're fresh. An unpreserved name lasts only a few days before everyone forgets it. I like to think of myself as sort of a living memorial, a human museum. Betty Bixby deserves a memory, but me, I've always been a sucker for the big bucks, which is why I chose Mountain, a man who had money the way most of us had misery."

"Who was she?"

"Betty Bixby? A poet. She won the last Pulitzer they gave for poetry. Betty's poetry will live by itself, but Mountain's money will dissolve back into nothing. Besides, Betty killed herself, and I've never been fond of suicides. The name always looks better than it fits. Doesn't take long to figure out why that person needed to die so badly. Then the fun is over. You should wear a new name only as long as it feels right. They can cause blisters. But I do recommend some of Betty's poetry. 'Avoirdupois, King of Troy: A Metric Verse' is one of the finest examples of post-Apathera poetry you could hope for. It'll knock your socks off."

We both turned simultaneously and spotted the twin flicker of headlights slowly approaching on the uptown track.

"Going uptown, Mr. Mountain?" I asked, standing up.

"Thanks, but no. I think I'll just finish my lunch right here. I've got several billion dollars to spend in the next day or so. A man can't do that on an empty stomach."

Wightman buzzed open the door and greeted me with a curt, calculated glance. "Less than two hours, Mr. Hughes. Not a bad time. Not bad at all."

"What's this about the case being closed?"

"I don't see why you should find it so difficult to grasp. The case is satisfactorily concluded."

"To whose satisfaction?"

"To mine, Mr. Hughes. To mine."

"You got the tapes back?"

He pursed his lips and nodded a nod which meant something other than yes. "Let's stop this ridiculous charade? We both know the tapes will never be recovered. Even if the thief hasn't already destroyed them, exposure to the atmosphere most surely has. If not stored in cyanide gas, the special coating on the tape oxidizes after three days."

"This is the first I've heard of it."

With a yawn he couldn't quite stifle he let me know he was already bored by our conversation. "I suggested as much the other day when I explained how the vault operates. I told you I had my reasons for not wishing the case to drag on, didn't I?"

"I don't swallow that, Wightman."

"And I don't care what you swallow."

"You didn't have to pay me for four days if three was all you wanted."

"It was worth the money. You'll get paid for the four days."

"That doesn't compute. You could have gotten someone a lot cheaper to run your charade for you."

"Wrong. You were the best I could buy for the money. Good actors always cost a little more. But don't fret because the play has closed earlier than you anticipated. You got good reviews and better results than I had hoped for. Two of our five unfortunate victims have no further need for time, and two of the other three have told me to have the investigation terminated. The fifth I can handle myself. You've done admirable work."

"Which two told you to close the case?"

Wightman curled his lip into a soft sneer. "Senator Sieg and the delectable Miss Bashcock. Your expression says you're surprised. I warned you about stepping on toes."

"Did Lea Dark say anything?"

"For once, I haven't heard a peep out of Mrs. Dark. I thought she'd be the first one you scared off. But don't worry about her. I've got her under control."

I didn't say anything right away, and Wightman reached into his desk and handed me an envelope. "This, I believe, makes us even." He waved the envelope at me, but when I didn't grab it, he dropped it on the desk. "But I don't understand your hesitancy. Surely you won't have much trouble accepting money? Or, maybe you've reconsidered? Can I talk you into opening an account in lieu of payment?"

"Not on my life. This isn't just a matter of money anymore."

"Come now, with professionals like ourselves, isn't it always a matter of money?"

"I'm out on a limb, Wightman, because of this case. The police have me implicated in Darling's death, and unless I come up with an alternative, my head will roll."

"I don't see how that's any concern of mine." He winked at me. "And, besides, the police should be no problem for a man of your considerable talents."

I stared into his eyes searching for some spark I could fan into fear. I couldn't let him cut me loose. It wasn't because I thought he'd save me when Murtaugh came knocking. But Wightman was the reason I was at Darling's house that night, and, if I let him off the hook, I'd be risking the only good alibi I had. I couldn't trust him to support my true story if I didn't have something on him. Hell, I didn't even have a real contract with Wightman.

"You know that's not true, Wightman. The police usually move like glaciers, but sometimes one loud noise will turn them into an avalanche. You know about avalanches, don't you? That's what you're really afraid of, isn't it? The police. You know as well as I do that Darling's death was caused by a transducer malfunction. You're afraid the police will figure it out too. Have they already been here? You won't get them off your tail by tossing me away."

"You're wrong. The police don't have anything to do with my decision. It's based on the requests of my depositors. And there is no way Mr. Darling's transducer could have mal-functioned. The safety measures aren't built in, Hughes, they're implicit in the operating principles of the transduc-tion process."

"No good, Wightman. You want to cut the link between us because you know Darling was killed by his transducer. Once that gets around, how long do you think your bank will be open?"

"It won't get around."

"I'll personally see that it does." I stared into the colossal blankness of his face to see if he was buying anything I said. Nothing. It was obvious bullying him wouldn't work, so the only other choice was to convince him I had the case solved. The bridge I had built toward Lea was still untested, but I had to run across it. It seemed the only road to Wightman, and I was beginning to feel that avalanche creeping up be-hind me.

"And what happens once people discover your security

system is so leaky? You've got a fine con going here, you wouldn't want to take a chance with it, would you? You see, I know who the thief is. I know how the tapes were stolen. I know why. The thief also killed Darling. You see, it makes a nice neat bundle. One the police will accept without many questions. One that gets both of us off the hook. Want to hear my case against her?"

When he looked over at me, raised his eyebrow, and asked, "Her?" I saw that I might have him.

"Lea Dark. The fifth victim, the only one who hasn't yet complained about her missing tape. Why? Because she stole it."

Wightman looked at me. He was genuinely surprised, and as I explained my case against Lea to him, he became more and more interested. Balancing the tips of his manicured fingers one on another, he sat there, occasionally swallowing, while a grin started to grow on his face. For the first time since I had met him, I was seeing honest emotion. When I was finished, he nodded slowly.

"I know parts of it are hard to accept, Wightman. But it makes more sense than that phony tale about Senator Sieg and Allison Bashcock ordering you to stop the investigation. I saw both of them today, and neither mentioned a thing like that to me."

For a few moments he sat tapping the tips of his fingers together. By then his smile stretched from ear to ear. "In fact, that part is true. I did get calls from both Senator Sieg and Miss Bashcock. And I've already had a visit from a policewoman named Murtaugh. She described the condition of Darling's body. Of course I denied any connection with the affair, but, as you said, the police are difficult to convince. Your case against Mrs. Dark sounds very promising. I may just reconsider my decision, and have you finish this task you have thus far so nobly advanced."

"That's more like it. Now, did the transducer kill Darling?"

"I don't see how. Transducer malfunctions are really impossible. Just as it is for one person to activate another's systems. Both principles are implicit in the transuction process itself."

"You keep saying that, but one of those principles isn't as implicit as you think. Allison Bashcock once succeeded in activating Darling's transducer. He knew quite a bit about the transuction process, too."

"What are you trying to say? That Darling deep-ended himself with the transducer?"

"It wouldn't surprise me."

"But you just got finished blaming Lea Dark for his death."

"I'm not changing that opinion, either, but I don't think she actually killed him. She only gave him the reason and the opportunity. Darling was too clever to get tricked into tinkering with his transducer, and I doubt if anyone could have forced him to kill himself, not like that. Lea put the idea in his head and the transducer in his hand, but he pushed the button."

"Why would she have done that?"

I told him and he almost applauded with satisfaction. "Very good. If that's true you might just pull it off. Though it seems you're laying a load of conjectures at her door. It'll take more than guesses to sic the police on someone as prominent as Lea Dark."

"I know. It'll take her confession. But that's only the last straw. I've already loaded everything else on her back."

"Indeed you have Mr. Hughes. That's what I like about you. You'll do what's necessary. You're a survivor. Like me. Even though we've been through hard times, we always manage to somehow land on our feet. That's what it takes to survive. Keeping your head up and your feet down. Go to it. And take this money with you."

I nodded, and it occurred to me I didn't dislike the man or his money as much as I thought I did.

20

After I walked out of Wightman's, I remembered I hadn't eaten since breakfast. I wasn't particularly hungry, but there's that sore that was once a bleeding ulcer to keep me honest about things like meals.

Culinary opportunities in that part of town are few. I found a Quikstop on Broadway that hadn't been boarded up, and I went right in. Normally, I avoid fast food chains because their food is invariably fast in a way the advertisements never mention. At that point, however, I was past caring.

I cajoled the dour-faced woman skulking behind the bulletproof window to dig through the heap of chicken wings and find me a few pieces that hadn't been prematurely embalmed in "FryAway." It took her a little while, but she got a nice tip for her trouble, and I got a meal that didn't leave grease rings on my esophagus.

While I gobbled those chicken wings, I rechecked the ammunition I planned to use against Lea. I also thought a little about Joan, and wondered why she hadn't called. It was early to start worrying, but not too early to wonder. I killed an hour before I gathered sufficient courage for my next move, and it wasn't quite eight as I rang the bell at the Dark residence. Edward greeted me with the same enthusiasm we once reserved for door-to-door missionaries.

"I'd like to see your mistress."

"Ms. Joan is not home," he said, staring at me down the full length of his aquiline nose.

"That's just as well. It's Lea I want to see."

"I'll tell her you're here." He left me blowing frost rings outside while he went to report my presence.

When he returned a few moments later, he opened the door and stood to one side. "You're to wait in the library." His displeasure was obvious even if the reason for it was not. I followed him through the dark corridors to the library, and thanked him as he closed the heavy oak door after me.

The library was a massive room, built at a time when the future of knowledge seemed secure. Three interior walls, at least five meters from the parquet floor to the ornately plastered ceiling, were lined with book shelves. The fourth wall, which faced the river, was blanketed by dark-red floor-to-ceiling drapes. A broad, leather-topped desk commanded the center of the room, forcing a not tiny leather couch to share the draped wall with an ancient wooden étagère dating from the French Revolution. I'm not a connoisseur of antiquities, but the previous owner of that piece once explained its history to me. It was made for an uncle of Alex's several greats removed. The fact that nothing in the room had changed in twenty years was more than my imagination working overtime. Since my last visit to it, nothing had changed; nothing except that it was alive then, a place where activity and ideas were generated. Now it was dead, an obscene archive with no more use than the ranks of law books that lined its walls. It was an empty set from another man's life story.

I walked over to a series of framed photographs on the étagère. They portrayed the usual pictorial progression of a family. There were candids of both Lea and Alex as children, a formal wedding pose, the obligatory shots of beach and mountainside vacations, and a color montage of Joan growing up. I had seen most of them before even though I was seeing them through different eyes. One picture, however, was unfamiliar. When I picked it up for a closer inspection, it left a frame-shaped bare spot in the gathered dust of several decades. Behind the picture, two gold wedding bands lay next to each other. They, too, left their imprints in the film of dust covering the Dark family shrine. One ring was engraved "Alex" but the other, for some reason I didn't understand, was engraved "Jacques." I found myself wondering if Lea had had a husband I didn't know about.

The photograph itself showed Alex and his young daughter seated at a table in front of what looked to be a French sidewalk café. Alex, casually dressed in light beige summer slacks and a cream-colored shirt, was smooth shaven, and his face, more bloated than I had ever seen it, underscored the top gloss of encroaching baldness. He was trying hard to be cheerful, but his weak half-smile failed to mask the obviously bleary desperation of alcoholic degeneration. Joan, seated to his right, was stiffly dressed in the dark-blue skirt and sweater combination of a French schoolgirl. She was frowing, not so much at the camera, but down toward the pavement. A half-empty wine bottle towered among the clutter of two wine-glasses and an ashtray overflowing with cigarette butts. A bottle of Coke and an empty tumbler lay among the clutter on the table in front of Joan, next to a stack of schoolbooks. The third chair at the table was empty, but an ecru sweater was draped jauntily over its caned back, and a briar pipe and leather tobacco pouch lay on the seat with an empty camera case and a crumpled pack of cigarettes. Alex's right arm was draped casually over his daughter's shoulder, and his left hand was raised in a greeting for the photographer. The picture had been snapped at an unfortunate moment when Joan seemed to be struggling out of her father's embrace. She had her face turned just enough for the camera to capture a flame in her eyes which reminded me of the one I had witnessed at her parent's divorce.

Across the bottom of the photograph, in a tight, uneven facsimile of the same script I had seen on a thousand legal briefs, Alex had written "just me and your darling daughter." It was, in my opinion, a photograph that flattered no one.

I heard the latch on the door turn, replaced the photograph, and looked around. Lea sat in her wheelchair, observing me with hazy curiosity. "If you've come to sniff my daughter's tail, Mr. Hughes, she's not home." Lea was wearing a blue brocaded dressing gown which covered her feet and billowed over the arms of her wheelchair. Her hair, pulled back in a tight bun, accentuated her face and long neck. In the dim light, the animal glow of her eyes was fearsome.

I made no move to leave. "I've come to talk with you, Lea. Not Joan."

"I find that difficult to believe. I was awake when my daughter came home this morning."

"Nevertheless, it's you I want to talk to."

Her eyebrows arched. She gave a shallow laugh, and let the door close behind her. "I'm sure I haven't the slightest idea what you're talking about, but, if you have something to tell me, you may as well sit down." She motioned toward the couch and rolled herself across the room in my direction. "I trust this isn't going to be one of those odious dramas. Stricken swain come to ask for the damsel's hand. If she wants you, she can have you. My daughter is long past the age where I feel the least responsible for any mistake she cares to make." Lea halted a meter from where I was sitting. At that distance, I could smell the faint, heavy musk of a perfume used for so many years it had become her natural scent.

I dragged out my most confident of smiles. "On the contrary, Lea. My visit has nothing to do with Joan."

I don't know if it was my smile or something I said, but one of the two struck her as amusing. "Now, Mr. Hughes. Chasing the daughter of a former employer is one thing. Chasing his widow is quite another matter. You exceed your expectations."

"I have no expectations. I'm here on business."

"Business? What legal matter could you possibly have to concern me?"

"We misrepresented my present occupation to you the other evening. For some years now, I've been a private investigator. At the moment, I'm working for a man named Ivory Wightman. I believe you know him." I wanted to dent that carapace of composure Lea wore, but I didn't get a nod, a quiver, or a goddamn blink out of her. So, like any good

American boy, I took another shot. "Wightman's had security troubles down at his bank lately. It seems several of the account tapes have been stolen. He hired me to get them back."

For a quarter of a minute, she sat staring quietly into my face. Then, her eyes riveted to mine, she raised her right hand, palm toward me. "Do you intend to continue or am I supposed to be guessing something? You haven't explained why you felt this intrusion on my privacy necessary."

"I suppose you don't know your account tape is among those missing and presumed dead."

Lea Dark was nothing if not a consummate actress. The mixture of shock and grief that flashed across her face was blended perfectly. Instinctively she raised both hands toward her face, caught them halfway, and forced them back into her lap. It would have been too easy to believe until that moment she had known nothing about the tapes having been stolen. She wasted several more seconds of my time before she asked, "You knew about this the other evening, didn't you?"

"Of course."

"And you lacked the common courage to mention it then?"

"Joan thought the news would be a shock for your weakened heart. I didn't know until later that wasn't a problem."

"My daughter is a congenital moron. For which, I suppose, I must accept some blame. What's your excuse?" She stared at me coldly for a moment. "You seem to be enjoying this, Mr. Hughes. Are you pleased I find this news so unsettling? I wonder, could you be casual had you just discovered one entire year of your life was suddenly missing? That's what it amounts to, you know. I've saved almost a year of my life on that account tape. Surely you're at an age where a year is no longer a trifle. How dare you sit there and so smugly enjoy my misery."

"It's not the misery I enjoy. It's the performance."

"The what?"

"The performance, Lea. It's very good. Almost believable. With a little polish, it might even convince a jury."

"Exactly what are you talking about? If you've got something more to say, say it. Otherwise, I would prefer you to leave."

"Aren't you interested in hearing what success I've had tracking down the tape thief? I'd think if a year of my life was missing, I'd be interested in hearing what efforts have been made to recover it."

"Of course," she said. And then, with venom in her voice, she continued, "But somehow, I don't have much faith in your deductive ability. I doubt you could follow a trail of bread crumbs through the forest."

"Oh, but I have. And the trail leads right to your door."

Her eyes dilated, her breath quickened, and her hands gripped the arms of the wheelchair until her fingers turned white. I felt like applauding.

"Mr. Hughes, I think it is really time you leave. I've heard quite enough from you. Shall I call Edward to assist you, or will you see yourself out?"

"It's no good, Lea. You won't act your way out this time."

For one moment, she regarded me with contempt. Then, slowly, she rolled her chair around and started for the door. I let her cover half the distance before I said, "I'll be glad to go, but I'll be back. And I'll bring some good drama critics with me. I'm sure the police are going to be very interested in the evidence I've uncovered."

She stopped but kept her back toward me. "Evidence?" she asked wearily. "Yes, of course, you must have had some reason for making an ass of yourself. Perhaps it would amuse me to hear this evidence you've come up with. Perhaps I can spare us both any further bother. But then, you might even be a bigger fool than I think." She turned her chair to let me see the mockery in her face. "But you must promise not to get violent. You see, I'm an old woman. You could snap my neck if you wanted. But you wouldn't do that, would you? You're just an old-fashioned fool, not one of the more recent violent varieties. When you commit suicide, you'll do it alone."

"Do you deny you stole those tapes?"

"Deny! What earthly reason would I have for stealing my own property?"

"I wondered that myself. If it was just your tape that was missing, it would be a good question. But four others are gone too, and that changes the situation entirely. But, then, you know all this already."

She smiled patronizingly. "Oh, of course I do. But why don't you humor me and relate the whole story." She winked. "We could both use the laugh."

"Several days ago, during a normal visit, one of Wightman's depositors discovered his tape compartment had been emptied. He reported the situation to Wightman, who then checked through all the compartments to see if other tapes were missing. He discovered four more empty compartments. Wightman waited for the ransom note he assumed would come, but nothing arrived. That's when he came to me. His security system is good, the best. A thief would need a compelling reason to go to the trouble of stealing something that couldn't be sold and had no value to anyone but its owner. But, given the proper motive, a depositor could have learned other people's securicodes, and, with relatively little difficulty, gain access to other compartments."

"How?"

"By showing up pretending to make a normal transaction. Instead of opening her own compartment, this thief would open her intended victim's compartment, remove that tape, conceal it, and present her own tape at the desk for processing. Then it would be a simple maneuver to leave with both tapes. The scheme is so simple, it's almost foolproof, at least until the thefts were discovered. But then all the thief has to do is sit pat, pretending to be one of the victims with an empty tape compartment. She'd wait until someone told her that her tape was missing, and, given the present state of the law, the chances are no one would ever suspect her. Of course, if you hadn't heard after three days, you'd get itchy. You'd go looking for a good reason for someone to break the news. Someone like Jeanette Dumbrey. Your performance the other day was brilliant."

"You said five compartments were empty. I assume you have a reason for singling me out of those five. Or have the other four already laughed in your face?"

"I have reasons. But, as you already know, two of your four victims will never laugh in anyone's face again."

"Such drama. Such suspense. It's you who are giving the good performance." She seemed to be amused by my efforts, much too amused, I told myself, for someone who's just lost a year of her life. "I haven't heard anything to make me confess to something I didn't do. You didn't suspect me at dinner the other evening. What have I done in two short days to warrant this treatment?"

"I saw you coming out of Wightman's office yesterday afternoon. You seemed very energetic for someone confined to a wheelchair."

Lea looked at me with muted amazement. Then she shook her head slowly. "Is this the brand of evidence you've collected? If so, we're both wasting our time. The sources you've chosen to believe are, to put it bluntly, inaccurate. I use this chair as an aid, but I am by no means confined to it." She stood and walked an effortless circle around the chair to prove her point. When she sat down, she said, "You see, I come and go as I please. Perhaps I do tire more quickly when I exert myself, but I am in no way bound to this chair. Nor have I ever claimed to be."

"How does your illness hamper you, Lea?"

"Hamper? It's killing me. Isn't that enough?"

"And that's why you got the idea to escape to a place as dreary as the orbiting colony will be?"

"Why do you say dreary? This earth we live on, Mr. Hughes, this is dreary. Filled with dreary people such as yourself. Yes, I am going to emigrate, but not only because of my disability."

"You realize there are regulations against your emigrating to Orbicol."

Lea sneered. "Regulations are impediments only for those who lack conviction."

I nodded. "Why did you go to Wightman's yesterday if you didn't plan on making a deposit or withdrawal?"

"How do you know what my intentions were?"

"If you didn't know your tape was missing, it seems natural you would have asked to get it from the vault. Since you didn't, you must have had other reasons. Unless, of course, you already did know."

"Splendid logic. But misconceived. I went to Ivory's to ask some questions about the new transducer he had made for me. Since I'm going to Orbicol soon, I will require a transducer with a very large storage capability. You see, I don't plan on returning, so I must be able to take my entire time account with me. Ivory called me several days before, but I didn't feel well enough to go in to see him until yesterday. I didn't know he was going to be out of town. Ivory has been very patient with me. I pay him well. The insolent slut he has for an assistant couldn't get it into her head that I had already arranged to pick up my new transducer."

"You treated her badly."

"Did I? If Ivory insists on employing his mistress for activities other than those for which she is suited, why should I suffer?"

"She thought you wanted a replacement because you lost your transducer."

"She is a dolt. I don't know where she got that misconception."

"May I see your transducer? Just to clear up the mistake."

She straighened in her chair and smoothed her eyebrow with her right index finger, continuing the motion behind her ear and along the soft skin under her chin. "I could show it to you, but I don't see what right you have to come here and make these demands. If you doubt my word, get yourself a search warrant."

"That won't be necessary." I stood and walked over to the desk. The desk calendar was turned to June 14, 1983, the day of the Dark's divorce. My back was to Lea when I said, "That was an attractive coat you were wearing yesterday. I've never seen one like it. Does it belong to you?"

"Don't be ridiculous. Of course it belongs to me. Do you think I'm in the habit of wearing other people's clothing? My late husband had it made for me. It's baby seal and quite valuable."

"That striping must be rare."

"It is, though I've seen similar coats."

I turned around and looked at her. "This afternoon, I spent an hour with Senator Sieg. Victor Sieg. You know him, of course?"

"We both know Victor. I don't know why that should be in question."

"He mentioned you've been lobbying for a variance of the Orbicol immigration regulations."

"He's a friend. That's what friends are for."

"Senator Sieg also told me you have also been, and I quote, 'badgering Carlo Mountain' to intercede on your behalf. Do you deny it?"

The question obviously delighted Lea, "Why should I deny anything? Both Victor and Carlo are friends. You've gone to some trouble tracking down my friendships with Senator Sieg and Carlo Mountain. Had I known your true intentions Saturday evening, I could have spared you some effort. Do you think I'm limited to those two resources? I have an abundance of friends in influential positions. At one time or another, I've asked most of them to help me. Would you like a complete list of them? But first tell me how you happened to single out those two?"

"Both have accounts with Wightman."

"I see. But you mean 'had,' don't you, at least in Carlo's case?" Her voice was as gentle and warm as winter in Wyoming, and I detected a cruel satisfaction in it.

"That's a strange attitude about the death of an old friend."

"One mourns the passing of a friend in proportion to the affection they shared while living. Carlo was never what you would call a loving person. But that didn't stop him from being a valued and valuable friend. I haven't seen Carlo in months though we did speak to each other regularly. Carlo has not been a happy man in recent years. But, then, who has? I knew he was a depositor, of course. He introduced me to Ivory in the first place. I wasn't aware Victor also subscribed. He was always such a closed child." She paused a second for to smirk. "Victor is about your age, isn't he? He's done so well for himself."

I ignored her. She was trapped and we both knew it. I wasn't going to let her wriggle away on a slug's trail of cheap insults. "Not only were they both depositors, but Sieg and Mountain also had their tapes stolen."

"I see. And you suspect I took their tapes to force their permission for my passage to Orbicol? Mr. Hughes, that's too obvious a motive."

"Some motives are obvious only to the person who commits the crime."

"That's it then." Her eyes flared with understanding. "You've always known I was guilty. You've been waiting for the proper crime, haven't you?" Neither of us said a word for a long moment. "But, this time, you're wrong. You claimed five compartments were empty. Who are the other two?"

"The fourth person is Allison Bashcock."

Lea searched her mind for the proper few seconds before answering. "Should I know her?"

"She's a writer, a novelist."

"I haven't read a book in years."

"Allison also works for Melray Johnson, a public relations firm."

"Her mother must be very proud of her."

"She's also the illegitimate daughter of Blanche Tarbridge and Gregory Darling."

Lea returned my steady gaze. "All Mr. Darling's children are illegitimate. So, I believe, are Mrs. Tarbridge's." There was real tension in her voice now. I felt I was on the verge of breaking her.

"Gregory Darling was victim number five. And also the person who discovered the theft in the first place."

Lea sat ramrod straight in her chair. When she spoke, she could hardly contain the quaver in her voice, and her hand begin to tremble, not much, but enough to tell me I was right.

"That does make five. At least you can count. Why was I chosen to be the guilty party? You claim you have evidence. I'd like to hear something other than innuendo."

"Did you know Gregory Darling died on Friday evening?" I said, boring in for the kill.

Lea nodded grimly.

"Did you know the man?"

She took a long time before speaking. "I did. Long ago."

"When did you last see him?"

Lea sighed and shook her head. Her eyes closed. She rubbed her forehead lightly with her fingertips. "It's been so long I hardly see how it could matter. Why this preoccupation with ancient history, Mr. Hughes?"

"I don't think three days quite qualifies as ancient history, Lea."

That got a rise out of her. "Three days! Have you lost your mind? I haven't laid eyes on Gregory Darling in over thirty years." Then, to ice her lie, she added, "Of that, I can assure you."

I got up, walked over to Lea, and laid the list Trigger had prepared on Lea's lap. "This shows each visit the five victims made to the bank in the last six months. You'll note your name appears far more often than any of the others."

"I assume I save more time than they do."

"If we look a bit more closely, we'll see a suspicious pattern to your visits." Then, continuing the logic as I had done with Trigger, I went through the list, narrowing down the possible suspects. As before, the same name was left when the others had been eliminated. When I was finished, Lea sat studying the list.

Her hand wasn't shaking anymore when she handed the paper back to me. "Well, that is evidence. And impressive deduction. But totally flawed. Based on circumstantial and arbitrary assumptions. You were once a lawyer, Mr. Hughes. You'll admit this would never stand up under cross-examination."

"I agree. Unless other details corroborated it. By the way, do you know the police think Gregory Darling was murdered?"

"No."

"There's a strong link between the person who stole the tapes and Gregory Darling's murderer. On the afternoon Darling died, he had two visitors. One was a woman who was with him when he died. Where were you on Friday afternoon, Lea?"

"I was here at home."

I nodded. "I was the other visitor. I was there when the woman arrived."

"If you saw this woman, then there's no mystery." Lea was cool, almost too cool.

"I didn't see her face, only her coat. The same coat you have already admitted you own."

"You're wrong. I was nowhere near Darling's home. You must have seen another coat that looks like mine."

"Perhaps, but I don't think so."

"Mr. Hughes, I don't care what you think. I do know you are mistaken in your every assumption. I also know that if you persist in these insane allegations, I'll make you regret it."

"But there's so much more, Lea. Don't you want to hear? Gregory Darling died from an enormous psychological trauma, a trauma caused by the infusion of another person's time into his system. The other person was Darling's visitor. You see, she left her transducer at his house. The police found it in his hand when they performed the autopsy that revealed his transduction disk. They still don't know the identity of that woman. In fact, they may not even know the transducer they found didn't belong to Darling. But I do. He kept his in a silver case. He showed it to me that last afternoon. Later that evening, I found the same transducer in his bedroom. You see, I also discovered his body, Lea. It was one of the most terrifying sights I've ever seen in my life. He was twisted by agony no one could imagine, distorted into a caricature of a human being. I'm going to see his face for the rest of my life. Won't you?" I reached into my pocket and took out Gregory Darling's transducer. "That's what's left of him, Lea. Don't you want it as a memento?"

She looked at me and a slow, victorious smile spread across her face. "The transducer can only be activated by its owner. So your theory about Mr. Darling's death is wrong."

"That's what everyone says, Lea. But we both know a transducer can be activated by someone's blood relative." I offered her the transducer a second time. "Don't you want this memento of your brother, Lea?"

Lea didn't even flinch. "You keep it, Mr. Hughes. Gregory and I ceased being brother and sister many years ago. As I said before, I haven't seen him since then. Besides, I have a transducer of my own."

She reached into the pocket of her dressing gown and held out her hand. "I trust this will end our ridiculous discussion. If you care, I'm sure Ivory will verify this transducer belongs to me."

She didn't stop speaking, but I couldn't take my eyes off her palm. The fact that Lea could produce a transducer didn't mean she was innocent, but it did blast a giant hole in my argument. Lea stormed right through that hole.

"This display of your incompetence surprises me. Any clearheaded infant would have seen through these arguments, but, because you managed to uncover a deep, dark secret, you seem to think the rest of your ramshackle creation becomes valid. It doesn't. Why would I want to kill my brother after not seeing him all these years? Did you ask yourself that?"

"There are several reasons. He was working on an auto-biography, which would undoubtedly reveal your true origins. All you've got propping up your feeble sense of class, Lea, is Alex's family name. Exposure by Darling would have destroyed that."

"Nonsense. Gregory was the one who always refused to acknowledge our common origins. He's the reason we haven't seen each other all these years. And, even if you were right, why would I want to steal something I already owned. The fact is, Mr. Hughes, I don't give a damn about that account tape. You see, Ivory has transferred all my stored time to my new, larger transducer. My account tape was already empty. Ivory has been most helpful with all these arrangements. The best friends are still the ones you buy. Ivory has already made the necessary arrangements for me to emigrate. Did you know that? The whole idea was his in the first place, and he's followed through. So that shoots your motive to hell. The man is brilliant, but I can't see why he employs incompetents. Miss Dobbson, I suppose, has her uses. But why he hired you, with your pathetic prejudice . . . "

"Prejudice?"

"What else? Were I you, with the obvious hatred you harbor for me, I would have required more than circumstantial evidence before suspecting you. You want me to be guilty. You have to convict me of something, don't you? The particular crime isn't important. In your eyes, I'm guilty. But your motives are so obvious they're pitiful. And, that's what you've become, Mr. Jack Hughes. A pitiful, crusading idiot. You're as bad as my daughter."

"It won't work, Lea. You won't get off by attacking me."

"You can't be that self-deluding. Didn't you think I sensed your hostility the other evening? You hate me. And why, I asked myself. Because I wasn't foolish enough to devote my life to the noble Alexander Hamilton Dark? But I have, you see, and in a way you never even guessed. You say you came here looking for the truth, well then let's have it. I ruptured your frail sense of right and wrong when I divorced my husband."

"You're wrong, Lea. The evidence led to your door. I only followed it."

"Now, Mr. Hughes, admit what we both know is true. You wanted to convict me of the first available crime because, twenty years ago, I divorced my husband."

I should have kept my mouth closed while thinking, but I couldn't. "You're right about one thing. I never ranked myself among your fans. But not because you divorced a man. There's nothing wrong with divorce, except the way you accomplished it. You chewed Alex to pieces before you spit him out, and some people call that manslaughter." I was cold, harsh, sure of my ground for the first time since walking into the room. "You took a man as solid, as kind, as capable as any I ever knew, and you tore him to bits. When you were finished digesting the soft humanity, Alex crawled into a corner and drank himself to death. By then, there wasn't anything left but the husk."

"Now you're the one who's being dramatic." Lea pursed her lips and whistled softly. "You do hate me, don't you? You think I'm a vampire." She hoisted her chin to show me the canine tips of her front teeth. Making a clicking noise in her throat, she slid her dentures forward along her tongue so they jutted over her lower lip. She let me stare into her empty mouth a moment before sucking her teeth back into place. "As you can see, my fangs were removed a long time ago. You were no better judge of character when you were a lawyer than you are now. To you, Alex was a great man, a kind and generous employer, a leader of his community, a stalwart, upstanding citizen. A good father and a better husband. A paramount." She snickered ironically as she ticked off each attribute. "Believe me, Mr. Hughes, my husband would rather have been your paramour than your paramount."

I stared at Lea, but she allowed me no other reaction before she continued. "You say I left a husk of a man when I divorced Alex. What would you say if I told you I married a husk and kept it together for sixteen years? Would you believe the Alex you knew and respected was a cheap facade, a hollow brickwork built to mask an alcoholic pederast, a whimpering faggot as incapable of feeling real affection as I am of growing a prick? The morning after my wedding night, how do you think I enjoyed discovering my admirable husband preferred wiggling his shriveled cock in the bellboy's ass to sleeping with his new bride? That was a rude awakening, as you say. And yet, I came north with him when he graduated from law school and tried hard to be the wife he could be proud of. Every day for sixteen years, I watched him pull on one of his well-tailored suits, go out, and show the world a complete lie. For sixteen years, I put up with his midnight trysts with the slimiest of scum this city held. And, when I could put up with him no longer, I divorced him. Don't you think I know everyone thought I was a southern chippie putting the screws to a good man? But, for all the things I did say in court, I let Alex escape with his reputation intact. I never said one-tenth of the things I could have. And, even after the divorce, even after the bastard had finally crawled into a gin bottle and died, I still honored the image of the man everyone thought I had married. So you see, I've remained faithful to that image even if I divorced the man." Lea paused to make sure she had my attention.

"Mr. Hughes, your disbelief is evident. But come, you're the one who loves proof. Would you like to see some? That picture you were staring at when I came in, the one that shows the poor remains of your dear, destroyed Alex. Have a closer look at it."

She stood up and swept the photograph into my hands. "Ask yourself who the cameraman was. Ask yourself why the loving daughter is so disgusted at the attention of her admirable father. Why is there a pipe on the table and a pack of cigarettes on the chair when you must have known Alex was allergic to tobacco. Did you notice the ring on Alex's hand? You didn't know about Alex's French husband, did you? Ask yourself why that noble scion of northern aristocracy sent me the goddamn picture in the first place. And, maybe, when you've answered all these questions, you'll be ready for more proof. Or maybe you'll realize how fortunate you were that my exalted husband kept his hands out of your pants long enough for him to escape with his saintly reputation intact. You think I was lucky to get the house and the money, Mr. Hughes? He was lucky to keep his ridiculous self-respect. I didn't kill him. His conscience did. Maybe, when you've finished hating me for all the things I said at the divorce, you'll consider all the things I didn't say. Maybe you'll find the courage to ask yourself why you were so anxious to convict me of a crime I never committed."

I looked at the picture rather than Lea. I could see all the things she mentioned, but you can't destroy a man's reputation on circumstantial evidence, can you?

Lea glared at me for a while. Then she said, "Do you wonder why I've preserved this room like a shrine? To remind myself of the high contrast between the reality of my husband and the lie the world remembers. I've earned my share of enemies, Mr. Hughes, I won't deny that. But I've also had the benefit of many I never deserved." She rolled her chair back a meter and anointed me with the last few drops of her poison. "You may kick Alex's corpse all you want, but you'll never get him to stand up and testify against me. He wasn't capable of standing up by himself when he was alive. He was so terrified of women, I don't know how he ever believed he could get anyone pregnant.

"But I suppose I was lucky to have found a fool of his caliber." She wheeled around and started toward the door. "You'll excuse me now. If you have anything else to say, it can wait until morning. This nonsense has quite exhausted me. I must rest up for my trip. I assume I can trust you to let yourself out. I won't worry about the silver. But please, don't feel you have to hurry away. Quiet reflection will do you good. You have such a long walk home. Perhaps, when my daughter comes back, she'll drive you."

I watched Lea leave the room. I let her leave, and I didn't say a thing. There was nothing to say. I listened to the wooden vibration of her wheelchair moving across the floor. Then, for a long time, the house was silent. I waited quietly. I was no longer in a hurry.

21

Hours must have passed before I heard the tumblers on the front door clicking open and the drum of leather heels punctuating the stillness. The sound of the heels moved down the hall, passed the library door, hesitated a moment, and then returned. Joan was well into the room before she was even aware of my presence.

"Oh Christ!" Her reaction caught her stiffly and she wrapped her arms around her chest as if to keep her breath from exploding away. "Jack, darling, you frightened me. I didn't know anyone was in here. I couldn't imagine why the light was on. We never use this room."

She wore a dark-green winter coat clenched tightly at the waist. The cold flush on her cheeks left the bloodless whites of her eyes in stark relief, and the room's half light emphasized the gray in her hair.

"Why didn't you tell me you were coming? I would have been home sooner."

I shrugged. "Your mother and I have been killing time. Besides, you were going to call me."

"You weren't home." She raised her eyebrows, stripped off her coat, and moved across the room toward me. Her gray velveteen ensemble clung to all the places it had been designed to cling. "You and my mother? I do hope she didn't bore you. She get's so tiresome when she rambles off on one of her tangents."

I shook my head. "On the contrary. I was hanging on her every word."

Joan shrugged, grabbing a hesitant breath like a shoplifter boosting a bit of air. "You have more patience than I do."

"I was surprised to learn how spry Lea is. I thought her heart slowed her down to a crawl. But I was wrong."

"What do you mean?"

"She ran circles around me."

Joan shook her head slowly. "I still don't understand."

"Was Alex a homosexual?"

In an instant, shock, realization, resentment, and hatred all marched across her face like the bucket brigade on their way to a ten-alarm blaze. "Is that what she told you?"

I nodded grimly.

"But, why on earth did . . ."

"Let's just say I wormed it out of her. Is it true?"

"Jack, what difference does it make now?"

I ignored her question. "Is it true?"

After a long moment, she nodded.

"Why didn't you tell me?"

"When I realized you didn't already know, I saw no good reason to tell you. Your memories of him were so warm." She became more aloof. "Besides, most of those memories were founded on the truth. Alex may have been a homosexual, but he . . ."

"There's no need to explain. I agree with you, but your father's sexual preferences wouldn't have made any difference to my memories of him. He was fair with me, and I don't care if he was wearing pink hot pants under his three-piece suits, he was a good lawyer." I stood up. "Your butler took my coat. Any idea where he might have hidden it?"

"In the hall closet. But Jack, you aren't leaving already, are you?"

I said nothing but walked out and found my coat. When I returned to the library, Joan was sitting on the couch.

"You know, my mother was a bitch for telling you." She avoided my eyes as I spoke.

"On the contrary. She was defending herself. I gave her a hard time. I accused her of engineering the theft of those tapes."

That surprised Joan, though I also caught an inexplicable flutter of amusement at the corners of her mouth. "My mother? But why?"

"Because I thought she was guilty."

"Whoever gave you that idea?"

"A lot of people. You among them."

"Me?" she asked in bewilderment. "How?"

"For one thing, you gave me the impression she was confined to her wheelchair."

"Did I? I may have said she had to spend a lot of time in a wheelchair, but, even if I did, it was an idle comment. I don't see how that gave you the idea my mother was a crook."

"It was an idle comment, all right, but what do you think I build cases out of? Idle comments, tiny inconsistencies, stray observations, slight incongruities, that's all there usually are. How often do you think I can find any evidence that doesn't demand logic or a creative interpretation to make sense? That's what a detective does; gather up mismatched details, sort them out, and create a case. It's a cut-and-paste job. I have to look for the patterns myself. Sometimes, the patterns I find don't fit right." I shifted my coat to my other arm. "I have a murderer to catch and not much time to do it."

I was halfway to the door when Joan caught my arm. "I know you're shaken just now, but call me in the morning when you've had time to think. My father . . ." She hesitated, searching for the right way to continue. "Despite what Lea said, Alex was always a fine man and wonderful father. Even at the end."

"Give me credit, Joan. I don't need the pep rally. It's not your father's homosexuality that bothers me. It's my own stupidity."

"What do you mean?"

"Your mother was completely right about one thing. I wanted to prove her guilty of this tape theft because I hated her. I shouldn't let personal feeling influence my work. When that starts to happen, I can quit pretending to be a professional and get a government job."

He smile was weak, ineffectual. "I understand, but call me in the morning."

"What good will that do?"

"What harm? Last night . . ."

"I remember last night, Joan. It was nice. Very nice, but tomorrow morning I'm going to be busy. Most likely, where I'm going I'll be allowed only one phone call, and not a lot of chatting time on that one.

"What are you talking about now?"

"There's a police detective grooming me to be Darling's murderer."

"You?" Alarm flashed across her face, and I let myself believe it was concern for me. "Why you?"

"Wonderful reasons. I discovered his body." Then I shrugged. "And, in a funny way, I did kill him. Darling was well through the back door when I got to his house, but I slammed the door closed after him. It doesn't make any difference now. The police need someone to toss in the volcano, and I'm as much a virgin as anyone."

"But, if you didn't murder him, what's your crime?"

"Getting involved. It's an occupational hazard."

"Jack, you're not really going to have to take the blame for that man's death, are you?"

"I don't have bright hopes of catching someone to take my

place before Murtaugh catches up with me."

"Who's Murtaugh?"

"Murtaugh's a firefighter who beats out little fires before they get to be big fires. In this case, I'm the blanket. Murtaugh's the cop in charge of investigating Darling's death."

"You don't have to give yourself up, do you?"

"Are you suggesting a mad dash for the border? If I'm not home when Murtaugh comes looking, there'll be an A.P.B. on me faster than you can say 'Jack Hughes.' The police aren't fond of taking prisoners. The price of a fair trial is regarded as an unnecessary expense down at city hall. Funerals are a lot cheaper and far more conclusive. That's why, when people started buying generic justice, the gas chambers started working overtime. Dead men cause no problems. As big as this city is, there isn't a hiding place high enough to keep them from finding me. Once an A.P.B. goes out, I'm as dead as thread. I honestly thought that when the Supreme Court ruled that any jury which condemned a criminal be present at the executions, people would be slow to hand out death sentences. But three weeks ago in Philidelphia, a jury gave the gas to a woman who let her daughter commit suicide. Thanks, but I don't want a trial before a jury of my peers."

"You could stay here." She tightened her grip on my arm enough to tell me what she meant. I wanted to turn, to ignore her intent, but her eyes held mine like a beggar's.

"I haven't got much time to locate the guilty party, Joan, but I think I'd better use it. Last chance, so to speak."

"Oh, I don't think you should be as worried about the police as all that. You can call this Murtaugh in the morning from here. If you think that's necessary. The police are reasonable people."

"If it's a hiding place you're selling, you can forget it. Murtaugh knows every move I've made in the last two days. The police department is never short of stooges. And, if it's a last meal for the condemned man, thanks, but I don't seem to have much appetite at the moment."

Joan dropped my arm and took a backward step. "Well,

at least you give me credit for being charitable." There was
no rancor in her words. She flexed her eyebrows and rolled
her head in a slow clockwise orbit. "Why, just think of all the
other nasty reasons I might have for helping you. You flatter
me, Jack. But not yourself. Don't question my motives. If
you want to leave, then go ahead."

"A fine speech."

"What makes you so skeptical, so full of doubts? Can't you
just accept my offer with the grace with which it was intended?"

I tried tempering my words but found just the proper
touch of flippancy elusive. "What makes you such an opti-
mist?"

She didn't answer, but neither did she loosen her grip on
my eyes.

"Joan, it's late. I've lived too long to believe in fairy tales,
or even that anything ever works the way we want it to."

She turned and took a confident step toward the desk.
"I'd accept that excuse from most people, Jack. But not you.
In many ways, you're just like me. I don't believe in fairy
tales either. I never have. You at least had a nice little 'once
upon a time' with Alicia." She laughed and looked around
at me with a slow, liquid smile learned at the hands of a better
teacher than I. "You know my mother is certain I'm a nym-
phomaniac."

"Are you?"

She shook her head energetically. "Not a chance. I'm much
too particular about whom I sleep with to be a sexual obsessive. The world isn't exactly teeming with desirable partners."

"I see. I make the grade? Is it my sturdy, silent masculinity
that bowls you over? Or my quaint, romantic sense of values?"

"Maybe it's because you seem to have a little self-respect
left. Not much, but it shows. Or, maybe it's because I sense
you're near the edge of venting your anger. There's a hint
of emotion left in you, a flicker of life. Jack, a few hours ago,
I could have said you reminded me of my father, and you
would have been flattered. But it's still true. You do remind

me of Alex. All the things I loved about him. Is that so wrong or hard to believe?"

"No, it's not hard to believe. We're all suckers who go looking for ideals we prized once upon a time. That's why living is disappointing. We continually get our noses rubbed in those ideals. Time, it seems, wounds all heels."

"But don't stop looking. Not yet. You call that cotton batting you wear protection against the pain of life. You're a liar. That batting is to protect you from the chill of the back door. But that door's always been open. We all live in its chill. Isn't it nice to get warm now and then?"

"It is. Now and then."

"Then stay with me tonight."

I let her lead me to the top of the stairs. She opened a door in the dark hall and whispered in my ear, "I'll be just a moment. Warm the bed." She was true to her word. I had hardly finished taking off my shoes when she joined me in the small room. "I just wanted to make sure they were asleep." Then she put out the light.

With few revisions, we reshot the film of the previous night. This version also ended with the angel of mercy taking one last long sigh, only this time, we all knew it was an act. The feeling was still warm, and wonderful, but no closer to real life than a love story in an Allison Bashcock novel.

In the early morning, however, I was perfectly content to lay watching dust motes careen madly in the spear of sunlight that split the curtains. While Allison slept, the silver and black of her hair wove a fine embroidery on my shoulder. I even allowed myself a moment to think all was right with the world. I was already untangling myself from that dream when Joan stirred in her sleep. I caught my breath, anxious not to wake her, but she rolled over luxuriously and slept on.

It's crucial for me to remember I was already walking calmly to the nearest exit before I left Joan's bed. Later, without that knowledge, I couldn't have separated my emotions as clearly nor been capable of divining the frail line between history and just another product of vistavision.

It's odd how often so much can hinge on an insignificant detail.

I pulled on my clothes and started down the steps. They creaked more loudly than they had the night before, or maybe this time I was the only one who heard their reproaches.

My coat was still draped over the edge of the étagère where I had dropped it. I was pulling it on when I noticed the photograph of Alex and Joan in Paris. I couldn't help one last look. Then something odd about the note Alex had scribbled across the bottom of the photograph caught my eye. His weak scrawl showed all the signs of mental deterioration; the upstrokes were foreshortened, the downstrokes flattened into bulbous tubers twice the width of each uneven letter. Only the word "darling" was smoothly executed by a determined hand.

Then I noticed something else. The cover of the top book on the stack in front of the blushing schoolgirl lay exposed to the private eye of the camera. In English, the title of that epic romance my wife and a million other women carried around in the mid-eighties was *Dark Shadows*. I recognized the cover immediately, even if I didn't the original French title, *Jeanette d'Ombre*. In an instant, the point of Alex's faltering, alcoholic message made perfect sense.

22

My body wasn't moving nearly as fast as my mind when I got outside. Half expecting to see a police cruiser waiting at the curb, half sorry when I didn't, I glanced up and down the street. I felt as if I were on a collision course with an uptown bus, and, in a curious way, Murtaugh was the only person who could prevent a crack-up.

Some things never change. You still can't find a cop when you need one.

I did find a cabby dozing peacefully on the corner of Seventy-seventh and West End Avenue. It wasn't quite eight when I dropped my hat on the desk in my office. I didn't bother to take my coat off before I sat down at the data console and began strumming the keys like the lady in the instruction film. Answers to my questions began parading across the screen and what could only be called a meaningful dialogue was played out between me and my electronic memory. When the fifteen minutes were over, there were only a few loose strands for me to weave into that shroud.

I got Wightman out of bed. He wasn't pleased, though from the lust in his voice, I knew he hadn't been sleeping.

"Hughes, where are you?" he asked when I told him who was calling.

"In my office. Alone."

"Lea Dark?" he asked, a broad note of optimism padding his voice.

"At home in her own bed, I assume. She's not our thief, but you knew that. Thanks. She told me you conned her into believing she could go to Orbicol. She told me the whole crazy scheme was your idea in the first place. Only she didn't use words like con, crazy, or scheme. That old woman really believes you. I almost find myself feeling sorry for her, something I never thought would happen. Weren't you satisfied with the money she was giving you for her time account? You had to give her a better reason to get hooked on your gizmo, didn't you?"

"I gave her a reason to live. That's got her this far, hasn't it? That was more than any doctor could have done. I kept her alive. I don't think there's anything wrong with that. Or with my accepting a reward she would have given any other doctor." He sounded genuinely offended.

"Relax, Wightman. Lea still thinks you're a genius. I don't even blame you for trying to take advantage of my stupidity. I deserved it. It would have been a good opportunity for you to get her off your back."

"You don't know half the story."

"I know I don't. That's why I want you to get a tape from the vault for me."

"A tape?" he asked.

"Jeanette Dumbrey. Run it through your console. I want to know if it's a real time tape or not."

"Jeanette Dumbrey!" He waited a few moments before speaking again. "It'll take some time. Will you wait? Or shall I call back?"

"Call back." I put the phone down and waited with mad thoughts racing through my head. When the phone rang, I picked it up. It wasn't Wightman.

"Jack? Are you all right?"

"Just fine, thanks." My voice was cool, but not cold.

"I woke up and you were gone. I didn't know what to think." She giggled like a French schoolgirl. "I thought maybe the police had snatched you out of my bed."

"I haven't seen the police."

"Why did you leave without waking me?"

"For the same reason you left without waking me the day before. I was going to call."

"Are you just going to sit there and wait for them?"

"Who?"

"The police. Sergeant what's-her-name."

"Murtaugh. There's no point in hiding."

"Jack, this is going to sound silly. When I got up, the first thing I thought was that you had run off because you felt guilty. Don't laugh. It's happened to me more than once."

"I'm not laughing."

"No, you're not, are you."

I realized I had a death grip on the receiver.

"Jack, I have to see you. There's something I must say. Something I didn't get to tell you this morning. I could be there in half an hour."

"Murtaugh could be here in two minutes." Then, as neutrally as I could, I said, "How about your office?"

Joan thought a moment before speaking. "If you think that would be safer, of course."

"That would be much safer. Murtaugh has no reason to look there yet."

"Jack, please be careful."

"Don't worry. I've made all the mistakes I'm going to make."

I cut the connection and dialed Wightman's number. He answered immediately. "Hughes? Your line was busy."

"A friend called to ask me to be careful."

"How sweet," he said cynically. "I checked Jeanette Dumbrey's tape. Cheap audiotape with no time-storage capacity at all. In fact, I ran it through the audiorecorder. There's a message on it. Would you like to hear it?"

"More than anything else in the world."

I heard Wightman fumble a tack-jack into the phone receiver. There was an even hum of taped silence followed by a woman's falsetto. "Hello," she said. "This is Jeanette Dumbrey. I'm out at the moment, but at the sound of the tone, leave your name and number. Maybe I'll return the call."

Then Wightman was back on the line. "That's it. Do you know what it means?"

"I was right the first time. The thief's name is Jeanette

Dumbrey." I waited a moment while he thought that over.
"Don't worry, friend," I said before I hung up. "I'll let you
know how everything turns out."

I wanted to make one more call before I left. I dialed the
number and listened to a sleepy male voice answer, "Yeah?"

"Detective Murtaugh, please."

"Missed her by a few minutes. She went to arrest some
guy. You want to leave a message?"

"My name is Hughes. If Murtaugh wants me, I'll wait for
her at 342 East Forty-second Street. Got that?"

"342 East Forty-seventh."

"No. Forty-second." A misunderstanding like that could
cost me my life. I laid the phone down and spent half a
minute looking for my coat before I realized it was still on
my back.

Only half a minute, the difference between meeting Murtaugh at my front door and going free.

She was out of her car before I was out of the building's
lobby. Both Slovinsky and Chick had come along for the ride,
but they stayed put. I could see the place between them
reserved for me.

"Stop right there, Hughes!" Murtaugh shouted, though
she didn't have to. "We got some talking to do."

I obeyed her gruff command as if I had a choice in the
matter. "I don't suppose you'd believe I was on my way to
meet Darling's killer?"

She stood a meter from me, raised her eyebrows know-
ingly, and shook her head. "Not one bit. The whole thing's
been taken out of my hands."

I nodded and held out my wrists for the cuffs, but she just
kept shaking her head. "You give up too easily. And too late.
Darling's case has been closed."

My arms refused to drop, and, almost of their own volition,
both hands began to tighten into fists.

She sniffed and rubbed her nose daintily with her paw.
"Darling's death was officially declared a suicide. Mountain

died a natural death, and all the vultures have already torn into his estate. We're off the hook. All of us."

My hands were clenched so tightly my arms were beginning to tremble. "Just like that?"

"Just like that."

"Mind telling me why?"

Murtaugh glanced quickly up Park Avenue. "What's the difference? You're off the hook. Consider yourself a lucky man."

"I don't get it, Murtaugh. Two days ago, you woke me in the middle of the night to threaten me with two murder charges, and now, all's forgiven. That didn't happen by itself."

"The Lord moves in strange ways, Hughes." She nodded at my trembling fists. "Put them in your pockets where they belong. I really thought you'd be glad to hear the news. Why do you think I came all the way up here again? Hell, you look so guilty now, I ought to lock you up on suspicion."

"What happened? Someone told you to forget it, didn't he? That has to be it. Someone with enough power to make it stick. Give me three guesses?"

She shook her head. "You know it doesn't made any difference who."

"But it makes a difference to me. It was a certain Senator, wasn't it?"

She turned a shoulder toward me and looked back at the two cops sitting dumbly in the cruiser. "Hughes, leave off. I'm being as straight as I can. Straighter than you've ever been with me. I don't know everything that's gone on. No one does. Still, I'm sure I could fill you in on a thing or two. But I'm smart enough to know when to go and when to stop. There's a red light now where that green light used to be. Isn't getting off the hook enough?"

"No, Murtaugh. It isn't. We both know there's more than a simple suicide to Darling's death."

She took a step back. "If you're too stupid to know what's good for your hide, then I don't feel sorry for you one bit.

You do what you want, but don't look for my help. You can run as far as you want. It's still a free country." She looked at me with something like pity in her eyes. "But you're a bigger fool than I guessed. You're on your own."

Murtaugh nodded briskly and got back in her car. She made a tight U-turn and moved the wrong way down Park Avenue. As the car pulled by me, Slovinsky leaned out the window.

"Hey, Hughes. This makes us even again."

As right as that was, it was a judgment I wouldn't have wished on my worst enemy.

The elevator in Joan's building wasn't scheduled to go up for ten minutes, and the lockmaster looked genuinely shocked when I started up the stairs that wound around the open shaft of the lobby. By the time I was out of breath, I was on the ninth floor, and higher than he'd ever climbed in his life.

I knocked on Joan's door, but no one answered. The lock on the door was a simple latchkey system, and I needed less time to pick it than I did to stop panting. Her office was as sparsely furnished as a nun's cell. A scarred metal desk, straight from some dried-up secretarial pool, was jammed up against a window that was covered by filthy venetian blinds. A filing cabinet squatted behind the door. Only two of the four drawers in the cabinet contained anything at all. One held a pair of black rubber boots, a folding umbrella with the initials "J.D." and a yellowed copy of the *Times/News* from the previous summer. The other drawer held some bottles of camouflage, a red wig, a box of dried fruit, and a pair of sunglasses, all the raw material from which evidence is constructed.

I tried the top drawer of the desk. It slid open easily but held nothing of interest: pens, pencils, a box of rubber bands, a few discolored paper clips, and a half dozen cubes of sugar, all the paraphenalia people have been shoving in top drawers as long as they've had drawers to shove things in. The bottom drawer was larger and much more interesting. I tugged at it tentatively, but it was locked.

Straightening one of the paper clips, I started to pick it open. I was too involved in the task to hear the door open behind me.

"The key is in the top drawer. All you have to do is look."

23

Joan stood transfixed, half in her office, half out. Her eyes were filled with a watery tension I would have taken for grief if I hadn't known better. But, like a pregnant bride in white, she wore her innocence badly.

After a long moment, she slowly pushed the door closed and went to the window where she drew up the blinds. "Now we'll be able to see something," she said officiously. When she looked back at me, she had donned a veil of disappointment.

"Well?" she asked.

"Well?"

"Don't you feel you owe me an explanation?"

"I'd rather hear yours. Mine's too long, too involved, and not very flattering to either of us."

"Jack," she said softly. "What are you talking about? I wondered why you wanted to meet here. I never guessed you meant to break in."

I got to my feet. "You can save me some effort. Where are the tapes, Joan? Or, would you prefer me to call you Jeanette?"

She didn't bat an eye. "I wish you'd quit playing this foolish game and tell me what you want."

"A confession would be nice."

"A confession? If you had stayed a little longer this morning, you would have had a confession." She reached into the top drawer and removed a key, which she held out for me. "But not one that has anything to do with whatever you're going to find in there. This key will open the lock."

I made no move to take the key from her, but several seconds passed before she let her arm fall to her side. "I was going to confess that I've fallen in love with you."

"What kind of fool do you think I am?"

She looked at me, and for the first time, I saw a gleam of bitterness in her eyes. "How many kinds are there?"

"Only two. Those who believe everything and those who believe nothing. Last night, I was definitely the first kind. Last night, I would have swallowed any lie. You should have made your confession then."

"The truth doesn't change from day to day."

"I agree. It never changes. You took the time tapes. I know you did, only I'm still not sure why. I've got an opinion but no way of knowing how right it is. That's where your confession would help."

"Forgive me, father, for I have sinned." Sarcasm flared in her voice though little of it heated her eyes. "Will that do?"

"Your motive, Joan. That's what I want. Your motive for all the lies, including this confession. Simple hatred? Jealousy? Thirst for revenge? Fear? Or maybe just a dab of megalomania? Any one would do."

She shook her head but said nothing.

"Don't make me go through all the gory details, Joan."

"I think you'd better. Just to humor me," she said evenly. "It seems the only way I can save my reputation. I can't disprove your accusations unless I know what they are."

"As you wish. Shall we begin with Lea? That's where you started, after all. It's easy to hate her for the rotten way she treated Alex, before, during, and after their marriage. You might even blame her for bringing out the worst in him. I know I did. He may have been everything she said last night; he could have been worse, and it wouldn't change her cruelty. Of course, you've probably picked up a few more things to hate about her in the last fifteen years. In the best of times, she'd be hard to live with. We could speculate about other reasons all day, but let's go with the one I'm sure of.

"Of course, once you convicted Lea, Carlo Mountain and Victor Sieg become accessories to her escape, so to speak. Two powerful men with the means to save Lea from her slow death she's living on earth, or at least that's how you and Lea saw them. That stumped me for a while. I could understand how your mother might swallow that scheme of Wightman's, but I gave you credit for being more astute. Of course, stealing the tapes had the added advantage of ruining Wightman too, by discrediting his bank and exposing him for what he is. You went to all that trouble to stop them from helping Lea and you didn't guess they were all conning her. It took me a while to convince myself you could be so gullible. I had even more trouble figuring out where Gregory Darling and Allison Bashcock fit in. Out of all the high-powered people Wightman services, they were about the most harmless. Of course, once I deciphered Alex's message on that photograph in the library, I realized you had more against them than either Sieg or Mountain. When did you discover that Gregory Darling was your mother's brother, Joan? Before or after you found out he was your father?"

Joan was stingy. She betrayed no easy emotion. Only the shudder that rippled faintly across her cheeks indicated the energy she kept surpressed. "You have no proof," was all she said.

"You're right. At least not the kind of proof your mother demands. You see, that's my problem. I've got all the evidence I need to prove your crime, but none to prove your motive. You'll have to help me there." I felt inside my coat pocket to reassure myself Darling's transducer was there. "You had no way of knowing I was at Darling's house when you arrived last Friday wearing that red wig and those sunglasses that make you Jeanette Dumbrey. You didn't know I saw your mother's coat in the closet. You didn't know Darling asked me to come back a few hours later. Of course you didn't. Otherwise, he'd be alive today."

"Tell me," she said dryly. "Does your code of honor permit you to take your suspects to bed?"

I wanted to ask her if her code required her taking her victims to bed, but I didn't want to hear another lie. I shook my head. "Last night, I was the first kind of fool."

"Then, did I say something in my sleep? Or was it something I didn't say?" Spite began to bleed into her voice.

"We're getting off the track." I realized I was raising my voice despite my best intentions. "We were discussing your visit to Darling's house. The poor bastard never suspected who was seducing him, did he? Why did you wear Lea's coat? Was that part of the ritual for murder? When did you break the news?" I pulled the transducer from my pocket and cradled it in my palm. For the first time, fear replaced the hurt in her eyes. "This belonged to Darling, but I don't have to tell you that."

"I've never seen it before in my life."

"Don't be silly. Darling showed this to everyone he could. This is the solid proof we're both looking for." I held it out for her to take, but she backed away, retreating until the filing cabinet stopped her. I took two steps and grabbed her by the wrist. "You didn't answer my question, Joan. When did you find out who your father really was?"

"You're wrong. You have no proof."

"I will when you press the button that activates the transduction circuits."

"What will that prove?"

"Like dunking a witch, it'll prove everything and nothing.

Either way, only the crowd goes home happy. Joan Dark abhors the idea of time deposits. This transducer can't do a thing to her." I jammed my thumb down hard on the button. "Just like it can't do anything to me. I haven't got a little disk of silver in my head. Can you say the same?"

"Even if I had one, I couldn't activate another person's transducer."

"Of course you couldn't." I forced Darling's transducer into her hand and closed her fingers around it. Her hand was cold, her face white, and her eyes distended with fear.

"Don't do this, Jack," she stammered, her voice less sure than ever. "It won't prove a thing."

"We're going around in circles, Joan." I was gripping her shoulder so hard with my other hand that my fingers ached. "If you survive our little test, if nothing else, it'll prove you love me. Of course, if you fail, it'll also prove you went to Darling's house intending to kill him. It'll prove you edged him as close to the deep-end as you could before giving him the final shove. What are you afraid of, Joan? Your father's ghost? Or his time?"

"It isn't what you think."

"Of course it isn't. You didn't masquerade as Jeanette Dumbrey, Jeanette of the shadows, Jeanette the feminine avenger. You didn't concoct an elaborate scheme to steal those tapes. You didn't carry out a ritual murder of your father. You didn't torture him with the revelation he'd been screwing his daughter, knowing he'd never forgiven himself for getting his sister pregnant thirty-six years ago. You didn't—"

"Jack, I swear . . ."

"Don't swear anything. Just press the button."

"It won't prove a thing," she repeated numbly.

"Then what are you afraid of? Look at it as a chance for you to prove what an ass I'm being. I have you wound in nothing but a long string of circumstantial evidence. Recently I found out how misleading that kind of evidence can be. Of course, if you can activate this transducer, I'll have some irrefutable evidence to support a few of these wild hunches. I'll know you intended to kill—"

"That's not true. I didn't intend . . ." Her eyes and mouth grew large, bloated with the memory welling up inside her. "I didn't know he'd . . . I only wanted to keep him from hurting me. He began screaming, pounding on the mattress like a wild man. He looked up at me and I knew he was going beserk. I ran out of the house. That was the last I saw of him until the paper the next day. I didn't know . . . I . . ."

"You're lying," I said harshly, struggling to keep a trace of business in my voice. "Why did you go back to his house that night? Why did you ransack the place?"

"I remembered I left my transducer lying on the living-room table. I thought he would have calmed down . . . I . . ."

"Poor girl. You probably spent half the night wondering what happened. You didn't know he died from an injection of another person's time, which short-circuited his whole system. Or, did you want to have another look at your handi-work? You waited so many years for your revenge. Did you enjoy watching death knit pretty designs on your father's face? Press the button, Joan. Let's see how accurate my theories are."

"You can't imagine I wanted him to die like that," she said desperately.

"How would you have preferred? Alcohol? No, I don't think you had the patience to sit through another alcoholic episode. The transducer's much faster and offers possibilities for exquisite torture. Press the button."

Joan stared dumbly at the transducer in her hand. As she shook her head slowly, she looked up at me. Then, taking one last breath, she just brushed her thumb across the button, and, instantly, the transducer's red light flashed on.

But, otherwise, nothing happened. I was sure nothing would. But Joan wasn't, and, after all, seeing the confession written on her face was the point of the whole charade.

Joan had steeled herself against the expected slap of indescribable pain, and when it didn't come, she couldn't mask either her surprise or her relief. When I let go of her arm, she slumped against the filing cabinet. Her third reaction was wonder. After a moment, she looked up at me. The tears in her eyes had turned to questions. I put Darling's transducer on the desk and answered her questions.

"Oh, you're Darling's daughter all right. You've got a transducer implanted in your head, and as we've seen, blood relatives can activate each other's transducers. But even Darling couldn't put any time into his life with that transducer. Without his account tape, he couldn't put time in or take any out. The storage circuits of that little wonder are in a state of equilibrium, and to operate either way, a transducer has to contain a concentration of time unequal to that of the user. You knew that, Joan. You stopped at the bank on your way to Darling's to make sure your transducer was loaded before you blasted him. That's premeditation, the difference between manslaughter and first-degree murder."

She said nothing while she searched for the shreds of her lost composure. "I never wanted him to die."

"Sure you didn't," I said cynically. "When did you hatch your plot? When did Alex tell you the truth about your parents?"

"Just before he died. He wasn't himself anymore. The knowledge he kept locked up all those years drove him crazy."

"It certainly drove him to drink," I said in a voice far older than my usual one.

She straightened herself slightly, ran a still-trembling hand through her disheveled hair, and looked into my eyes. "You think you've got the whole mess sorted out, don't you? You think you can just wash your hands and walk away." She smoothed the folds of her suit. "But you're wrong. I want you to know how wrong. I did want to torture my mother, Gregory, and the others. But I didn't want him to die. I wanted him to stew in his shame as long as Alex stewed in his. But when I told him who I was, he started throwing things. I locked myself in the bathroom to get away from him. Soon after, I heard him scream horribly, but I stayed locked where I was until the house had been quiet for a long time. When I went downstairs and saw him, I panicked and ran. Later, when I realized I had left my transducer there, I forced myself to go back. Gregory was gone and I couldn't find it. I didn't know how he died until you told me. That's why I was so surprised when you said he suffocated. I never knew blood relatives could activate each other's transducers. If I did, I certainly wouldn't have let you bully me into pressing that button. I don't suppose this makes any difference now, but you said you wanted the truth." She looked at the door. "Isn't this when the police are supposed to burst in? I guess you'll enjoy telling Detective Murtaugh the whole story."

"I would enjoy it. But Murtaugh wouldn't. She doesn't give a damn what happened. Not anymore. This morning, Gregory Darling's death was officially declared a suicide. That'll be as close to the truth as the police care to get. Our noble Senator Sieg decided there was too much commotion down in the barnyard, so he penned up the hounds." I didn't doubt Joan was being honest this time. There was no more reason for her to lie. Besides, I was past doubting. Darling had been tightly wired when I saw him in the afternoon. I could imagine something in him snapping after Joan dropped her bomb. He knew one sure way to find out if she was telling the truth. When he proved it to himself, he could easily have gone deep-end. He was holding the ticket in his hand. Or maybe he started something he couldn't stop. The distinction doesn't alter the eventual outcome.

Joan took a step toward me. "But, Jack, if the police aren't looking for Darling's killer, what purpose . . . Why did you put me through this?" She took my hand and I was surprised when I realized how soft her hand was.

I thought about my answer a long time before I spoke. "When you called this morning, I didn't know the police had already terminated their investigation. I was already on my way over here when Murtaugh gave me the happy news.

After that, I wanted to get the tapes back. That's why Wightman hired me."

"They're in the bottom desk drawer," she said, laying the key in my hand.

"Yeah." I weighed the key a moment. Somehow, it seemed heavier than any key ever had. "None of the owners really gives a damn about the tapes. Two are dead, a third is glad to be rid of her time, the fourth is going to be President. The fifth person thinks she's moving to space. Everyone has his own private fantasy." I fitted the key into the lock and opened the drawer. "I don't think Wightman even cares about these tapes anymore. If they aren't stored in cyanide, the coating that makes them capable of storing time decays. He can't reuse them. So I'll take them along as a memento. I'd like something other than money to remind me of the job I did. That's my private fantasy, that I can do what I claim to. I don't get the satisfaction of bringing my quarry to justice. Hell, I don't even get the girl."

"Jack, my first confession was true. I know my falling in love with you is ridiculous, but no more than your asking me to kill myself to prove it."

I smiled weakly and rubbed my ear. My legs were beginning to itch. I pulled the pitiful stack of cassettes from the drawer and stuck them in my pockets. "What do you think love changes? My stupidity or your lies? Does it change the theft of these tapes or Darling's death, suicide or not? You're still guilty even if you're going to have to come up with the punishment to fit the crime all by yourself. Don't you remember? Truth never changes."

"But people change. The last few days have changed me. And I know they've changed you. The simple truth is that I love you. And you love me. I know you do." Joan halved the distance between us with a single step, but there was no way in the world she could eliminate it all.

I shook my head slowly. "That simple truth," I said quietly. "The shortest distance between two lies."

"It's the only future either of us have."

"Joan I have nothing left in my life to hate." I forced myself to smile, even though I knew the smile was a lie. "What makes you think I want anything left to love?"

"You're afraid. Don't be. Trust your instincts."

"My instincts? My instincts told me your mother stole those tapes." I was struggling hard to keep my smile aloft. "And why shouldn't I be afraid? I know how little I have left to lose. The myths I live by seem to be dropping like flies. All that's left are a few rags of self-respect. Everything else was traded in to satisfy that promise of a newer, ever better to-morrow."

"Those myths are killing you. Let them go."

"They're all that are keeping me alive. Sorry. No more trades. Did you ever hear the joke about the ship-wrecked sailor in the North Atlantic. Out of nowhere, a shining ocean liner appeared. They sent down a rope, but the sailor refused to let go of the miserable piece of flotsam that kept him from drowning. 'But you'll die,' the people on deck called down. The sailor looked up at the name of ship, which was *Titanic*. 'Thanks just the same,' he called up. 'But I've seen this movie.' "

"I've heard that story before. It was stupid then, too."

"That's my problem. The only stories I remember are stu-pid. They all have these sad endings."

"Jack, trust me. . . ."

"Trust you? I'd trust Wightman before I'd trust you. He's reliable. He's only interested in survival and money. That's how you tell professionals like us from amateurs like you." I removed her hand from mine and squeezed one last smile around my lie before I left the room.

I pitched the tapes in a dumpster outside my building. They were far too heavy to drag up all those steps to my office. When I got there, I heated a cup of water and pre-pared a dose of my regular brand of coffee. Just as I was sitting down to enjoy it, the telephone began to ring. It rang twenty times, but I never considered answering it.

Later, long after the ringing had faded into another black-out, after I had finished my coffee, I strolled into my office. That's when I noticed the blue teacups lined up in a neat row across the floor and remembered my prisoners still waiting for me to decide their fates.

One by one, I lifted the cups. I had clemency in my heart, but the bastards had already escaped.